IMMORTAL

Pati Nagle

Evennight Books
Cedar Crest, New Mexico

Immortal

copyright © 2011 by Pati Nagle.

ISBN: 978-1-61138-062-0

Published by Evennight Books, an imprint of Book View Café.

Cedar Crest, New Mexico.

For Debbie

Acknowledgments

Many thanks to my helpmate, Chris Krohn.
Thanks as well to Plotbusters and the good
folks of the Oregon Writers Network,
especially Kris Rusch and Dean Wesley Smith.
You know why.

= 1 =

He came up to my station at the university library desk, eyes green and earnest, and a bolt of lightning shot through me and settled in my abdomen. He was absolutely freaking gorgeous.

Understand, I am not the starry-eyed type. More the shy, geeky, can't-get-a-date type. In fact, my parents are already despairing (loudly) that they will never have grandchildren.

It's not that I don't like guys, it's just that I'm picky — maybe unrealistically so. But this guy was so exactly my type, it was scary.

High cheekbones, skin fair and smooth with the slightest golden tinge. His eyes, as they held my gaze, seemed to shimmer from deep green to gold-green. His voice was soft and had a slight lilt to it, as if he might be foreign, though he spoke perfectly.

"Can you help me find this book?"

I didn't want to look away from his face, but he was holding the note out to me. I took it and glanced down.

The handwriting was graceful, not your usual undergraduate's scrawl. The book was one I'd never heard of, but the call number told the tale. I offered the note back.

"It's in the Kathryn Wesley Collection, in the west hall. They'll need your student I.D. and one other form of identification, and you'll have to use it in the library, you can't check it out."

Listening to myself, I sounded like a some awful character in a TV drama — the hide-bound librarian. What I was really thinking was if I offered to buy him a drink, would he laugh? A soda, of course. I wasn't twenty-one yet. Counting the 116 days left.

He was frowning again, staring at the note in his long

fingers. Pale pink paper with the words of some forgotten flyer on the back.

"I don't have a student I.D."

Irrational disappointment went through me. Not a student, harder to connect with. He didn't look any older than me, but I wasn't a good judge of age. I saw my fantasy receding. No surprise.

I put on my cheery librarian smile. "Do you have a Community Borrower's card?"

He shook his head, looking troubled. My chance to be a hero, a little bit. I pulled an application form from one of the slots under the counter and laid it down facing him.

"It's twenty dollars a semester. Fill this out and turn it in with your payment and you should get the card within a week."

His frown deepened as he scanned the form. He looked up at me, and again I felt like I'd been sucker-punched.

"I cannot wait a week. May I not see the book today?"

"I'm sorry, you need either an I.D. or a Borrower's card to use a rare book."

He stood still, frozen in disappointment. I wanted to run get the book and hand it to him, he looked so heartbroken. I watched him breathe three times before he met my gaze again.

"Please, it is important. Can you not help me?"

He had spoken in a whisper, but the intensity of it almost turned my legs to jelly. I gulped a breath as a tingling washed slowly through my body from head to foot.

All attraction aside, this was not a normal reaction. I leaned the heels of my hands on the counter, wondering if he had pulled some kind of hypnotic trick on me, but if so he didn't press the advantage. He simply waited, watching me with those amazing eyes.

I swallowed and answered quietly. "Well, I could request the book. You could come with me and look at it, but it would have to be after I get off work."

"When is that?"

"Four o'clock."

"Then I will return at four o'clock. I should come here?"

"I'll meet you over by the history display."

I nodded toward the alcove a few yards along the building from the main desk. He followed my gaze to the glass-encased artifacts and images, currently depicting the history of the Rio Grande, then looked back at me and smiled like the sun rising. I swear I could almost hear birds singing.

"Thank you." He gave an odd little nod, almost a bow, and headed for the front doors.

"Hey, what's your...name."

I hadn't been fast enough, and I couldn't raise my voice in the library. His long, graceful strides took him through the metal detectors and the glass doors and out into the autumn sunshine. I just had time to register that his backpack was unusual—soft leather with fringe on the flap and a leather string lashed around a large blue bead instead of a buckle—and that the sun lit his long, russet ponytail almost to red, before he was out of sight.

Amanda, working the next station over, said softly, "Wow, Len."

"Yeah," I answered shakily.

"Who was he? I had a customer so I couldn't listen in."

"I don't know. Not a student."

She pushed up her glasses, gazing out the front doors. "Maybe he's an actor. There are lots of movie crews in town."

"Maybe."

Someone came up to my station with a stack of renewals, ending the conversation. Amanda might well be right, I thought as I processed the books. Our current governor liked Hollywood people and had arranged for lots of incentives for movie companies who shot on location in the state, so it was hard to get around Albuquerque without tripping over a film crew these days.

And an actor might have the kind of charisma that had just bowled me over. My pulse sped up again as I recalled the few moments he'd been in front of me. I closed my eyes, remembering his face, his voice. My heart did a slow flip as I realized I was going to see him again in just a few hours.

"Everything all right, Miss Lenore?"

I flinched back, opening my eyes. Dave Wharton, my supervisor, had come up beside me and I had been so damn preoccupied I hadn't heard him. The antithesis of my ideal, Dave was stocky, hairy just about everywhere I could see and I'm sure in places I didn't want to imagine, and full of himself.

"Everything's fine." I grabbed the unused application and put it back in the slot, though for an insane moment I wanted to keep it.

"What did Pretty Boy want?"

"Looking for a book, but it's in special collections."

Stupid! Too much information. I was giving things away and I shouldn't. If Dave got too nosy and felt like interfering, he could prevent me from keeping my promise to the gorgeous guy.

Technically I shouldn't have offered to give that guy access to the book, though it wasn't *specifically* against the rules to do what I'd suggested. Stretching them, yes.

I ran through the renewal records I'd just updated on my screen, for the sake of looking busy. Dave watched for a minute, then went away. I breathed a sigh of relief.

For the next three hours I tried unsuccessfully to keep from checking the time. I knew it was hopeless to try not to think about the gorgeous stranger with whom I had made a date, albeit a really tame one. I replayed my few minutes with him over and over in my mind, savoring every impression.

Yes, I am obsessive, and probably too romantically inclined, especially for a wallflower. Guys who fit my taste for pretty men (clean-shaven, thank you, and more sleek than muscle-bound) aren't all that common, and are usually taken by the time I notice them, if they're not gay. They don't often notice me back, either. I'm nothing extraordinary, and I'm shy with strangers, so that's two strikes in the attract-your-dream game.

I wished I'd written down the title of the book he wanted. It was in Spanish, and I thought it had something to do with colonists in northern New Mexico, but beyond that I couldn't remember. We had *lots* of books that fit that description.

To pass the slow times during the afternoon, I surfed the catalog trying to spot the entry. No luck, though I compiled a list of titles that I thought might interest my glorious researcher. Maybe if I was helpful he'd be grateful, inclined to take pity on a poor geek and spend a little time with her.

By three-thirty I was quietly going nuts with anticipation. Amanda had left at two, and the only other person who had seen my researcher was Dave, so I had no one to talk to about him. That was probably for the best, because I was getting too worked up.

The last five minutes of the hour I was useless. Kept staring at the doors, watching for him, terrified he might come and go before I could clock out and go to meet him.

I should have told him five after four. I should have explained that it might take me a few minutes to get to the history display. I—yi yi

At 3:59 there was no one in line. I logged out, grabbed my pack from under the counter and dashed back to the staff room to punch my time card. Dave was pouring end-of-the-day coffee into his mug, and glanced up at me.

"See you tomorrow, Miss Lenore."

He drawled the words, lingering on my name, trying to piss me off. No way was I going to get into it with him today.

"Right. Bye."

I shouldered my pack and stepped out, forcing myself to walk and not run to the history display. My heart sank when I saw there was no one there.

Swallowing, I stood in front of a case showing photos of the Rio Grande over time, staring at the pictures without registering them. I should have known better than to get my hopes up. Probably the guy had decided it was too much trouble, or maybe he'd found his book at the city library's special collections branch. I hadn't even thought to suggest that. Some help I was.

"Hello."

I jumped. Heart drumming, I turned and saw my dream researcher standing a few feet away, smiling tentatively.

"Oh! Hi."

I laughed, self-conscious and delighted and sure I was blushing. His beauty floored me all over again.

"I'm Len, by the way," I said, considering offering a hand, then chickening out and shoving it in my back pocket instead.

"Len?"

"It's short for Lenore. And you?"

"Caeran."

I paused, wondering about the origin of the name. Sounded vaguely Celtic, but I could be wrong.

He watched me, waiting expectantly. I gestured toward the west hall of the complex.

"Well, we should go. The Wesley Collection closes at five."

He fell in beside me, his nearness making me tingle. I glanced at him as we walked, picking up a few more details to treasure. He wore a loose-weave cotton shirt and trousers—earth-tones—and knee-high moccasins. Very hippie, but not in the sixties throwback sense. The clothes might have been Guatemalan or some other ethnic style, but I couldn't pinpoint them.

We got in the west elevator and I punched the button for the third floor. No one joined us, so I had him to myself in a confined space for a few seconds. I was all too official about it, mainly because I was feeling shy.

"Did you bring your citation?"

"My what?"

"Your note with the book title."

"Oh. Yes."

He dug the scrap of paper out of a pocket. I reached for it.

"I'll put in the request, and it'll take them a few minutes to pull the book. Then you'll have until five to look at it."

He nodded, handing over the slip. "Thank you again."

"My pleasure." I smiled, then glanced at the citation. "You speak Spanish?"

Another nod. He sure wasn't outgoing, but that was something I could definitely understand. Fighting my own shyness, I kept trying to be friendly.

"That'll come in handy if you visit any of the rural areas of the state. If I'm not mistaken, you're new here, right?"

"Yes." He glanced down, his gaze going distant.

The doors opened and I led him down a short hall to the Wesley Collection's home, a broad, low-ceilinged space that took up the entire third floor of the library's west wing. Metal detectors flanked the doors. At the front desk was Barbara Collier, a nice, honey-haired woman who'd helped me with a paper my freshman year.

"Hi, Barb. Can you rush this one for me?"

I handed her the slip and pulled a request form toward me, hastily filling it out. Barb glanced at the note, brows rising as she typed the call number into her keyboard.

"It's been years since anyone's requested this. It might have gone upstairs."

I signed the form and pushed it toward her along with my ID. She just glanced at my card and handed it back. That was an advantage of my being on the library staff; ordinarily she'd make a copy of the I.D. and the paperwork would take a while. Too bad my guest didn't know how lucky he was.

"Go ahead and put your bag away and I'll pull this. Is this gentleman with you?"

"Yes, we're using the book together."

"Well, it's a gloves-on item. You'll show him the protocol?"

"Of course. Thanks, Barb."

I stepped to the bank of lockers along a nearby wall, pulling some quarters out of my pack before sticking it in an empty locker in the top row. My guest—Caeran, I reminded myself, savoring the name—was gazing at his surroundings.

"You'll have to lock up your pack," I told him. "No pens or anything allowed."

He turned a bewildered look on me. I suddenly wondered if he had money issues. He didn't look homeless—too clean—but nothing about him screamed wealth. A point against his being an actor, though not all actors were rich.

"We can share, there's room."

I shoved my pack to the back of the locker and invited him to add his. He hesitated, then set the bag inside, watching with a slightly anxious expression as I shut the door and fed in quarters.

"You can hang onto the key if you like."

I held out the key, bulky with its numbered plastic tag. He hesitated, then took it. A shock went through me as his fingertips brushed mine.

He smiled. "Thank you."

Oh, man oh man. I had it bad.

I led him into the research area, where several large tables were available for using materials from the collection. Two of them were occupied, one by a grad student poring over some ancient maps, another by a faculty member looking through a four inch thick tome. I walked to the counter where a box of clean cotton gloves sat next to a stack of letter-sized paper—goldenrod, so the library staff knew it was from their supply—and a box of sharpened pencils. I poked through the gloves and pulled out a pair, offering them to my guest.

"See if these fit you."

He put the locker key in his pocket and took the gloves, looking doubtful. I chose a pair for myself, and explained.

"The book's old. The oils on our skin could damage the paper. We have to wear these when we're handling it."

Caeran nodded. "I see."

I picked up a few sheets of the goldenrod and a couple of pencils. "You'll want to take notes, I assume?"

"Yes."

"We'll use these, and of course we try not to mark on the book. OK, then. We're all set. Choose a table."

For a long moment he stood still, apparently giving the

selection serious consideration. Finally he moved toward the table farthest from the entrance, and took a seat from which he had an oblique view of the door and the front desk. I sat down next to him, since the tables were too wide to work across. I kept a couple of sheets of the paper and placed the rest in front of Caeran.

Lull time. Quick, think of something to say! As usual, this demand froze my brain.

I swallowed, deciding not to ask him if he was an actor. I'd already tried "you're new here" with poor response, and "so what's the hurry to see this book?" seemed rude.

"What brought you to New Mexico?" I blurted, sotto voce for the sake of the other patrons.

"An airplane," he answered softly.

"Ha, ha. I mean why did you come here? Were you here for the balloon fiesta?"

He frowned slightly, then shook his head. "W-we wanted to see the trees. Aspens."

"Oh, yeah. I love them, too. You're here at the right time, they're just turning. If you want a guide or anything...there's also one valley of maple trees in the Manzanos, if you like those."

He answered with a polite smile. I had a feeling I was striking out.

"So, you're here with friends?"

"Family."

"Ah."

While I was struggling to come up with another question, Barbara appeared with the book. It was smallish, bound in leather that was starting to crack with age. I couldn't quite read the title on the spine. She laid a blotter-sized sheet of white paper on the table in front of us, pushing the goldenrod out of the way, and tenderly set the book on top of it.

"There you go," she said in hushed, slightly reverent tones, her gaze flicking to Caeran's gloved hands. "Let me know if you need anything else."

"Thanks, Barb!" I whispered as she went back to the front desk.

Caeran hesitated, and I thought it might be because I was right there, so I picked up my pencil and started making a grocery list on one of my sheets of paper. After a moment he opened the book. I kept my eyes on my list and counted to sixty before daring a glance.

The print was old and fairly dense, and in Spanish. I'd taken a couple of semesters in high school, not enough to really be able to comprehend text without the company of a Spanish dictionary. I figured if I was curious I could always request the book another time and puzzle through it. What I didn't want was to make Caeran uncomfortable, so I didn't try to read over his shoulder. I worked on my list, and drank in my impressions of him as he sat beside me.

I wasn't quite close enough to register his smell, at least not consciously, but pheromones or something were making me high. I was falling for him, which was probably not a good idea but sometimes your body doesn't give you a choice about these things. I was hypersensitive to his every movement, all of which were graceful. He never coughed or fidgeted, just sat there silently turning pages.

He scanned them quickly. I guessed he was skimming, looking for something to catch his eye. He was halfway through the book before he paused to make a note. I glanced up as he picked up his pencil. Nothing special on the page as far as I could tell, but his gaze, his whole attitude, had intensified.

He wrote down one word—a name—then kept reading.

I had finished my grocery list, so I made a list of things to do. When that was done I gave up and started doodling.

Every now and then Caeran would make another note. His page looked like a list, too; a list of surnames, a couple with annotations of place names, I thought. I tried not to snoop too blatantly, but I was curious. What could be so urgent about this centuries-old history? Why couldn't it wait a week?

Maybe it hadn't been the wait, but the twenty dollars that

had bothered him. Except that if he could afford airfare, then twenty bucks shouldn't be a problem.

Where had he come from? I wondered. The UK? Europe?

And why come to New Mexico for aspens, when the Colorado Rockies were right next door? Aspen-viewing, and then suddenly an urgent need to research New Mexico's colonial history? I must not have the whole picture.

Barb came out from the front desk and started going to each of the patrons, quietly informing them that the facility was about to close. I glanced at my watch, which read 4:55. Caeran seemed not to have noticed, but when Barb came over to us he sat back. He'd gotten about halfway through the book.

"We'll be closing in a few minutes," Barb said.

Caeran nodded, made a note of the page number, then closed the book and handed it to her. "Thank you."

She smiled and headed for the guy with the maps. I pulled off my gloves.

"Did you get what you needed?" I asked softly.

A slight frown creased his brow. "Perhaps."

"We could come again tomorrow if you want to finish."

He turned his head to meet my gaze. "That is kind of you. Thank you."

I smiled. "Glad to help."

He removed his gloves and picked up his notes, carefully folding it in half. We stood up and I gathered the unused paper, pencils, and the gloves and carried them back to the counter.

Caeran took the key from his pocket, then stood frowning at the row of lockers.

I joined him. "I think it's number four."

I pointed to our locker and watched him try to fit the key into the lock. He turned it over a couple of times before he got it to go in. I bit my tongue on an offer to help. He wasn't stupid, just unfamiliar with the format. My curiosity about him grew.

He slid his notes into his pack and followed me to the elevator. The map-guy grad student joined us, to my silent regret. Ignoring him, I smiled at Caeran and took my heart in my hands.

"So, can I buy you a cup of coffee?"

Caeran looked surprised, then gave me his polite smile. "Thank you, but I must return to my kindred. My family."

"Ah. OK."

Hiding my disappointment, I folded my page of lists into quarters and stuffed it into my pocket. The elevator opened and we walked out. I waited for the map guy to get out of earshot, then turned to Caeran with a friendly smile.

"Well, see you tomorrow maybe, if you want to go through the rest of that book. I'll be working 'til four again."

He turned to me, his glorious face showing mixed emotions that I wasn't sure I was reading correctly. Doubt? Speculation? He seemed to be looking at me, really looking at me, for the first time. My heart suddenly tried to fly up out of my chest.

The small crease on his brow faded, as if he'd reached a decision. "If I return, shall we meet in the same place?"

I nodded. "History display. Yeah."

He kept gazing at me, and I stared back, mesmerized. He made me feel like I was floating in an exquisite limbo. I didn't know if he was doing it on purpose, and I didn't care. I did get the feeling that he was examining me as if I was some interesting specimen. Didn't care about that either. I could have stood there for hours.

Suddenly he smiled. "Thank you for your help."

I sucked in a giddy breath. "Any time."

He turned and strode away. End of interaction.

I walked after him, knowing it was hopeless to play the moth drawn to the flame, but unable to resist. He went out the doors and turned west, heading for University Boulevard.

His stride was long and I had to hurry to keep him in sight. At the same time I didn't want him to catch me following him, so I kept a few other students between us. That got harder as we moved toward the edge of campus and the crowd thinned out. I dropped to a stroll and tried to look like I was just walking along enjoying the day.

Leaves were turning orange and gold, the fallen ones swirling on the sidewalks and in the gutters. Roses in front of the older buildings on the street were showing a last, glorious pre-winter bloom. It was sunny with a cool breeze, perfect weather.

Just before reaching University, Caeran turned south along the street that loops the campus. I followed at a careful distance, composing excuses in case he caught me following him and confronted me. If he was aware of me—and it was quite possible he was—he chose not to show it. He walked to the south side of campus, crossed a lawn to Central Avenue, and went to the bus stop.

I sat down under a tree, watching him, debating whether to join him. Instinct warned me that would be a bad move. Not good if he were to get the idea I was stalking him. Which, basically, I was.

It didn't matter anyway. In a few minutes a bus arrived and he got on it, heading for downtown. I watched it roll away.

I might see him again tomorrow, if he decided to look at the rest of the book. Should I be so lucky, though, it would probably be the last I saw of him, unless I was somehow able to connect with him.

I rubbed my eyes. I wasn't good at this. I should let it go— let him go, and just enjoy the memory of his incredible beauty. Maybe tomorrow I'd try to sneak a photo of him as a memento.

Laughing at myself, I got up and slung my pack over my shoulder. A few yards away a weathered man in filthy, beat-up denims turned bloodshot eyes toward me. Street dudes hung out along this stretch of grass fairly often. I looked away to discourage him from panhandling me, and strode briskly back the way I had come.

I needed distraction. I had the novel I was currently reading in my backpack, but I knew I'd be too restless to sit and read. A movie might do it, but none of the titles in the theaters interested me. There was always fun, off-beat stuff showing at Student Union Building, but that wouldn't be until later in the evening.

And I didn't really feel like a movie. I wanted something more breathtaking, some environment in which I could fantasize about being with Caeran, since fantasy was likely to be as close as I got.

I wanted to ride the tram to the top of the mountains and stand looking out over a hundred miles of beauty. Since tram tickets were pricey, I settled instead on a visit to the bosque. Fall color was just coming in along the river, and the leaves of the cottonwood forest would be all green and gold. I'd have to hurry—the Nature Center would be closed—but I should still have about an hour to wander around on the trails before the sun set.

Walking across campus to my dorm to get my car, I thought about Caeran. Not only was he gorgeous, he seemed to have a lot of the qualities I liked. He was graceful, and modest. Elegant? Nothing about his appearance said that, but I had to add it to the list of his merits. He *felt* elegant. Like he'd come from a more gracious time. Or maybe I was just reacting to his slightly unusual behavior—maybe it was a cultural thing.

So, OK, what did I *not* like about him? Anything? Other than the fact that he wasn't as nuts about me as I was about him?

I couldn't think of anything. Knowing it was unwise to be so obsessed with a stranger, I tried to think of things that, while I might not mind them, could be warning signals.

Possibly he didn't have a lot of money. He'd been reluctant to spring for a Borrower's Card, and he'd taken the bus. He had also mentioned coming here by plane, but that could have been a lie.

My besotted soul instantly objected to the thought that Caeran could possibly be deceitful. Gut feeling told me he was honest. Gut feeling might well be partial, though, so I tried to ignore it.

Could he be trying to take advantage of me somehow? I didn't think so. It would have been pathetically easy for him to do so, but he'd declined my offer of coffee. If he'd been looking for a mark, he'd have said yes.

True, he asked for my help, but only in getting to the book. Which brought me back to wondering why the book was so urgently important. All he'd taken from it was a list of names of people who were long dead.

Identity theft? Nah—there had to be easier ways. Crooks didn't draw attention to themselves by requesting rare books in libraries.

Although...I had done the requesting. I didn't even know Caeran's last name.

I was stumped, and I had reached the dorm parking lot. Giving up the puzzle for the moment, I got in my car and drove through the city toward the Rio Grande.

= 2 =

The sun was headed toward the volcanic escarpment west of town, and the late afternoon sunlight slanted through the trees of the North Valley, setting yellow leaves aglow. I parked on a side street near the entrance to the Nature Center, which was already locked up. A gap in the fence nearby gave access to the bike trails along the bosque, via a wide path with cottonwoods behind the fences on either side.

Grand old trees, going golden for fall, a few leaves already dropping to brighten the cinder path. I inhaled the dry-leaf smell of autumn and sighed with pleasure.

The path gave onto a walking trail that ran along a flood-control ditch. I crossed the ditch on a footbridge and headed up to the bosque proper—the forest that ran along the Rio's flood zone, all through the city. A paved bike trail ran between the bosque and the ditch. I crossed it and went into the woods, turning south, away from the most frequented trail.

Dust rose up from my footfalls to hang in the late afternoon sunshine. Birds chattered and fussed; I heard some geese calling as they flew over, heading for the pond at the Nature Center. I looked up through the tree branches, peering into the blue beyond the golden leaves, hoping to catch sight of a passing "V" of sandhill cranes. I didn't see any, nor hear any when I paused to listen.

I closed my eyes, thinking of Caeran, picturing him beside me, thanking me for showing him these trees, which were nearly as beautiful as the aspen groves up in the mountains. I laughed softly at myself, then walked on, content with the fantasy.

The sun was heading toward the escarpment and would set before long. I could feel the air getting cooler as the sunlight retreated. I kept going, though, giving myself permission to walk until the sun was actually down. Then I should head back. The bosque was fairly safe, but I didn't care to walk alone there at night, and I was a bit off the beaten path. Still on a trail, though, even if it was little more than a dusty track through the undergrowth.

I came around a bend where the trail skirted a thicket of olive trees, and stopped. A few yards away a homeless guy was squatting in the dirt, whittling on a stick with a knife. I was about to back away when he turned his head a little and I saw a familiar jawline. My heart jumped.

"Caeran?"

He looked up at me in surprise, and I saw that it wasn't Caeran. It was someone who looked a whole lot like him, though.

"Oh—sorry! You must be one of Caeran's family. Is he here?"

He stood up and faced me, and I saw that what I'd taken for ratty clothes were a shirt and loose trousers a lot like what Caeran wore. This guy was every bit as gorgeous as Caeran, but not as trusting. He was still holding the knife, which didn't make me as nervous as it had at first, but I took note of it. He frowned at me.

"How do you know Caeran?"

"H-he came to the library where I work."

The stranger stared at me intently, reminding me of how Caeran had done something similar, though it felt more like a threat with this guy. He didn't smile at all.

A tingle started at the back of my neck. The guy's eyes— green, but darker than Caeran's—bored into me, and for a moment I thought I saw a faint glow around his head. I felt like he was trying to see right into my heart. Something like a whisper went through the back of my mind. I couldn't make out the words.

Then he looked away, leaning against a tree trunk and whittling at his stick again. "Caeran is not here."

I blinked. The glow was gone, or I had imagined it. "Oh.

Well...when you see him, tell him I said hi. Len, from the library."

No acknowledgment. Only the long scrape of the blade along the stick. A curl of pale wood fell to the ground.

OK, fine. I could take a hint. I went back the way I'd come.

By the time I got back to my car it was twilight. I paused to inhale one last breath of autumn, and to gaze at Venus blazing above the escarpment in a sky of deep, glowing blue.

I'd satisfied my itch for the outdoors, but I had even more questions now. Who was Caeran's look-alike, and why was he so unfriendly? He'd radiated "leave me alone" vibes. Most people who hiked in the bosque were pretty outgoing, but then, he wasn't from around here.

I drove back to campus, musing about having met not one, but two drop-dead gorgeous strangers in one day. Weird that I had run into the second one, but then, Caeran had said they were interested in fall color, so the bosque wasn't an unlikely place for them to go. I hadn't been thinking about that when I decided to go there—at least, not consciously.

I wondered if it was just the two of them in town, or if there were more. The actor scenario seemed less and less likely.

Maybe they were staying at one of the B&B's in the area. That would make a kind of sense, except why had Caeran taken a bus instead of a rental car?

Or could be they were visiting friends...but that felt unlikely. A local friend would have told Caeran what to expect at the university's library, would have given him a ride. No, the more I thought about it, the more Caeran struck me as someone finding his way through a culture that was foreign to him.

And that might explain his family member's unfriendliness. Fish out of water, instinctively defensive. Made sense.

Back at the dorm, I took a long, hot shower. I didn't feel like going out again for a movie, so I worked on a paper that was due the next week, then read until it was late enough to try to sleep.

Caeran dominated my thoughts as soon as my head hit the

pillow. I let myself daydream about him, hoping to fall asleep. It took a while, and the fantasies got elaborate and a little far-fetched, before my brain finally gave it up.

I dreamed about him, or maybe my memory got fuzzed with the daydreams. At any rate, when I woke up I was clutching my pillow. I got up, ate a carton of yogurt, went to my early class, then headed back to the library for my shift.

Amanda didn't work Thursdays, so again I had no one to talk to. The first couple of hours were busy, though—lots of folks in on their lunch hours.

I hoped Caeran was going to show up, but if he didn't, I'd look through the book and try to figure out what he was after. I might have to resort to a Spanish dictionary. There was probably one in the Wesley Collection that I could use.

I did better at not looking at the clock, but I was still antsy the last hour of my shift. There was a real chance that Caeran wouldn't come back. He hadn't said for sure that he would. I kept telling myself that, trying to stay cool, but my brain was already picturing us sitting together.

I tried pretending he had said he wouldn't be returning. That sort of worked, at least so far as allowing me to appear unconcerned. I was very concerned, of course, but was able to hide it.

I watched the digital clock on my monitor tick away the last sixty seconds of my shift. At four precisely I picked up my pack and logged out. No Dave to harass me in the break room, for which I gave silent thanks. I slung my pack over my shoulder and headed for the history display.

Caeran was there. My heart jumped with glee. I slowed down, wanting to look at him for a moment before he noticed me.

He was looking at a section of the display that covered the bosque. He seemed intent on it, but maybe he was just intent about everything. I remembered his look-alike from the evening before and wondered if they had talked about me.

He sensed my presence and looked up. I smiled.

"Hi. Back for more?"

"Yes."

"OK, let's go."

We went up to the collection. I'd hoped we would talk in the elevator but there were some exuberant freshmen riding it with us, headed for the stacks. Caeran ignored the glances the girls threw at him, and the surly looks from the guys. I was pretty sure he'd noticed, though he gave no sign of it. I mean it would be hard not to notice the giggling.

We escaped into the quiet of the Wesley Collection. Barb had the book waiting at the counter and we sailed through checking in. Caeran even had some quarters ready for the locker.

He seemed completely confident now, unlike his hesitance the previous day. It reinforced my impression that he was dealing with an alien culture. He seemed to be adapting well.

I sat doodling again and watching him covertly, wishing we had talked more. Afterward, I promised myself. I would start a conversation, find out his last name at least. Maybe try again to ask him for coffee.

He made another list of names. Shorter, this time. He got through the rest of the book with ten minutes to spare, then leaned back in his chair, frowning at his notes. I sneaked a peek and saw that one of the names was circled. It looked like "Madera," and there was a note beside it that I couldn't read.

"Find what you need?" I whispered.

"I hope so."

"If I can do anything to help..."

I stopped when he looked at me. The intensity of his gaze made my stomach flip over. For a long moment I gazed back, then he whispered to me.

"Does the library have information about local transportation?"

"Uh—some. Student Union Building's a better bet. Or the Internet."

He'd been on the bus, so he must have information for the

city's routes, or know where to find it. What more did he need to know?

He made a note on his page and sat frowning at it. I watched him, holding still, almost holding my breath.

He looked at me once more, the searching-your-soul look that had held me spellbound before. Worked again; I couldn't move, not that I wanted to. It scared me a little, but I liked it.

Finally he looked away. I sucked in a breath.

"May I call you?" he said, and my heart lurched. "If I need more information?"

"S-sure. I'll give you my cell number."

He laid his list down on the table and I scrawled my name and number at the bottom of the page. I was really proud that my hand didn't shake.

"Thank you."

He folded the page and stood up. I shoved my doodles in my pocket and followed him to the lockers, bringing along the book, which he seemed to have forgotten. I handed it over to Barb, thanking her, then accepted my pack from Caeran.

We got in the elevator. Panic time! I might not see him again.

"Could I have your number too?"

He blinked at me. "I don't have a phone."

"Oh, OK. Well. Do you have time for coffee today?"

He looked like he was about to say no, then changed his mind. "Perhaps. Could we find transportation information at the same time?"

"Sure. SUB's got an espresso stand."

I smiled and he smiled faintly back. My heart was trying to fly. I kept my mouth shut, not wanting to spoil my luck by saying the wrong thing. Caeran didn't always react the way I'd expect.

We left the library and I started toward the SUB. Caeran kept pace with me, his stride graceful and silent.

"It is far?" he asked after a moment.

"No, that's it right ahead."

I led him inside the big building. As always, the place was bustling with students, chatting, surfing the Web, doing homework in the big dining rooms or at cafe tables in the halls.

The information booth was close to the entrance we'd used, in a slightly less trafficked area. The espresso stand was farther in. I walked over to the racks of leaflets by the wall, hoping not to have to talk to the girl manning the info booth. It was early enough in the semester that she had a couple of people standing at her counter.

I turned to Caeran. "What did you want to know?"

He scanned the flyers, wearing his intent expression. "How to get to the north of the state."

"Well, there are maps here—"

"Not directions. Method. Are there buses that go there?"

"It depends where you're trying to go."

He took his page of notes out of his pocket and unfolded it. "Guadalupita."

"I never *heard* of Guadalupita. Where is it?"

For the first time that day, he looked hesitant. "North."

"We need the Internet."

I walked over to some empty chairs and pulled my netbook out of my pack. The SUB's wireless was dog slow—too many users—but I was able to call up a map. Guadalupita was a tiny spot on a tiny road north of Mora, which itself was a far cry from downtown Albuquerque.

"It's in the middle of nowhere. There won't be bus service. Closest you could get is probably Taos."

Caeran sat next to me and peered at the screen. "Perhaps I could walk from Taos."

"It's over fifty miles! Through the mountains!"

Caeran frowned slightly. "Then it might take too long."

"Look, the best way to get there is gonna be by car. A one-day rental wouldn't cost too much. Most of the car places have Internet coupons—"

"I don't drive."

He said it very quietly, as if he didn't want to be overheard.

I glanced at a couple of guys walking past and lowered my voice.

"Does anyone in your family drive?"

He shook his head. I had trouble wrapping my brain around an entire family that didn't drive, but then, if he was from Europe or someplace where they didn't use cars so much...

Caeran was still staring at the map. I got a crazy idea. I tried to fight it down, but I was too hooked on him and I wasn't thinking rationally. It was a damn good thing he showed no signs of being a psychopath, though that might not have stopped me.

"I have a car."

He looked up at me, his face suddenly lit with hope so intense it took my breath away. The next moment he shook his head.

"I cannot impose on you."

"You could cover the gas. I wouldn't mind driving."

He looked incredulous. "You would undertake to drive strangers that far?"

"Well, it depends how many strangers. My Saturn holds four—five if you squish."

I wondered belatedly if his surly look-alike was going to be included. Not that I could back out now, or wanted to. My heart was pumping at the thought of spending several hours with Caeran, though the family chaperones would be a damper.

He was frowning again, staring into space. It gave me time to realize just how crazy I was acting. He and his family could be criminals. They could steal my car and desert me in nowhere's-ass, New Mexico. Or worse.

But not Caeran. I knew in my soul he wouldn't hurt me.

"You know nothing about me," he said softly.

"That's true. You could tell me your last name."

He seemed to find that funny. "Woods."

Too ordinary a name for him. "OK, so now I know something about you."

He was still smiling, and frowning at the same time,

shaking his head. "If you drove us to Guadalupita, you would learn more about us than you want to know."

"Are you kidding?"

He looked at me, surprised.

"I want to know *everything* about you."

His eyes went wide. I had the sudden sensation of falling into them, of being absorbed into his being. Then he looked away, leaving me with residual vertigo.

"Len, I shouldn't."

It was the first time he'd said my name. I wasn't even sure until then that he remembered it. A tingle went through me.

"Why not?"

He surprised me by burying his face in his hands. The gesture, his posture, spoke of distress. I wanted to fold my arms around him. I clutched my netbook instead.

"Look, it's a long drive. We can talk on the way. I'd like to...I know it sounds like a cheesy line, but I really would like to get to know you."

He was still for a long moment, then suddenly sat up. "I need to make a phone call."

I offered him my cell. He looked at it, looked at me.

"Want me to dial it? What's the number?"

"I don't know yet. I need to look it up."

I brought up a search engine on my netbook. "Name?"

He didn't bother to look at his notes, but gazed at me, slightly worried. "De Madera."

"In Guadalupita?"

"Yes."

I typed it in, not feeling hopeful. Tiny town like that, guy might not have a phone. And that was one of the names Caeran had pulled from that old book—who knew if the family was still there?

The name came up, though. I punched the number into my cell phone and handed it to Caeran.

He stood, pacing while the phone rang, then he stopped and said, "Señor de Madera?"

The next moment he turned away, and I couldn't understand the rest of what he said. It didn't sound like Spanish, unless it was some ancient colonial Spanish or something. I should recognize that, though. New Mexico's Spanish vernacular had a lot of colonial influence.

The conversation was brief, but evidently satisfactory. Caeran returned, eyes blazing as he handed me back my phone.

"You are sure you wish to do this? To help us in this way?" he said softly.

"Yeah. I am."

"So be it. I will do all I can to repay you. When do we leave?"

"Uh...well, it'll take about four hours to drive, maybe more. If we left now—with the time to pick up your family—we probably wouldn't get there until after ten."

Caeran shook his head. "That will not do. I must stop at the bar to ask directions, and it will be closed by then."

Guadalupita had a bar?

"OK. I have a class in the morning, but it gets out at 11:30. We could leave then, be there around four or five."

"Very well. Should I meet you here?"

"Would it be easier if I picked you up?"

"Yes. Thank you."

He looked relieved, and I wondered again what the urgency was. Didn't quite have the nerve to ask.

"How many of you are there?" I asked instead.

He rubbed his chin, frowning slightly. "It will be me and two of my cousins."

"OK." I put away my netbook and took out my notes from the library. "What's the address?"

He looked at me. "You met one of my cousins last night."

So he had heard about that. "In the bosque, yeah."

"Come there."

"To the *bosque*?" I glanced around, making sure no one was listening, and lowered my voice anyway. "Caeran, are you living in the bosque?"

A smile tugged at one corner of his mouth. "We are used to camping."

I began to wonder if I'd made a mistake. The more I learned about Caeran, the weirder the whole thing sounded.

Maybe he was homeless after all. But he didn't set off my creepazoid alarm the way most homeless guys did.

"Can I ask you a question?"

Caeran glanced toward a loud gaggle of kids coming down the hall. "Shall we walk?"

"Sure, OK. Let's get that coffee, if you're still interested."

We hit the espresso stand—latté for me and hot tea for Caeran—and went outside. It was heading for six o'clock, and the sun was starting to set. Air was cooling down already. We strolled back past the library toward the pond, sipping our drinks, not talking until we stopped at a bench under some trees.

Sparrows swarmed toward us, then hopped away into the bushes when they saw we didn't have any food. We sat down and looked out at the pond, where the ducks were lazing around by the banks, stuffed full of bread crumbs and popcorn.

"So...what's the rush to get to Guadalupita? I bet you didn't even know about the place until this afternoon."

I held my breath, hoping he wouldn't be annoyed by my nosiness. Though he didn't answer right away, he showed no sign of anger.

"One of my cousins is ill." He glanced at me. "Not contagious, but we cannot take her to a hospital."

"Why not?"

He was silent, frowning at the paper cup in his hands.

"No ID?" I said softly. "The University hospital will admit her, even without it. They have a budget for charity cases—"

"That is not the issue." He turned the cup in his hands. "The...healer...in Guadalupita knows what to do for her."

"What, is he some kind of curandero? We have those here, too."

"Not just any healer will do. He has the skills to help her."

My turn to frown. I watched him, trying to figure it all out. A money issue? Religion? Too many weirdnesses, too many possibilities. I was trying too hard to guess, and when it came right down to it, this was none of my business.

"OK. So, I pick you up at the bosque. But I can't drive my car in there."

"There is a place—a turning of the street—"

"By the entrance to the Nature Center? That'll work. If I don't see you I'll park at the Center."

"We will be there."

"It'll probably be close to noon by the time I get down there."

Caeran nodded. "We will be waiting."

"OK."

I stared at him, not wanting to leave. He was looking at the pond, but after a minute he turned to me with a smile that melted my heart.

"I am grateful for your help, Len."

"Sure. Glad to. I, uh—I'm sorry your cousin is ill."

He just smiled. I could have gazed at that forever. His face, so beautifully sculpted—not soft, but just right in all its angles. No heaviness, only classical perfection.

I think, in that moment, I would have done absolutely anything he asked.

Fortunately for me, he was apparently a gentleman. He stood up and shouldered his pack. Hiding my disappointment, I did likewise.

"So, see you tomorrow." I stuck out my hand.

He took it and raised it to his lips. The brush of that soft warmth on the back of my hand sent a rush straight down to my toes.

"Tomorrow." Still smiling, he turned and walked away.

I watched him skirt the pond, heading for University and the bus stop, no doubt. With a small groan I sat down again.

I could have offered him a ride. Why did I always think of these things when it was too late?

My fingers touched the back of my hand where he'd kissed me. Still tingled.

I sat there a long while, sipping my tepid latté, thinking back over everything that had happened that afternoon. The healer in Guadalupita was just plain bizarre. How had Caeran been so sure he would find someone there, based on the mention in that book? After probably two hundred years, to find someone with the same name, who was also a curandero...it seemed so weird.

I could rationalize it, sort of. That kind of tradition was often passed down in a family, and small towns in New Mexico didn't change much through the years.

But man. Caeran had been really lucky to find the guy he wanted, just like that.

Of course, it might not have been as easy as it looked. He'd had that whole list from the day before. Maybe he'd found a phone book, or gone to the public library or something, and gone through that list without finding anything. Maybe.

Guessing too hard again.

I got up and walked to my dorm. Spent the night picking away at my homework, with absolutely no enthusiasm. Went to bed and couldn't sleep. I lay there thinking about Caeran until exhaustion finally took me out.

= 3 =

I was late to my physics class. My least favorite course; the professor was awful. He mumbled and meandered in his lectures, and responded to questions with unconcealed impatience. Consequently, I wasn't doing great in the class. I almost decided to ditch, except that that would leave me killing time until I went to meet Caeran.

I had my netbook open, ostensibly taking notes, but I soon drifted to looking over the map I had downloaded and saved the night before. There were two possible routes to Guadalupita, one through Santa Fe and winding through the mountains on state highways, the other on I-25, branching off toward Mora at Las Vegas. I decided to take I-25, though the other way was probably a prettier drive. Better to get Caeran's sick cousin to her curandero as fast as possible.

I was out of my seat the minute class let out. Hustled back to my dorm, grabbed a sweater in case it was cold up north, and jumped in the car. Bought gas, granola bars and a six-pack of bottled water, then indulged in a junk burger and fries on my way down to the Nature Center. Nerves.

Caeran was there, leaning against the fence by the entrance to the bike path, reading a book. I didn't see anyone else. I pulled the car around and stopped by the curb.

He looked up, then turned toward the bike path and called something I couldn't make out. Another guy came out of the path, carrying a girl wrapped in a dusty-green cloak. It took me a second to realize he was Caeran's look-alike, the one I'd met before. Not so surly today; he glanced at me, looking kind of anxious. I went around and opened the door to the Saturn's back seat, then watched him tenderly place the girl in the car. He turned to me.

"Thank you."

Caeran joined us. "Len, this is Nathrin, and that is our cousin, Mirali."

Weird names. I'd have to ask what language they were from. Scandinavian, maybe?

I nodded to Nathrin. "We've met, I think."

"Yes. Forgive my unfriendliness, then. It was my duty to guard our camp."

I waved a hand in dismissal, then glanced at Mirali. Nathrin had lain her along the back seat. She looked a lot like him and Caeran—the family resemblance was obvious. Same hair, same beautiful features, though her face was a little softer and her chin more pointed. Her eyes were closed; she didn't look obviously sick, but she didn't look happy either.

"She'll have to sit up and fasten her seat belt, I'm afraid. It's the law. I've got a blanket she could use for a pillow."

Nathrin got Mirali settled while I dug the blanket out of my junk-filled trunk. Good thing they hadn't brought any luggage. The guys each had a pack, that was it. I put my own pack in the trunk and shoved my wallet in the pocket of my jeans. Tucked the blanket behind Mirali's head and buckled her in, then got in the driver's seat. Nathrin sat in the back with her, and Caeran took shotgun.

"Buckle in, everybody. We don't want to get a ticket."

I fastened my own seat belt, then helped Caeran with his. I watched in the mirror while Nathrin fumbled with his belt for a moment, then got it fastened.

"Anybody need anything before we head out? Food, bathroom?"

"No," Caeran said. "Thank you."

"OK, then. Guadalupita, here we come."

I drove north on Rio Grande, taking the scenic route through the valley to Alameda. Nobody talked. Glancing in the rearview, I saw Nathrin's attention fixed on Mirali. Maybe they were a couple.

Caeran was watching the scenery, golden cottonwoods along most of the way. I realized I had deluded myself—I wasn't going to have any deep conversations with him, not with the other two in the car.

Still, I was with him, side by side, close enough to touch. That was worth it, right? And I was doing him a favor, so maybe he'd be grateful.

Maybe I was nuts.

Well, it was a beautiful day for a drive. Couldn't beat that. We'd gas up in Las Vegas, take a break at the raspberry farm in Mora.

I glanced in the mirror. Breaks would depend on how well Mirali weathered the ride.

I wondered what was wrong with her. Couldn't ask—that would definitely be too nosy. Caeran had assured me she wasn't contagious. Beyond that, it wasn't any of my business.

I pulled onto I-25 and accelerated. Caeran shifted in his seat and I glanced at him. He was staring ahead, looking tense. Not used to freeway driving, maybe. I turned on the CD, which held a disk I liked to listen to in traffic—mellow guitar music, to keep me from getting to angry with idiot drivers—and turned the volume to low.

"That OK?" I glanced in the mirror. Nathrin looked oblivious.

"Yes," Caeran said after a second.

I tried to think of a question that might start a conversation, but wouldn't offend. Came up with nothing for several long minutes. It was Caeran who spoke first.

"This is very pleasant music."

"Oh, thanks! It's an Australian guitarist. I really love his stuff."

"It reminds me of—our music, somewhat."

"Are you a musician?"

"Merely as a pastime."

"What do you play?"

"A flute."

"Classical?"

He glanced at me and I felt a whisper of the tingle his

intense look always gave me. "Ancient. It is a style of reed flute created by our people."

"Oh, cool. I love folk instruments."

We lapsed into silence. Not wanting to lose the interaction, I blurted the first question I thought of.

"Did you bring your flute with you? I'd love to hear you play."

"Yes, I have it with me."

"If I'd known, I would've brought my guitar. I'm not that great, but I can play a few songs."

Caeran didn't say anything, but I felt his smile. I could guess what he was thinking: that he was glad I hadn't brought the guitar, glad he wouldn't have to listen to me trying to play and then say something polite and kind and completely false.

Caeran didn't like falsehoods, I'd gathered. He wasn't great at lying—it always seemed to make him uncomfortable. Even the little polite lies that most people uttered without thinking, like the customary phrases of greeting and farewell; conversational pit stops, places where everyone could breathe and regroup. The words might have no literal meaning, except that to Caeran they must have, or why would he keep stumbling over them?

The silence stretched. There was enough traffic on a Friday afternoon between Albuquerque and Santa Fe to keep me plenty busy. Though I wanted to talk more, I decided not to stress out about it. Better to get Zen and just enjoy the moment than to be anxious that it was less than perfect.

Caeran was apparently comfortable with not talking. Nathrin hadn't participated at all anyway; he was totally absorbed with Mirali. I kept an eye on them in the mirror, not that things changed much in the back seat. I didn't know if Mirali was asleep, or in pain, or what, but she never opened her eyes.

As we approached Santa Fe I asked again if anyone wanted to stop. Again, Caeran said no, so I stayed on I-25, bypassing the city and striking east through Glorieta Pass. I offered my guests water and granola bars; Caeran and Nathrin both accepted the water and turned down the munchies. Mirali was still out of it.

"Have you spent much time in these mountains?" Caeran asked when we were well into the pass.

"I used to go to summer camp up in the Pecos." I gestured north, toward the mass of the Sangre de Cristo Mountains. "It's beautiful country."

"Are there many people there?"

"The towns are pretty tiny, but there are a lot of cabins, especially along the river. People like to fish the Pecos in the summer, and there's hiking and hunting. There's a huge wilderness area. I guess you'd say it's sparsely populated, but there are lots more visitors than residents."

"Ah."

"Forget about using your cell phone up there, though. Oh —you don't have one. Never mind."

Caeran smiled again, appreciating the joke, however lame. I liked him a lot in that moment. He was generous.

By the time we got to Las Vegas I needed a pit stop. I pulled into a gas station and hustled in to use the bathroom, then came out to pump gas. To my surprise, Caeran was already filling the tank.

"Hey, you didn't have to do that!"

He shot me an inquiring look. "You suggested we buy the gas."

"Well, yeah, but you don't have to pump it."

"I don't mind."

"Well, thanks. Need anything from the store?"

He shook his head. I looked in the back seat window and saw Nathrin holding Mirali's hand. Her eyes were open, so I opened the door.

"Hi. How are you feeling?"

She gave me a startled deer look. Nathrin answered for her. "She is somewhat tired."

"I bet. Traveling's no fun when you're sick. You could use the restroom while we're stopped, if you need to."

They exchanged a look. I backed out and gently closed the door, leaving them to talk it over. As I straightened I noticed Caeran watching me with the intense look that was becoming familiar. It still made my gut clench, and I couldn't look away from his eyes. He looked like he was about to say something, then Nathrin's door opened and he got out, helping Mirali out of the car.

When I turned back to Caeran, he was putting away the gas pump. Moment lost.

I followed the sweethearts into the store. I was restless and craving salt, so I picked out some chips and a soda. Very naughty, especially after the junk burger for lunch. I'd have to exercise more control over the weekend.

Suddenly it occurred to me that I had no idea where I'd be spending the night. I hadn't brought a change of clothes or a toothbrush or anything. Feeling stupid, I found an overpriced toothbrush and carried it to the counter with my snack. Through the windows I saw Caeran standing by the car, as if he was guarding it. I paid for my stuff, then walked to the back of the store where Nathrin was waiting outside the ladies' room.

"She OK?" I asked.

He nodded. I went away but stayed in the store, just in case Mirali might need help. I looked at the newspapers, then at the maps. When she came out of the restroom I headed back for the car.1

I got in and opened my chips, indulging in a mouthful of salty decadence. Caeran waited for the others before climbing in.

"Want some?" I offered him the chip bag.

He surprised me by reaching in and carefully extracting a potato chip. I watched him examine it before eating it. Sure looked like he'd never tried one before.

Who was this guy? What planet was he from?

And how could I get there?

Nathrin had Mirali settled again. She sank back into the corner of the seat, looking exhausted by her visit to the store. I gave her a smile but she'd already closed her eyes.

"Seat belts, everyone. Last call for food or drinks."

It took Nathrin a minute to get himself and Mirali buckled in. I picked out another CD—Deuter's *Land of Enchantment*, fairly soothing—and swapped it into the player.

We were making good time, but we were leaving the freeway now so the driving would be slower. Heading northwest toward Mora, we left urban civilization behind and started climbing into the hills and high meadows of north-central New Mexico. The mountains to the west loomed larger, patches of aspen showing in vast, golden splotches against the blue of the evergreens. The air was cooler here. I'd definitely want my sweater later.

Watching the countryside slide by, driving at a slower pace, I began to relax. Caeran listened intently to the music; flute music, and he'd said he played the flute. I waited about halfway through the disc, then on a song he seemed less interested in, I posed a quiet question.

"Do you know if this curandero is planning to put all of us up?"

Caeran looked at me, wearing the frown that meant he was confused. I rephrased.

"If there's no place for us to stay in Guadalupita, we might have to go back to Las Vegas. No problem, we should be able to get rooms."

He nodded, apparently trusting me. That gave me a good feeling but it also made me want to laugh.

We reached Mora and I glanced in the mirror. Nathrin was watching Mirali, who was conked out again.

"Anyone like raspberries? There's a farm we could stop at, if we need a break."

Nathrin didn't respond. Caeran answered after a pause.

"Perhaps we should continue. How much farther is it?"

"Probably about half an hour. I brought a map, but it's in my pack in the trunk. Heck, I need to stop and get it out anyway. I don't know the number of the highway we're looking for."

I pulled over at the raspberry place and hopped out. Raspberry picking season was over or I'd have been more tempted to linger. As it was, I was good and didn't even step into the store, just got the map and came back.

I showed the map to Caeran. "Here's the road we need—434. Did we pass a sign that said that?"

"I did not notice."

I handed him the map and started the car. We drove around a bit and found the road (Mora's a pretty tiny town, though bigger than where we were headed.)

The sun was dipping toward the mountains. Sunset would be earlier because of them. I felt anxious, which was strange. Maybe the uncertainty of what would happen when we reached our destination was bothering me. Or maybe I was worried my adventure with Caeran would end before it had really begun.

"Hey Caeran?" I kept my voice low, glancing at him for his reactions.

"Yes?"

"Do you date much?"

"Date?" Frowning.

"Are you seeing someone. You know, a girlfriend?"

He was silent for a moment. "Are you asking if I have a lover?"

"Um—well, I was trying to be more subtle than that, but I guess yeah."

"I do not."

"Oh."

I could feel my face burning. I was such a klutz! I tried to think of something else to talk about. Caeran didn't help, he just sat there brooding. I'd been too nosy, damn it.

"So, how about them Dukes?" I muttered to myself.

"Pardon?"

"Nothing. Stupid joke."

"You know dukes?"

"It was a baseball team. In Albuquerque. They're gone,

though—they went up to Portland and turned into the Beavers. We've got the Isotopes now."

That shut Caeran up good, not that it had been my intention. I couldn't tell whether he was offended or just hopelessly confused, and I didn't want to make it worse so I shut up too. We arrived at Guadalupita in silence.

"Town"—even "village"— was a generous description. It would have been nothing more than a handful of ranches if it hadn't been for the post office. One house, right on the road, looked like it used to be a store.

The bar looked like it had been a house, up until, say, day before yesterday. Old adobe, the sort of old farmhouse that had started as one room and had more added on over time. The tin roof sported patches of rust. Black-on-white cardboard sign in the dusty window: "Open."

Two pickups were parked in the driveway. I stopped the Saturn on the shoulder of the road, turned the engine off, and looked at Caeran.

"I think this is where we ask for directions."

He looked at the building, doubt in his face.

"Shall I come in with you?"

He nodded, frowning, and got out. I joined him and walked up to the building, pulling open the ancient, blue screen door. The door behind it was painted blue also, which I actually took as a good sign. Someone had wanted to protect the house from evil spirits.

I glanced at Caeran as I opened the door, a silly thought fleeting through my mind that perhaps he wouldn't be able to enter. He proved that wrong right away, stepping through the door and looking around in silent wonder at the dim interior of the house.

A neon Budweiser sign on the wall behind the bar and a TV mounted high in one corner provided the majority of the light in the place. There were two tiny cafe tables—empty—and six tall, backless stools in front of the bar. Three of them were occupied by two men and an overweight woman, all Hispanic. They stared at Caeran in belligerent silence. I got a glance or two, but apparently I was normal enough to dismiss. Caeran was hard to ignore.

The bartender was a bleached blonde chica with hoop earrings and long, red nails. She looked at Caeran with more curiosity than animosity, then after a minute turned to me and raised an eyebrow.

I put on a smile I didn't feel as I stepped up to the bar. This was going to take some diplomacy.

"I'll have a Bud," I said, glancing at the single tap mounted on the bar.

She snapped her gum once, then pulled a glass out of a cooler set into her counter and filled it. "What about your friend?"

"He'll have a Bud, too."

I paid for both beers, then picked mine up and sipped it, trying to look like I enjoyed it. My taste runs more to ambers and dark beers. I guess I'm a snob, but to me Bud tastes like sour water.

I caught Caeran's eye and summoned him to join me with a nod. He took the stool on my left, as far as possible from the locals. The bartender put his beer in front of him.

"You look like someone I know."

Caeran gave her a startled glance, then looked at me as if seeking help. I nodded and tilted my head toward her. Caeran turned back to her.

"Would his name be Madera?" His voice was rough. He was nervous.

"Yeah. You know him?"

"We came here to ask his help."

"Oh." She looked at me, as if trying to figure out what my problem could be. "He's very good."

"Can you direct us to his place?" I said, impatient to get on with it.

Her eyes narrowed a little. "What's your name?"

"Caeran," said my companion. "I called him yesterday, and

he told me to ask here for directions."

"Hang on."

She walked over to the far corner of the bar and consulted a spiral notebook next to a phone. The people at the bar exchanged a few words in Spanish. I detected no outright obscenities, but couldn't catch the gist. Caeran shifted slightly on his stool, though. I glanced at him, but his face was neutral.

"OK." The bartender came back and handed Caeran a business card with an address scrawled on the back. "Go north eight miles and turn left at the carved owl. You can't miss it."

"Thank you."

Caeran accepted the note with one of his quaint little bows, then slid off his stool. He hadn't touched his beer. I took a gallant swig of mine—dinner—and followed him out, leaving a tip on the bar.

Just in the time we'd been in there, the sun had set. There was already a nip in the air. I thought about getting out my sweater, then decided to wait until we got to Madera's place.

"Can't miss it" turned out to be a slight exaggeration. I was looking for a number or a mailbox, but there was only a gap in the fence, and I would, too, have missed it if Caeran hadn't pointed it out. The carved owl sitting on a fence post looked like a hawk to me at first glance. I had assumed it was alive, watching for supper to run by.

The driveway was half a mile of dusty, rutted road. I took it slowly, trying not to jostle Mirali too much, but I couldn't keep her from feeling some of the bumps. Finally a house came into view. More old, sprawling adobe. This one sprawled more than usual; it was a pretty big place, and had probably housed a big ranch family at one time. I wondered if Madera had a family.

The house faced east, and a deep portal ran its length, to provide shade from the fierce morning sun. An antique-looking amber glass porch light shone beside a large zaguan door—big enough for a wagon to roll through—with a smaller door set into it. Beyond the house, Venus hung above the mountains like a jewel in the velvet blue evening.

I parked near the door and shut off the engine, then hurried around to the trunk to grab my sweater and my pack. Nathrin and Caeran helped Mirali out of the car. She looked pale, and after she took a couple of shaky steps, Nathrin swept her up into his arms and carried her to the door.

No doorbell, unless you counted the giant brass bell hanging on the wall nearby. Caeran pounded on the door instead. I stood behind them all, feeling superfluous.

I was expecting the curandero to be Hispanic. Silly me. When he opened the smaller door within the zaguan gate I nearly gasped.

He was tall and lean, with fine bones and an unconscious grace. Sure, his hair was black and his skin was a shade more tanned, but he could have been a cousin to Caeran and his friends.

His gaze went to Mirali and he said something in a flowing language I didn't recognize. Caeran stepped forward.

"Señor de Madera?"

The healer stopped talking and looked up at Caeran, suddenly guarded. His gaze flicked to me for an instant, then returned to Caeran.

"Yes."

"May we come in?"

He looked at me again, a little longer, as if trying to decide if I was dangerous. His eyes were a piercing blue, and for a second I felt a shadow of familiar dizziness.

"Of course. One moment."

He stepped back inside the house, and some clunking noises followed, then the zaguan gate swung back. Good thing, because Nathrin would have had a tough time squeezing through the smaller door with Mirali.

The space we entered was wide and filled with plants, surprisingly humid. Evening sunlight streamed through windows to the west, looking out on an enclosed courtyard, a *plazuela*, standard hacienda style. The curandero led us through a doorway on the right, into a long room that looked like it served as both living room and dining room.

We left the humidity behind; here it was dry and a bit cool, though a fire was burning in a kiva fireplace in one corner. The furniture was all carved wood, beautifully made with designs that were traditional, but the carver had given them a twist. Images were more flowing than static, if that was possible in carved wood. Edges were softened, polished smooth.

Navajo blankets covered the seats of chairs and benches, and hung on the walls. The room smelled of cedar and sage, and in one corner I saw some bundles of herbs hanging from the ceiling to dry. I wanted to gravitate toward the fire, but tagged along after Caeran and the others instead.

"Bring her in here."

Nathrin followed the curandero through another doorway at the far end of the room. Caeran paused, giving me an uncertain glance.

"I'll wait," I said, waving him on.

He smiled briefly at me, enough to double my pulse, then went through the door. I drifted over to the fireplace and sat down on the banco, warming my hands and staring into the little cave full of flames.

This was my chance to regret my impulsiveness, and also my lack of planning. I should have packed a bag. I should have brought a coat. I should have made *some* kind of plan for what to do after I'd delivered Caeran and his friends here. How long would they need to stay, and would they expect me to hang around and take them back to Albuquerque?

What a klutz I was, and all because I was nutty on a total stranger. I was lucky something bad hadn't happened.

I drew a long breath and let it out slowly. It was worth it, I guessed. Being around Caeran, however unromantic the circumstances, was worth it. I knew I would never forget this trip.

I sighed. "Ah, Caeran."

Footsteps startled me and I looked up to see Caeran returning to the room, gently pulling the door closed behind him. I felt my cheeks go red, though he couldn't have heard me. Could he?

He stood by the door for a moment, watching me. Hesitating. At least I'd gotten to know him well enough to tell.

I smiled and gave a little shrug. "Warmer by the fire. Come on over."

He smiled back and joined me, sitting on the opposite side of the fireplace. For a minute he watched the flames, and I watched the firelight dance on his face and in his hair. It made his eyes gleam like liquid gold.

"Thank you, Len, for bringing us here," he said softly, still gazing at the fire.

"My pleasure."

"I would like to repay you—"

"You bought the gas. That's fine."

"This has taken much of your time, though."

I shrugged. "It's the weekend. Pretty drive, good company. What more could I ask?"

Silence hung between us, and I suddenly suspected he knew what more I wanted. Embarrassed, I picked up a log from the wood bin and added it to the fire.

"How's Mirali?"

Caeran glanced toward the door. "The healer is—beginning to work with her. It will take a while."

I nodded. "Hope he can help her."

"I am sure he can." Caeran leaned his elbows on his knees and laced his fingers. "He has offered us beds for the night."

"Oh, good. Wish we'd thought to stop for groceries."

"He can feed us. Are you hungry now?"

I shrugged, though in fact I was. I figured the curandero was busy.

"He said there is a stew in the kitchen, and that we might help ourselves," Caeran added.

"Oh, really?" I tried to sound casual. "You want to go get some?"

He looked at me briefly, then smiled as if amused. "Yes.

The kitchen is across the way."

We headed out to the plant room and through the opposite door. The kitchen was long and narrow, but cheerful. Blue tile ran around the edges of the counters, and the tile backsplashes were painted with aspen leaves. A small table and two chairs—obviously made by the same artist who had carved all the rest of the furniture I'd seen—sat by the window.

The place smelled like heaven in the form of green chile stew. I headed for the stove, an antique gas model, probably running propane out here.

A large cast iron pot was simmering on a back burner. I lifted the lid and inhaled the steam fragrant of chile and onions, and my mouth started watering.

Caeran found a couple of bowls and some spoons. A search through the drawers produced a ladle, and we dished up servings of steaming heaven.

I noticed a pottery dish that looked like a tortilla warmer, and peeked inside. Yes, tortillas, and they felt like homemade. I pulled out one for each of us and joined Caeran at the table.

I glanced out the window. It had fallen dark by now, and the stars were starting to come out. I promised myself I'd go outside and look at them before crashing, even if I froze my ass off. In Albuquerque only the brightest handful of stars and planets were visible, but out here there was no light pollution to interfere. The Milky Way would be spectacular.

A couple of bites into the stew, Caeran stopped eating, looking alarmed. He sat blinking, eyes watering, almost as if he was about to have trouble breathing.

I got up and went to the fridge. The curandero had milk, fortunately. I poured a glass and brought it back to Caeran.

"This'll help."

"Ah—thank you," he said in a strangled voice.

He drank half the glass. I watched him for a second and decided that some tissue would be useful. Unfortunately, I didn't see any in the kitchen. There was a small stack of cloth napkins on the counter, though. I grabbed one for me and two for Caeran. By that time his eyes were streaming.

"Not used to hot chile, eh?"

He shook his head. "It tastes good," he said, mopping his eyes.

I smiled. Little did he know, he was on the verge of an addiction. Most of New Mexico's population would suffer withdrawals without regular doses of chile.

Caeran sipped his milk and took tiny, cautious bites of stew while I gobbled my serving. I mopped my bowl with the last of my tortilla and thought seriously about going back for seconds. With a momentous effort of will I refrained, and poured myself a glass of water instead.

"More milk?"

"No, thank you."

Caeran was tearing his tortilla into bite-sized pieces and dipping them in his stew. I sat down across from him again, watching him eat.

"Maybe we should take some to Nathrin," I suggested.

"Not now. He is helping the healer."

"Oh." With a fingertip, I traced the damp circle my glass had left on the table. "Can I ask you a question?"

He froze for a second, then ate another scrap of tortilla and nodded. Took a bite of stew and a sip of milk, all without looking at me.

"How did you know you would find this healer here from reading a two-hundred year old diary?"

Caeran finished chewing a bite of tortilla and swallowed. I waited.

"It would be better if I didn't explain."

I stared at him, dissatisfied. He still wouldn't meet my gaze.

"Family secrets?"

That made him look at me, and I thought I saw a tinge of guilt in his eyes. He sighed, and his brows drew together in a frown.

"I am sorry, Len. If it were just me..."

"Sure, I understand. I'm really not trying to pry into your business. It's just that it's—well, pretty remarkable. I mean, that curandero looks like he could be your cousin."

Caeran gave a wistful smile. "He is, in a way."

"But you didn't have his address."

"No."

End of subject, apparently. I took a swallow of water. There was an ache under my ribcage, and it had to do with frustration. Caeran just wasn't going to let me get close. If he couldn't confide in me about his library research, he probably wasn't going to share any deeper secrets.

Well, not like I hadn't expected it. Hope and expectation are two different things.

Suddenly unable to sit still, I got up and carried my dishes to the sink. Washed the bowl and spoon and set them in the wooden dish rack to dry, then refilled my water glass. I tidied as I drank it, washing the ladle and wiping up a couple of drops of stew that had hit the counter. When there was no more busy-work I chugged the rest of my water and washed the glass. It was a heavy, Mexican glass. Señor de Madera favored traditional styles.

Madera. It clicked in my memory all of a sudden. Madera meant "wood." The last name Caeran had given me was "Woods."

Cousins, eh?

It didn't fit, though. If they'd been in touch he wouldn't have needed the library. There was something he wasn't telling me.

I put the glass in the rack, carefully because I was angry. I turned to head for the door and saw Caeran watching me, his face showing distress that I couldn't quite pinpoint—guilt, or grief.

Or indigestion.

I shoved my damp hands in my pockets.

"Think I'll go outside and look at the stars. Do you need anything from the car?"

He shook his head. Part of me wanted to smooth the frown off his forehead. Instead I went out.

The air was sharp, the sky magnificent. I walked away from the house, out into an open field knee-high in wild grass. The dusty-sweet smell of old alfalfa told me it had once been a working field, but it hadn't been harvested in a long while.

Hugging myself in my inadequate sweater, I looked up at the sky. The Milky Way was a pale swath across the void, bejeweled with pricks of brightness. A single cricket mourned for warmer evenings and company. Beyond that, the night was silent. No machines making noise anywhere nearby. No cars, no generators. No planes. Blissful quiet.

Orion was rising, a sign of the coming winter. I watched, wanting to see his belt come above the horizon, knowing I'd wimp out and run for Señor Madera's cozy fireplace before that happened. As I stared at the hunter's shoulder, a meteor streaked upward, leaving a trail of sparks. I leaned back to watch it, nearly losing my balance. A warm hand steadied my back.

I yelped, stumbling away. My heart thundered.

"Forgive me." Caeran's voice. "I thought you might fall."

"I still might. God, you startled me! Make some noise next time, or something!"

"I am sorry."

In the darkness, I couldn't see his face. I looked back at the sky.

Falling star. I was supposed to make a wish. I closed my eyes and imagined Caeran's arms around me. Weird, when he was standing right there, and my feelings were still a conflicting jumble of resentment and desire. I didn't care; my self-indulgence wouldn't hurt him. He'd never know.

"This is glorious," he said. "We did not see this many stars in..."

"Where you came from."

"Europe," he said softly. "We were living in Europe."

"'Were?' You're not going back?"

"No."

A tingle started in my shoulders and flowed down my arms. Did he mean they planned to live in New Mexico?

I didn't voice the question. Wasn't sure I'd be able to stand the answer.

It occurred to me to quip that if he wanted to live in the bosque he should buy land, but I figured the joke would fall flat. Caeran had the literal thought patterns of a foreigner.

I felt...raw. I'd been teasing myself with wanting Caeran, knowing that I couldn't have him; he was too different, too distant. Then out of the blue, this announcement that he was here to stay. Thinking about it made me giddy, almost sick. I hadn't felt like this since my last hopeless high school crush.

I stared at the sky, wondering what the hell I'd done to myself. I felt so adrift, I could almost imagine floating off the planet, up toward those incredibly beautiful and cruel, cold stars. As I zoned on the void, a scatter of meteors—at least a dozen—fell like sudden tears.

"Oh!" Without thought, I turned to Caeran. "Did you see?"

"Yes. Beautiful."

I smiled, even though it was dark, and turned back to watch the sky, as happy as I had been confused a moment earlier. That didn't make any sense, I knew, but I'd worry about it later. This was a moment of magic.

I shivered, but I didn't want to go back inside. I wanted to stay here with Caeran a heartbeat away and stars streaking across the sky.

A swish and tiny crunch of dry grass told me Caeran was moving closer. I held still, scarcely daring to breathe. Another shiver went through me.

"You are cold."

I jumped at his voice, though he'd barely spoken above a whisper. He was so near that the hairs on my skin stood up.

"I-I'm OK." Shivering more.

"This will help."

Something thin and soft draped around me. At first I

thought it was a blanket, but Caeran twitched it into place along my shoulders and I realized it was a cape—a long one, brushing the ground. With it came a smell—his smell—that lit a fire in my belly.

He wrapped the cape around me and I was instantly warmer. His arms lingered, holding the fabric in place. What was left of my annoyance faded.

"Thank you," I whispered.

His arms tightened and pulled me back against him. My eyes fell closed; suddenly shooting stars were pale compared to what was going on in my heart.

"Len."

"Yes?"

His cheek brushed against my hair. I felt dizzy and opened my eyes, trying to steady myself. Darkness and stars.

"I should not be doing this," he murmured.

"Why not? I like it."

"I like it too."

I turned my head toward his, trying to rub against that cheek. I heard him draw a sharp breath, then he began to kiss my face, moving toward my mouth.

I turned in his arms, heart thundering. The cape slid from my shoulders; he caught it and wrapped it around us both, then kissed me.

Sweet, long, lingering kiss. I was floating. I cared about nothing but the feel of him, the taste of him. He could have whatever he wanted from me.

He stopped abruptly, pulling back, though the cape swathed around us kept him from moving far.

"What?" I said.

"You don't mean that."

"Mean what?"

"What you were you thinking."

"H-how do you know what I'm thinking?"

"Ah...you think pretty loud."

Was he joking? I couldn't see his face. The porch light was

behind him, and even though it was a way off, it blinded me.

"OK, then." *Kiss me again.*

"Len—"

Kiss me now.

His hand cupped my face, then he bent toward me. I stopped thinking straight, or much at all. He tasted better than he looked, if that was possible.

"Caeran!"

We startled apart like guilty teens. Caeran slid out of the cape and wrapped it around me, leaving me warm and lonely.

Nathrin stood on the porch of the house, backlit by the amber light, but I had recognized his voice. Caeran spoke in a husky whisper.

"We should go in."

He started toward the house. I followed, too confused to string a sentence together, angry with Nathrin—what the hell business was it of his?—and deeply, deeply frustrated. I had a fleeting thought of just climbing in the car and heading back to Las Vegas, but my pack was in the house, and anyway I wasn't going anywhere. Not until Caeran and I finished the wordless discussion we'd begun.

Nathrin fell in beside Caeran and muttered something I couldn't distinguish. They went into the house and I followed, kicking the door shut behind me. Nathrin glanced at me, but said nothing as he pulled Caeran into the living room.

Madera was there, standing by the fireplace. I noticed that his black hair was long, almost to his waist. Hadn't realized it before because it was tied back in a ponytail. At a glance he looked native, maybe with some Cherokee blood to account for the height. But the planes of his face were the same as Caeran's. Definitely some DNA in common there.

He looked up at me and smiled slightly. "Thank you for your patience. I have a room where you may spend the night."

He gestured toward the doorway at the other end of the living room. I glanced at Caeran but he wasn't looking at me. Nathrin was watching, though.

There was nothing for me to do but pick up my pack and follow Madera.

The door opened into a hall that ran west along a wing of the building. The place really was a hacienda, built in a square around the open courtyard in the middle. The hallway had probably been open to the outdoors once, but the side facing the courtyard had been enclosed with a wall of windows. I wondered how old the house was; the adobe was thick and irregular, and the doorways of the rooms didn't all look the same.

A couple of the doors we passed were closed, and guessed Mirali was probably behind one of them. Thought about inquiring after her, then decided not to bug the healer.

"Here you may rest," he said, gesturing to an open doorway.

I looked into a tiny bedroom, softly lit by a squat lamp on a bedside table. It looked cozy, but lonely.

"Thanks."

"You had something to eat?"

"Yes. Great stew. Thank you."1

He nodded, smiling. "Rest well, then."

"Yeah. Good night."

I went in the room and closed the door, feeling like I'd been herded. Sat on the bed and noticed I still had Caeran's cape wrapped around me. It was the deep blue of early evening, I saw by the bedside lamp. I buried my nose in the collar and inhaled, reveling in the smell of him.

His cousin, Nathrin, apparently disapproved of me. Madera seemed to want to keep us apart too, or maybe he was just being a proper host, officially giving me my own room but willing, in the spirit of Miss Manners, to ignore nocturnal comings and goings in the hall.

There would be some of that, if I had anything to say about it. I'd have to find Caeran, though, and I should probably wait a bit. He might be talking with his friends.

I collapsed backward onto the bed with a sigh. This whole

day had been weird. Too many mysteries, and I was too tired to puzzle them out. Instead I indulged in reliving Caeran's kisses.

I woke up cold, with my bladder insisting on relief. Sat up stiffly and looked around. My room had one door besides the front one, obviously a closet. I dug in my pack for the toothbrush I'd bought, then went out into the hall.

Had we passed a bathroom on the way to my room? I retraced my steps, looking at each door. One stood open to a dark room smaller than my own. I reached in and fumbled for a light switch, then noticed a glint of metal—the weight at the end of an old-fashioned string pull hanging from a ceiling light.

I pulled it, lighting up the welcome sights of a bathroom. Bingo.

A few minutes later, much more comfortable, I returned to my room and dug in my pack for my cell phone to check the time. It was almost eleven, and there was no signal so I turned the phone off so it wouldn't run the battery down trying to roam. I'd forgotten to bring the charger, of course.

I poked around in the pack some more and turned up a couple of condoms I'd picked up at the Student Health Center at the beginning of the semester. Stuffed one in the back pocket of my jeans, and decided to go in search of a glass of water and whatever else I might find.

The living room was dark, though by the time I got there my eyes had adjusted well enough that the faint starlight coming through the windows was enough to keep me from tripping. I went through to the entryway and on to the kitchen, also starlit through windows. Señor Madera didn't seem to believe in curtains, though to be fair there wasn't much need for them out here in the middle of nowhere.

The dish drain was empty. I got out a glass and filled it with water, then walked over to the table where I'd sat with Caeran.

I missed him. It was like an ache, and I knew that probably wasn't healthy, but it was how I felt. Short of going down the hall knocking on doors, though, I didn't know how to find him.

Had he really read my mind?

I shivered, not just from the chill of the night or the cold water I'd drunk. Things Caeran wasn't telling me—things they were all hiding from me—made me worry. It wasn't my imagination; I was sure of that. Too many weird things had happened. Who were these people, anyway?

I sat down and took a long swig of water. I could walk away. Couldn't I?

No. I didn't want to. I closed my eyes.

Caeran. I want you.

I listened, and only then noticed how silent the kitchen was. A tiny hum from the refrigerator, that was it.

Caeran, come and find me. Please.

I felt foolish. Spent a few minutes slowly drinking the rest of my water and realizing Caeran wasn't going to rush to my side.

Finally I got up and refilled my glass. Before going back to my room, I decided to see what else was in this wing of the hacienda. I went to the far end of the kitchen and opened the door on the west wall.

A hallway, its courtyard side a wall of windows, just like the other wing. This looked more utilitarian, though. Fewer ornaments. An open doorway proved to be a laundry room. Other rooms had closed doors. No lights showing anywhere.

I opened the first door and peeked in. A pantry. Lots of pottery jars and baskets. Not a single tin can—it looked like a museum display. Apparently Madera was one of those back-to-nature, do-it-all-yourself dudes, although the electricity had to come from somewhere.

I wandered on down the hall until I reached a door in the glass wall. I opened it, figuring it would be shorter to cross the courtyard to my room than to go back around through the kitchen and living room. It was bitter cold outside and I instantly wished for Caeran's cape, which I'd left in my room.

The courtyard was beautiful, with vines climbing up the pillars between the windows, beds of greenery, and flagstone pathways. Patio furniture sat in the shadows beneath bare-branched trees that would be deliciously shady in summer.

A fountain stood in the courtyard's center—a classic round, three-tiered number, ornamented with Mexican tile—very traditional. The water was flowing, though the temperature had to be below freezing. Maybe Señor Madera had a heater in the fountain. Or maybe it was magic.

I shook my head. Getting too punchy. Sleep would restore my perspective.

I started across the courtyard toward my room, but the door on that side opened before I got to it. For an instant my heart leapt at the thought that Caeran had come to me after all, but it wasn't Caeran. It was Mirali.

She looked pale and drawn, though that could be from the starlight. She leaned out, clinging to the open door with one hand. She wore the clothes she'd had on all day: cotton pants and a woven jacket. Not warm enough for this time of night, up here at seven-thousand-whatever feet.

She frowned at me and said something that sounded like Martian. I had no clue at all what any of it meant.

"Honey, you should get back inside," I said. "It's too cold out here."

She talked more gobbledegook. I shifted from foot to foot, starting to shiver.

"Let's go in, OK? I bet Señor Madera wouldn't like it if he found you out here."

I started toward her, intending to gently guide her indoors. When I got close she shouted something and flung her arm out toward me.

The world went white, and I felt like I'd been slammed by a flying door.

= 4 =

I heard a crash, tinkle. My water glass, I realized as I stumbled backward, blinded. I bumped against a patio table, heard it scrape on the flagstone.

Someone was shouting—a man's voice. I was too busy trying not to fall down to pay attention. Realized I was going to lose the battle, and opted for sitting rather than collapsing. My knees were rubber. I made it to the ground, ungracefully but without major damage.

More shouting, more voices. I wondered vaguely what they were saying. Stars were flying around in front of my eyes. Meteors, I thought, and giggled.

The next instant, warm hands grasped my shoulders and a voice—familiar, comforting—spoke to me. I struggled to pay attention.

"—at me. Look at me, Len."

I managed to focus on Caeran's eyes. The meteors faded away.

His beautiful face was contorted with worry. "Can you stand up?"

Wanting to reassure him, I opened my mouth, but all that came out was a croak. He hauled me to my feet and let me lean on him.

"Come inside," he said, coaxing.

Great idea. I was all for it, but my legs wouldn't cooperate. Caeran tried to help me walk, but after a couple of wobbly steps he scooped me up in his arms and carried me inside.

Madera closed the courtyard door after us, looking grim. Mirali was nowhere in sight. Nathrin must have taken care of her.

Caeran carried me to my room and gently put me on the

bed. He sat next to me, smoothing my hair back from my face.

"I am so sorry, Len. So sorry."

"No," I croaked. I really could have used that glass of water.

He leaned closer, speaking softly. "She did not mean to hurt you."

I heard another voice, Madera's. Couldn't tell what he was saying. Might have been that foreign language. Caeran looked at him, then back at me. He squeezed my shoulder, stood up and walked away. Madera took his place.

The healer laid a hand on my brow and another on my breastbone, very impersonal, though gentle. His hands were incredibly warm—so warm I felt drowsy. Pleasant enough, but I wanted Caeran. I fought to stay awake, but the warmth and the shock I'd taken were too much. I slid under the rising blanket of darkness.

The next time I woke, it was morning. Sunlight slanted in past the partly-open door. I saw cotton-clad legs, someone sitting in a chair by the bed. Looked up hoping for Caeran, and was disappointed to find Madera's blue eyes watching me.

"Are you feeling better?"

"Dunno."

My throat was parched. I sat up carefully. My head swam a little but settled down after a second. I looked at the nightstand and saw, to my delight, a full glass of water. I gulped it down and gave a sigh of relief.

"Yes, better. Thank you."

He smiled. "You are welcome. There is bread and fruit in the kitchen if you are hungry."

"Sounds good." I eased my feet to the floor and bent down to put on my shoes, which someone must have removed for me. "Don't suppose you have any coffee?"

"No, but I could make tea."

"Tea's good."

I needed some caffeine. The format didn't matter so much.

Madera led the way through the courtyard to the kitchen,

pausing to hold the door open for me. Sunshine lit up the flagstones and glinted from the fountain. A rosebush I hadn't noticed had two cream-colored blooms on it, even this far north and this late in the fall. There was no sign of broken glass or disarranged furniture.

I followed Madera across to the kitchen, which was warm and smelled like fresh baking. My stomach instantly demanded to sample the product. While Madera filled a kettle, I hacked a slice from a still-warm loaf that was sitting on the table, smeared butter on it, and gobbled it down. It tasted fantastic. I cut another slice, trying a dab of some jam on it this time. Apricot. Heavenly.

Madera must not have spent the whole night watching me. Not if he'd baked bread.

Hah. My brilliant powers of deduction were still in order.

Of course, someone else could have baked the bread.

I glanced at the sink, where Madera was washing some pears. Two small plates in the dish drain. Madera's and Caeran's? Nathrin's and Mirali's?

What had happened last night, anyway? Being the one that got knocked on my ass, I felt like I had a right to know, but instinct kept me from asking Madera. I had a feeling he wasn't going to be forthcoming.

If anyone would explain, it would be Caeran. I looked out the window at the fountain, wishing he'd show up.

"Mirali will need to stay here for a few days."

I glanced at Madera but he had his back to me, standing at the counter slicing the pears. I picked up the bread knife and started on thirds.

"It was very kind of you to bring her and her friends all this way," he continued. "She asked me to tell you she is grateful."

"That so?"

Could have fooled me. She'd looked angry, last night.

"She—was quite ill. Is still quite ill. She knows she is fortunate to have had your help."

Madera brought a plate of sliced pears to the table and sat

across from me. I bit into a piece of pear and its sweet, juicy softness exploded in my awareness. Either my taste buds were hyperenthusiastic this morning, or I was hungrier than I'd thought.

"These are wonderful!" I helped myself to more.

Madera smiled slightly. "I will send some home with you."

I looked at him. Had that been a not-so-subtle hint? I chose to ignore it.

"Did you grow them?"

He nodded. "I have orchards to the west. Pears, apples, apricots—"

"So you made the jam, too?"

"Yes."

"Wow. And nobody's married you?"

He looked disconcerted. I picked up the last slice of pear and ate it, watching him. He returned my gaze thoughtfully. I had a feeling I was being studied.

The kettle started to whistle. Madera got up, breaking the stare-off. While he fixed my tea I had ample time to kick myself for the marriage comment. What if he was a widower?

"Your furniture's really beautiful," I said, trying to make up for it. "Was it all made by the same craftsman?"

"Yes."

"Same person who did the owl at your gate, right?"

"Yes."

"Well, whoever made it's really good. They could sell this stuff in Santa Fe for big bucks."

He put the lid on the teapot and turned to face me, leaning against the counter. A small, wry smile slid onto his face.

"Thank you."

I paused in the act of picking up bread crumbs with a fingertip. "*You* made the furniture?"

He dropped his gaze. "I have a lot of free time."

"I thought you were a curandero."

"Yes, but this community is small."

How could he afford this big place, then? I didn't voice the question. Maybe I'd guessed right, and he was selling his furniture in Santa Fe. Bottom line, it was none of my business. I didn't want to cross from chattiness into nosiness.

I looked out the window. "Your fountain is beautiful."

"Thank you."

"Don't tell me you made that, too."

He laughed. "No. I did the tile."

"It's lovely. Reminds me of Mexico."

"You have been to Mexico?"

"When I was little. I remember lots of flowers and fountains. Have you been?"

He hesitated, reminding me suddenly of Caeran. "A long time ago. Your tea should be ready."

He turned away to get out a cup for me, a slim, pottery piece with a gorgeous glaze in shades of green, and no handle. He set it before me along with a cream pitcher and honey jar, then poured tea from the pot.

All the pottery matched. Had he made it?

I decided not to ask. It was getting too weird.

I picked up the cup and blew on the hot tea, then took a sip, burning my tongue. To give it time to cool down, I added some honey and stirred it with the spoon Madera had provided, which looked like real silver.

"I will fetch you some pears."

He left, rather hastily I thought, through the west door. I turned over the spoon and peered at the back of the handle. Old maker's marks. They looked hand-incised, not stamped.

Old money? That might explain some things. I still felt like I didn't have the whole picture.

And he was fetching me pears, so it definitely had been a hint. He wanted me to leave.

OK, well I knew better than to outstay my welcome, but I was going to see Caeran before I went. That was all there was to it.

I realized I was frowning, clenching the spoon handle. I put it down and tried the tea again. It was the perfect temperature, and tasted better than any tea I remembered. The honey had added a fragrance of flowers.

Everything about these people seemed hyper-wonderful. It wasn't just my imagination.

I drank the tea and poured more. Stared out the window at the fountain, trying to decide what to say to Caeran.

Ask for an explanation of the whammy Mirali had laid on me. Ask if he had really read my mind.

Ask when I'd see him again.

I swallowed, thinking I probably wouldn't like the answer to that last one. But I'd ask it anyway. If he was going to push me away, I wanted to know why. The disapproval of his friends wasn't a good enough reason.

I finished my second cup of tea and poured a third, thinking that might bring me up to a cup of coffee's worth of caffeine. It sure was taking Madera a long time to fetch those pears.

The door to the entryway opened and Caeran stepped in. He was carrying his pack, and smiled when he saw me, lighting up the room like the rising sun.

"Good morning. You look much better."

"I feel better, thanks." A lot better, as of that moment.

"Are you feeling well enough to drive back to Albuquerque?"

"I think so."

"Good. Nathrin is staying with Mirali, so I will be your only passenger."

Be still my heart. I smiled and nodded, hoping my delight wasn't too obvious.

"Want some tea? Bread?"

"No, thank you. I ate earlier."

He sat across from me and set his pack on the floor. I watched him, mesmerized. He gazed back at me and I was absolutely certain of the affection in his eyes.

"Caeran—"

He shook his head and put a finger to his lips, glancing

toward the west door. A moment later Madera came through it, carrying a small, intricately woven basket filled with pears. He glanced at Caeran, then set the pears on the table beside me.

"For you."

"Thank you! Do you have a grocery bag I can put them in?"

"The basket is for you also. A gift of thanks."

I looked up at him. "Seems like I'm the one who owes you thanks, for your hospitality, and for helping me last night—"

"You owe me nothing." He picked up my empty plate and turned away.

Caeran spoke softly. "We are all grateful to you for bringing Mirali here."

His eyes got the intense look I was getting used to, and I had a feeling he didn't want me to say anything more. I finished my tea and put down the cup.

"I guess I'd better get my things."

Caeran nodded. When I stood up he rose also, and followed me to my room, carrying the pears. Nice to have him staying close for a change, but I wished we could talk.

It only took me a minute to collect my miscellany into my pack. I slung it over my shoulder and turned to the door, where Caeran waited. I had a million questions I wanted to ask him, but they could wait. We'd have the whole drive back to Albuquerque.

We walked along the hall to the living room. Mirali was behind one of the doors we passed, I was pretty sure. Looked like she and Nathrin weren't going to see us off. No big surprise.

Madera was waiting in the entryway. With the sun still in the east, the room was shaded and a bit chilly. I summoned a smile and offered to shake hands.

"It was nice meeting you. Thanks for putting me up, and for—well, for everything."

"You are welcome."

He nodded, but didn't shake my hand. I stuffed it in my back pocket, felt the condom still riding there, and blushed. To hide my reaction I started for the front door.

Caeran and Madera exchanged a few murmured words behind me. I opened the small door within the zaguan and stepped out onto the portal. Blinked at the bright sunlight bouncing up from the wooden floor. I wanted my shades, but they were in the car.

The door closed behind me. Caeran joined me, smiled briefly, and said, "We should go."

I glanced back at Madera's hacienda. Nothing super-extraordinary from this direction, just a big old sprawling adobe house. Full of secrets.

I headed to the car and put my pack in the back seat. Caeran did the same, and carefully set the pears in the footwell behind his seat. The car was warm from the morning sun, so I rolled down my window and turned on the fan.

"Can I ask you a question?"

A frown fleeted across Caeran's face. "Let's wait a while."

"OK."

I was willing to humor him for now. I started the car and headed out the long, rutted driveway.

The morning was gorgeous. Trees that I hadn't noticed on our arrival flanked the driveway at intervals, still wearing autumn colors, and the sky was an incredible shade of blue. The air was cool and deliciously clean, with just a hint of wood smoke. It would be depressing to go back to breathing city muck.

I drove through Guadalupita and all the way to Mora without talking. Caeran seemed content with the silence. I pulled over at the raspberry place.

"I'm going to get a bottle of water. Want anything?"

He shook his head. I went in the store, bought water and a jar of raspberry jam, and came out to find the car empty.

Panic hit me as I thought Caeran had ditched me, then I saw him wandering in a garden beyond an adobe wall. I remembered the garden from past visits—it was gorgeous in summer, a riot of color—though now most of the flowers were done for the year. I went through the gate and joined Caeran by a bed of rosemary. He was staring down at it, frowning slightly.

"You OK?"

"Yes. No."

"What's the matter?"

He closed his eyes, shaking his head. "Nothing that can be fixed. Are we leaving?"

"Yeah, I guess. Unless you want to talk."

His frown deepened and he stood absolutely still for a moment, then turned and headed back to the car. I followed him, put my jam in the back seat and got in the driver's seat, where I paused to open my water and take a swig.

"So what happened last night? Did I piss Mirali off?"

"No. It was a defensive reaction."

"That's some defense! What is she, a black belt?"

Caeran shook his head, looking unhappy. "She was confused. She should not have been up."

I took another swig of water. "I was looking for you."

He closed his eyes. "I know."

"You know? How do you know? Were you watching me?"

His brow creased, but he didn't answer. It made me angry. "More mind-reading?"

"Len—"

"Well, what? All of you are acting like I'm some kind of leper or something. I thought we had—reached an understanding—"

"Len, you are a wonderful, wonderful girl, and I—can't. I can't be with you."

My gut tried to sink through the floor, and my throat went dry. I swallowed.

"Why?"

"I can't go into the reasons."

"That's not fair!"

"I don't want to hurt you, all right? And I would, so it is better that we just...don't."

I stared at him. He looked miserable, and he was making me feel miserable. There had to be some way to get him to trust me.

"I don't believe you would hurt me."

He gave a pained laugh. "Oh, I would. Inevitably."

"No," I said softly. "No, you wouldn't. I'm not a mind-reader, but I know that much."

"I would not mean to," he whispered, "but it would happen."

"That's crazy."

"It sounds crazy, yes."

"How could you hurt me if you don't want to?"

"By being who I am."

I took a deep breath. "OK. Who are you?"

He looked at me and shook his head. His eyes were haunted by sadness.

"Is it your family? Your friends—whatever they are? I know they don't like me."

"They do like you, Len. But they also see you as...a risk."

"Because you're not citizens?"

He looked out the windshield. It had been a guess, and his silence seemed to confirm it.

"I would never rat on you, Caeran. I don't care if you're here illegally—"

"That is not the issue."

"Then what is?"

"I...am not free to explain. We are too different, Len. That is all I can say."

Deeply frustrated, I started the car and lurched onto the highway. Drove too fast to the junction, by which time I had calmed down enough to know I shouldn't commit vehicular murder-suicide. Caeran sat in tight-lipped silence, and I didn't know how to restart the conversation without returning to the argument.

I drove toward Las Vegas, holding to the speed limit, unable to enjoy the scenery. There was a knot in my stomach that seemed to get bigger by the mile. I couldn't accept that Caeran wanted to walk away. I was pretty sure he didn't want to, but that he felt obliged to, and that it was his friends who were making him do it.

I thought of our embrace beneath the stars and my throat went hollow. Tried to think about something else, but I was too worked up and to my dismay I felt my eyes begin to burn with tears.

Crying would just exasperate Caeran. Blinking hard, I turned on the music to cover my erratic breathing and tilted my head toward my window. Tears spilled down my left cheek and dripped onto my arm. I hoped Caeran wouldn't notice. At first I thought he hadn't, but after a couple more miles he spoke.

"Stop the car."

I sniffed, trying to quit crying, and kept driving. Caeran punched the stereo power button, killing the music.

"Len, please stop the car."

I gave up and pulled over, and promptly lost it. Couldn't control myself any more; I sat there sobbing, wiping at my running nose. Totally unattractive.

Caeran reached over and turned off the ignition. He handed me a handkerchief—a real, cloth handkerchief, neatly folded—and waited patiently until I had pretty much stopped blubbering.

"I am sorry to have made you unhappy," he said. "I should not have let things go as far as they did."

I couldn't answer that one, so I just wiped my nose. Caeran kept talking, his gentle voice soothing, calming me.

"I know it seems unfair, but this small disappointment is much better than the hurt you would suffer later, believe me. I wish I had not caused you any pain at all. Indeed, I did not mean to. I am most grateful to you, Len. You have helped me and my kin more than you can ever know. You have probably saved Mirali's life."

That surprised me into a laugh. "I just gave you a ride. If someone saved her life it was Madera."

"But I would not have found Madera without your help."

I looked at him, remembering the first time I saw him

coming up to my counter in the library, his incredible beauty and the anxious hope in his eyes. Had that only been three days ago?

Three days, in which time I'd made a complete fool of myself over a man who was still, essentially, a stranger. Way to go, Len.

I sniffed and gave my eyes a final swipe with the soggy handkerchief. They were sore, probably red. I allowed myself one sigh, then started the car again and continued south.

We didn't talk until Las Vegas, where I stopped at the same gas station for a bathroom break. Didn't need gas yet, so I parked in front of the store, and Caeran and I both went in. I took the time to wash my face and give my hair a wet finger comb job, trying to make myself slightly more presentable. Couldn't do much about the red eyes, though I pressed a damp paper towel to them for a minute and they looked less puffy.

I decided to indulge in a junk food frenzy. If I was going to wallow, I might as well go whole hog.

When I came out, Caeran was paying for a bottle of water, a chug of my favorite soda, a bag of chips and a bar of dark chocolate. He put everything but the water in my hands.

"How did you do that?" I demanded.

He looked startled, then guilty. He didn't answer as we went back to the car.

I opened the soda and took a swig, cold bubbles biting my throat delightfully. I sighed. "You are a mind-reader."

Caeran looked away, buckling his seat belt. "I thought you might be hungry."

"Bull." I shook the chips, rattling them in their bag. "This is exactly what I was planning to buy for myself."

A corner of his mouth twisted up in a smile. "Like I said, you think pretty loud."

"Oh, man."

I tore open the bag and shoved a handful of chips into my mouth. Put the chocolate aside for later, and started the car.

I wanted to talk, but couldn't figure out what to talk about.

It was either trivialities or the danger zone, and if I kept resurrecting the latter it would be I who was hurting Caeran. He'd apologized so sweetly, I couldn't keep pestering him.

We stopped for gas in Santa Fe. Caeran insisted on paying. I asked if he wanted lunch, but he said he wasn't hungry and I was still stoked with junk food, so we headed on to Albuquerque.

The knot in my stomach came back. The closer we got to the city, the bigger it got. I didn't want to think about what was coming, so I turned the music back on and sang along, not caring what Caeran thought about my caterwauling.

The disc ended as we were approaching the Alameda exit. I swallowed.

"So. Back to the bosque?"

"Yes."

I nodded and took the exit and the slow way, wanting to delay, wanting a few more minutes to soak up everything I could remember about him. My damn eyes started watering again. I blinked to keep it back, determined not to subject Caeran to another scene.

I turned onto Rio Grande, cruising past the big homes. Cottonwoods dropped golden leaves on the car.

"You guys really shouldn't be camping in the bosque."

"It will not be for long."

"Gonna find a house?"

"Perhaps."

"We could stop and pick up a real estate guide—they're free—"

"Not here."

"What?" My brain didn't want to register what he was saying.

"Albuquerque is too big. Too many people. We need a quiet place."

So he was *really* leaving, as in inaccessible, as in no possibility of changing his mind. The knot in my gut swelled.

Nothing more to say. I drove to the Nature Center and

stopped by the bike access path where I'd picked him and the others up the morning before. Turned off the engine and got out, helplessly watching Caeran get his pack from the back seat.

"Want some of the pears? They'll go bad before I can eat them all."

He looked at me, eyes more golden than green now, like the leaves. My heart flipped over at his smile.

"All right. Thank you."

I picked up the basket and offered it to him. He chose six pears and slipped them into his pack.

"Take more."

"This is enough."

I put the basket on the seat. He stood gazing at me, pack slung over his shoulder. I couldn't stand it. I threw myself at him, hugging him tight, breathing in the smell of him. After a moment his arms closed around me.

"Caeran—"

"Shh."

"I'm never going to see you again, am I?"

He gently extracted himself from my embrace and kissed my forehead. "No."

"Well," I said shakily, trying to smile, "at least I had this much. I'm really—glad I got to know you."

He raised a hand to touch my cheek. "Be safe."

With a faint smile, he stepped back, then turned and walked down the path beneath arching cottonwoods. I watched him all the way, tears running down my face. He never looked back.

When he'd turned the corner out of sight I still saw him in my mind: crossing the bridge over the ditch, heading toward the bosque, turning south. I stood there for a long time.

A car coming out of the parking lot jolted me back to reality. I hurried around to the Saturn's driver's seat and got in.

Driving back to campus, I felt numb. A tightness started in my temples, growing to a full-blown headache by the time I reached my dorm. I parked and cleared out the car.

As I was picking up the empty junk food wrappers I came across Caeran's crumpled handkerchief. I picked it up, thinking about washing it and then taking it for a walk in the bosque.

No. Caeran wouldn't want me to do that. He wanted to be left alone.

A souvenir, then. I stuffed it in my pocket.

When I got to my room, I was too zonked to do anything but take some aspirin and collapse. I lay on my bed, thinking of Caeran until I fell asleep. Woke up in darkness, confused.

The clock said 6:30. My head still hurt, though not as bad. I drank a glass of water and felt slightly better.

Food was probably a good idea, though I didn't feel hungry. There was still a knot in my stomach. I looked at the basket of pears sitting on my desk.

Pears for dinner, and I really hadn't had lunch. It wouldn't cut it. I needed some protein, so I'd have to go out.

Easiest choices were the Student Union Building or the Taco Bell on the corner. I didn't care what I ate, so I opted for the SUB, thinking it might do me good to bump elbows with some other students. I put my wallet and other necessities into a fanny pack, grabbed my coat, and headed out.

Dark was falling early these days. Leaves blew around the broad concrete sidewalks, catching in the corners of the steps and piling up against planters and hedges, their dry smell reminding me of Halloween. I huddled in my coat and hurried to the SUB.

Light, music, and jabbering voices washed over me as I entered the building. The smell of coffee evoked a growl from my gut, so I hit the espresso stand first. The first swallow of latté was ambrosia.

I debated going through the cafeteria line or just grabbing a slice of pizza. The cafeteria would be healthier—I could get a salad, some meat.

I went for the pizza, and ordered a side salad to assuage my conscience. I figured I was still entitled to wallow for a while. Twenty-four hours at least. Then I'd straighten up.

Caeran. My chest tightened as I remembered his touch. His farewell. I wasn't hungry any more, but I tried to eat anyway.

I sat at a café table in the hallway outside the pizza place and watched the world go by. Groups of friends grabbing a bite before the seven-thirty movie. Maybe I should watch the movie—it would distract me—but I just couldn't summon any enthusiasm for it.

What I wanted most was to be with Caeran, which I couldn't have, so what I wanted next most was to be alone. Sitting here with happy people all around wasn't going to make me happy. I didn't know what I'd been thinking when I decided to come to the SUB.

I finished my pizza and ate a few bites of salad, then gave up on it, anxious to get back to my room to be alone in my misery. As I was getting up to dispose of my trash, I saw a man walking toward me and nearly gasped.

Tall, slim. His hair was ice white but he looked young—my age—so maybe it was a bleach job. He wore a battered leather jacket, a t-shirt for some heavy metal band, and jeans. Perfectly reasonable student attire, but he wasn't a student. I was sure of it.

The lines of his face, his posture, his stride, all rang very familiar. They reminded me of Caeran and his family.

I stood staring like an idiot. The stranger's gaze shifted to me and he slowed.

All at once I knew he wasn't like Caeran. He was

dangerous.

A stab of fear shot through me and I looked away, blinking as I shuffled to the trash can, watching the stranger from the corner of my eye. My heart was pounding.

I could feel his gaze boring into me. I moved toward the nearest exit, silently hoping he'd keep going the other way.

"Len! Hey, are you going to the movie?"

I nearly jumped out of my skin, but I was so glad to hear Amanda's voice I didn't care. She was coming in the doors with Don, a guy she'd dated a few times and whose last name I couldn't remember. He was a swimmer.

"Hey, guys!" I said, forcing a smile. "Yeah, I was kinda thinking about it."

The white-haired guy was past. I turned sideways a little so I could watch him down the hall, heart still hammering. I wondered if he could read minds.

Movie, I'm going to the movie. What movie was it anyway?

"You want to sit with us?" Amanda asked.

She was smiling, just friendly. Don's smile lacked enthusiasm, and I figured he didn't really want me along.

"Um, maybe," I said.

"Let's go, then. I want to get seats up front."

I followed them to the ballroom where the free movies were shown. All the way I kept watching for the white-haired guy, but I didn't see him again.

The movie was *The Wicker Man*, the original one with Christopher Lee. I'd seen it and liked it, but I'd had enough creepy-weird in real life lately that I wasn't hot to see it again. I also didn't want to be trapped in the ballroom, though that was probably one of the safer places I could be.

I showed my I.D. and lagged behind Amanda and Don going in. The crowd made me uncomfortable. More than ever I wanted to escape back to my dorm room.

I spied two seats together in the third row, touched Amanda's arm and pointed. "You two grab those."

"But—"

"I'll find a spot. I might have to leave early anyway—didn't sleep well last night and I'm kind of tired."

Don smiled, happier. Amanda looked disappointed.

"Well, OK. You want to get dessert, after?"

"If I'm still here. If not, I'll call you tomorrow."

"OK, hon." She gave me a quick hug and went off with Don, leaving me tingling. Still a little zotzed with adrenaline, I guessed.

I drifted toward the back of the ballroom. Saw empty seats here and there but felt no inclination to squeeze along the rows to get to them. I stood at the back, and when the lights went out and the film began, I took a long, leisurely look out the doors, trying to spot white hair in the milling SUB populace. Didn't see any.

I waited five minutes, then left. My eyes darted around as I walked through the SUB, searching for threats. I paused by an entrance, bracing myself to leave the warmth and light of the building for the walk across campus to my dorm. I took my pepper spray canister from my fanny pack and put it in my coat pocket.

A group of students burst in, laughing and shushing each other, late for the movie. I jumped out of their way, then went out before the doors could close.

A cold wind smacked me in the face. I shoved my hands in my pockets and hunched my shoulders, shivering as I hurried toward my dorm.

Any movement drew my attention. With the wind, there was plenty of movement from the shrubs and trees, so I kept looking from side to side. I passed some students, most of them headed for the SUB, hurrying to get out of the cold.

The skin between my shoulders was tight. Cold, fear...maybe both. Though I was more watchful of my surroundings than usual, a part of my mind whispered that if the white-haired guy had wanted to sneak up on me, he could have.

I fixed my eyes on the blue light atop an emergency call

box ahead. They were scattered around the campus—places where you could call for an escort if you were afraid. I thought about doing that, and probably should have, but the idea of standing still waiting for a campus cop to show up scared me worse. I kept moving.

Shortly after I passed the call box I could see my dorm. I almost broke into a run, but decided it might attract unwanted attention. Walking as fast as I could, I kept my eyes on the dorm doors. I breathed a sigh of relief as I went through them.

Made it. Up the stairs to my room, jittery with the key but got it into the lock and shut myself in. I threw the bolt and stood for a moment, shivers subsiding.

What had just happened? Had I freaked myself out? Had I made it all up?

I might have thought so a week earlier. Now I was sure I had not imagined it. The white-haired guy was like Caeran, and unlike him. While I knew in my soul that Caeran would never hurt me, this guy was a threat.

I took the pepper spray out of my pocket and put it on the desk, then took off my coat and proceeded to clean out the rest of my pockets. Keys, condom, handkerchief. I held the latter up to my face, wondering if it might hold any lingering smell of Caeran, but no.

Sighing, I dropped it on my desk and kicked off my shoes. I hadn't been out of my jeans in over twenty-four hours, and I needed a hot shower. I stripped and left my clothes in a pile on the floor, then grabbed the handkerchief as I headed for the bathroom I shared with my neighbor. Might as well wash the thing now.

I soaped it in the sink, rinsed it, and hung it over the towel bar. Took a long, hot shower and washed my hair, and felt a lot better for it. I was sleepy when I came out, but I made myself stay up and do homework until ten o'clock, then turned on the TV.

"Breaking news—a university student was attacked and killed tonight on the UNM campus—"

A sinking dread spread through me as I listened to the rest of the story, which didn't give much detail. A student had been brutally murdered some time after six. Name withheld pending notification of next of kin. Police asking any witnesses to come forward.

I sucked a sharp breath. I hadn't witnessed anything, but I had my suspicions. If I made them known, though, I'd be laughed off campus.

The white-haired guy. He'd terrified me with a glance. Had he been looking for a target?

A fit of shivers came over me. I moved to turn off the TV, then decided to leave it on. I needed some normal stories. The weather. I watched, zombie-like, until the sports came on, then turned it off.

Silence filled the room, allowing me to think again. Possibly, I had just missed being the killer's target. If so, then Amanda and Don had saved my ass, and I owed them big time.

Oh, how I wanted Caeran there—to complain at him, to demand information about the white-haired guy—but mostly to have him put his arms around me and make me feel safe. A completely stupid reaction; as if I suddenly had no ability to take care of myself.

I crawled into bed and read my English Literature assignment. Woke up with the book across my thighs and my cell phone buzzing its way across the desk; still on vibrate from my brief stint at the movie. I wallowed down the bed and grabbed it. 11:30.

"Hullo?"

"Len, oh, thank God!" Amanda said. "I just heard about the attack, and we didn't see you after the movie—"

"Wasn't me, obviously. But thanks for worrying."

"Did you hear?"

"Yeah, I watched the news. It's awful."

"They haven't said but I think it was a girl."

"I think you're right. 'Brutal' tends to mean rape in that context."

"Oh, God!"

"Are you in your room?" She lived in the dorm next to mine.

"Yes, Don walked me back."

"Let's meet for breakfast, OK? Nine?"

"OK. Call me first."

"I will. Take an antihistamine." Our poor man's sleeping pills.

"Y-yeah. You too."

"Thanks for calling, Amanda. See you in the morning."

I switched the phone back to ring and put it on my nightstand. Looked at the textbook and decided I'd been virtuous enough for the night. I put it on the floor, rolled over, and despite all the paranoia, fell asleep.

By morning the news story had been fleshed out a little. Female student, and the attack took place in the northwest area of the main campus, near the frats and sororities. Too close to home.

Amanda and I discussed the attack over breakfast, sharing what details we had picked up from various news sources. So far no witnesses had come forward.

I poked at my breakfast burrito with my fork. "You know, when you and Don ran into me last night I had just seen a guy who gave me the creeps."

"You're kidding! Did you recognize him?"

I shook my head. "Never saw him before. Tall, with white hair. I was really glad to see you guys. I was scared of him."

"Ohmigod! You should tell the police!"

"Tell them what? That I saw a creepy guy in the SUB? Come on."

"No, no, you should tell them! Anything could be a lead. You might be the only person who saw the attacker!"

"Only *living* person." I grimaced. "Maybe he wasn't the killer, though. He could just be some scary guy."

"Well, you should still talk to the cops. They could have you do one of those composite pictures, and put it on the news."

Oh, yeah—that would be good. Caeran would love that. "Nah."

"Len, it could save somebody's life!"

I bit my lip. She had a point—if my white-haired guy *was* the attacker. That was a huge "if."

I changed the subject, and we never got back to it. Instead we made plans for protecting our personal safety. We decided to spend the day studying together in Amanda's room, which was bigger than mine, and agreed to walk to classes and our library shifts together as much as possible in the coming week. It seemed like overkill to me, but I wouldn't mind the company. Amanda was a good friend, and with luck she would keep my mind off of Caeran.

The next few days were fairly uneventful. Gradually I relaxed, though Amanda and I faithfully escorted each other as much as possible.

The victim's name was released: Emily Barela. Neither of us knew her. She had been in the SUB early Saturday evening and had walked back to her sorority alone. She never made it there.

A few other details leaked out in the news. Emily had been raped and her throat was cut. She bled to death. Her sorority raised five thousand dollars for a reward for information leading to an arrest.

Amanda continued to nag me to talk to the police, and finally on Wednesday she dragged me to the north campus substation during our lunch break. Embarrassed, I spent fifteen minutes talking to Officer Dusenberry, a ginger-haired giantess in uniform who seemed suspicious of me right from the start.

"Are you here because of the reward?" she asked.

"N-no. I wasn't sure I should come," I told her. "I mean, I don't know that this guy had anything to do with it. I just got a bad vibe off him."

She peered at me over her wire-framed glasses. "We pay attention to bad vibes. Where exactly did you see him?"

I described it all: pizza, trash can, and my fortuitous meeting with Amanda and Don. I gave her every detail I could remember about the guy, except his resemblance to Caeran. That couldn't matter to the cops.

"You didn't happen to snap a picture with your cell phone, did you?"

I shook my head. "I was just anxious to get away from him."

"And you haven't seen him since?"

"No, ma'am."

"If you do see him—"

"I'll take a picture."

"—don't go near him. Call campus police."

"OK. I've got the number programmed in."

She had me read over her notes and sign them. I rejoined Amanda, who was waiting for me out front. We were late, so we ran back to the library.

Dave met us in the lounge, frowning. "Service slow, ladies?"

Amanda opened her mouth. I didn't want her to get in trouble, so I talked over her as I punched my time card. "We were at the police station. I was reporting a suspect for the murder."

His eyebrows shot up. "You witnessed the murder and you didn't say anything until now?"

"I didn't witness it. I saw a guy in the SUB who might have been the killer. He gave me the creeps."

"Sugar, if you called in every creepy guy on campus the cops would be overwhelmed."

I bit back a comment on the subject of creepy guys. Instead I nudged Amanda toward the door. Dave stepped in front of us.

"Well, since you're late, you can stay and shelve for half an hour after your shift."

"Sure," I said, hoping he wouldn't saddle Amanda with the same grunt work. My agreement surprised him and he stepped out of our way.

We went to our stations at the counter. Tony was the only clerk working, and a line had built up in our absence. Dave was too important to help with it, apparently. The three of us quickly cleared it up, and Tony waved as he took off for lunch.

Amanda began to tidy her station. "So, did the police do a picture?"

"Nope. She asked if I'd taken one with my cell. It's a good idea—wish I'd thought of it."

I wished I'd thought of taking one of Caeran. All I had to remember him by was the handkerchief. I had it in my pocket, and occasionally slid my hand in to touch it. That was self-torture and I knew it, but I just wasn't ready to let him go.

Amanda's shift ended before mine on Wednesdays. She had an afternoon class, one of the few to which I couldn't escort her. Dave had either forgotten this, or decided not to make her shelve.

"Be careful," I told her as she closed up her station. "Keep your eyes open."

"For the white-haired guy. I will."

"If you see him, run. I'm not kidding."

She grinned. "Where should we go for dinner? I'm tired of the SUB."

"Taco Bell? Or we could try the new Mediterranean place."

"That sounds good. Meet you back here and we'll walk over."

The afternoon passed slowly. At four I closed up and said goodbye to Tony and Marietta. She worked the four to eleven shift, and as I was leaving I turned to her.

"Do you have someone to walk you home after work?"

She nodded. "My boyfriend's been coming in at ten thirty and hanging out in the study carrels until I get off. Says he's getting more homework done these days."

I smiled. "Good."

"Thanks for asking."

I collected a cart full of books for the third floor and rolled it into the elevator. I'd get the shelving over as quickly as possible. It was pretty mindless work, and didn't really distract me from my inner thoughts. I worked as fast as I could, hoping to keep my mind off of Caeran. Thinking about him would just make me sad, so I tried not to do it. Didn't succeed all that well.

I had the cart three quarters empty when I pulled it around the far end of a row of shelves and stopped, frozen. The white-haired guy was standing halfway down the aisle, peering at a section of the shelves.

= 6 =

I grabbed a book from the cart and retreated to the aisle I'd just come from, heart thundering. My hands shook as I took out my cell phone and got it ready to take a picture. I remembered to turn off the flash, and hoped the fluorescent lights would be enough. Book in one hand, phone in the other, I slowly stepped back around to the cart.

He hadn't moved. I tried to keep my mind blank—tried to go Zen—as I reached up to put my book on a shelf, hiding the phone behind it. I turned and quickly shot a picture, then kept moving, pushing my cart past the aisle.

Had his head started to turn as I was leaving? The skin on my back prickled.

I moved faster, wincing at the rumble the cart made. Tried to keep my dread from showing in my thoughts. Books, shelve the books, got to finish that. I stared at the numbers on the aisles, not really registering them.

When I reached the end of the section, I abandoned my cart, grabbing my pack from the bottom shelf and making a beeline for the restrooms. Maybe white-hair wouldn't care about that taboo, but it made me feel a smidge safer.

Still shaking, I called downstairs to Tony. He answered on the second ring.

"Tony, I need a big favor. I'm in the ladies room on the third floor and there's a creepy guy in the colonial history section. Could you come up and walk me downstairs?"

"Sure. Which ladies room?"

"By the study carrels and the green chairs."

"OK. Stay put, I'll be right up."

"Thanks."

I felt slightly better. If I died, someone would at least know

89

what had happened.

I fumbled with the phone until I managed to bring up the photo I'd taken. It was better than I'd hoped; not crystal clear, because of the distance, but a fairly good shot of his profile. My stomach twisted, looking at it. I wanted never to see him again.

I called campus police and told them I wanted to email it to them. They gave me an address and promised to send someone to the library at once.

"Do you want someone to come escort you out of there?" said the officer who'd answered.

"I've got a friend coming for me."

"Make sure they stay away from the suspect."

"Right."

I hung up, silently cursing myself for not thinking to warn Tony. The white-haired guy wouldn't be interested in him, I hoped.

I moved closer to the door, keeping the privacy wall between me and it. Shoved my cell back in my pocket and dug in my pack for my pepper spray. My hands were a little steadier, but my breathing was still shallow, panicky. I leaned against the wall and listened.

My pulse distracted me. I couldn't exactly hear it, but I could feel it. Nothing going on outside came through as clearly.

I tried closing my eyes and taking some deep breaths. I heard footsteps and stopped breathing altogether.

"Len?"

Tony. I let out my breath in a sigh and left the restroom. He was standing just outside, looking suspiciously around.

"Let's go," I said, shoving my hands in my pockets and starting for the nearby door to the back stairs.

"That way?"

"Yes."

The elevators were too far away; I didn't want to cross that much open ground. I paused inside the stairwell door to listen. Heard nothing, so I ran down, my footsteps echoing loudly. Tony muttered something, probably a complaint, but he kept up with me. Two flights of stairs were nothing. I could have been shelving up in the stacks.

We came out the door on the ground floor and wound up face to face with a wide-eyed cop. I yanked my hands from my pockets and held them up.

"I'm Lenore Whiting. I called it in. Tony and I work here."

The cop frowned at us, then nodded and let us by. Neither of us fit the suspect's description.

Tony glanced back at him. "I thought you just saw some creep. What's this about?"

"Let's get to the lounge."

We strode through the reference section toward the main entrance and the counter where we worked. I kept my eyes open for the white-haired guy, but there were three more cops at the front entrance and if he had any brains he'd gone to ground.

I led Tony into the employee lounge, where Dave was talking with yet another campus cop. Dave scowled as we came in.

"There she is. *She* can explain it to you."

The cop, a nice-looking Latino guy, turned to me. "You're Lenore Whiting?"

"Yes. Thank you for coming so quickly."

"What part of the building were you in when you saw the suspect?"

I grabbed a copy of the library map and drew a circle around the section. "Third floor. He was in this aisle," I said, adding an "X" about where I'd seen him.

"OK. We'll check it out."

He walked away with the map. Dave tagged along after him, to my relief.

"Suspect?" Tony asked. "As in, murder suspect?"

"Maybe." I opened my cell phone and showed him the picture. "This guy."

"Who is he?"

"I don't know. I saw him in the SUB Saturday night. He gave me the creeps, so I told campus police about him and they said to call if I saw him again."

Tony frowned. "Marietta should see this."

"Send her back here, OK? I don't want to go out front."

Tony left, and a minute later Marietta came in. "What's going on?"

"I saw a guy upstairs who might be a suspect in the attack." I showed her the picture and gave her a brief explanation. Her eyes widened.

"I saw him come in! He asked where to find books on the early Spanish colonists!"

I stared at her, pieces clicking into place inside my head. The white-haired guy was looking for the same thing Caeran had been looking for. Family?

"What did he say to you?"

"He just asked where to find the section and I gave him a map. I offered to help him with a catalog search but he said he just wanted to browse."

"And then he left?"

She nodded. "I was glad—I didn't like him."

"Neither do I. You should tell the police about it."

"All but one of them went upstairs with Dave."

I glanced toward the door. A tiny voice inside me was fretting: *You're wasting everyone's time, this guy might have nothing to do with the murder, what if he's a friend of Caeran's?*

"I guess we should wait, then."

"Well, I have to work."

She moved slowly toward the door, looking unhappy. I sat down at the lunch table, ready to wait out whatever was happening upstairs.

"Let me know when they come back down, OK?"

She shot me a look, then nodded and left. I picked up a magazine from the messy stack in the middle of the table. It was one I'd already read, so I threw it back. I was fishing for another when someone moved into the doorway.

I jumped, then saw that it was Amanda. "You scared me!"

"There are cops outside. What's going on?"

I showed her the picture of the white-haired guy and told her the details. "I think I'd better wait until they're done up there, since I called it in. If you're hungry, go ahead without me."

"No way! I want to know what happens!"

She joined me at the table. We didn't have long to wait, fortunately. About ten minutes later Dave was back, giving me a sour look.

"There's nobody up there who looks like your suspect."

"He must have slipped out, then."

"Yeah, or he was never there."

I held up my phone with the picture showing. Dave ignored it.

"You didn't finish shelving."

I gritted my teeth to keep from yelling at him. "No, I didn't. When I see homicidal maniacs I tend to leave my work unfinished."

"You don't know he's a homicidal maniac."

"You don't believe he exists, so why worry about it?"

Amanda flashed her eyes at me, warning me to cool it. Usually I didn't let Dave get to me, but I was feeling stressed.

The nice Latino cop came back, looking apologetic. "He's not on the third floor. We've cleared it."

I bit my lip. "I'm sorry to have wasted your time. He must have left right after I saw him."

"We're doing a walk-through of the other floors, but we don't have the manpower for a thorough search."

"I understand."

He turned to Dave. "We'll have people watching the entrances until you close. If he comes out, we'll catch him."

Dave glared at me. "Good luck with that."

"Thanks for your help, Officer...?"

"Martinez. You're welcome."

"I hope I haven't led you wrong—"

His face hardened. "We take every legitimate lead seriously. Don't hesitate to call if you see him again."

I smiled, grateful for the reassurance. He left, and Dave went out front to talk to Tony and Marietta. Amanda and I followed him out and continued out of the building, past a pair of campus cops flanking the front entrance.

The sun was setting, and the air was getting cool. I wished I'd brought my coat.

"Is the SUB all right with you?" I asked Amanda. "I don't really feel like going off campus."

"Yeah." She nodded agreement, her brow creased. "Sure."

We crossed the plaza to the SUB and went downstairs to the New Mexican restaurant for killer green chile burritos. Comfort food, and it helped, though I still felt pretty edgy. I kept thinking about the white-haired guy looking for Spanish colonial books. He had to be following the same lead that had brought Caeran to my station a week earlier.

Should I try to let Caeran know about him? It would mean going to the bosque, and I'd sort of promised not to. Caeran might be gone by now anyway. The thought made my chest tighten.

If he was gone, he wouldn't care about my being in the bosque. If he was still there, he might appreciate knowing about the white-haired guy. Armed with this rationale, I decided to go the next day. I'd still have some daylight after I got off work—or maybe I'd call in sick. Let Dave worry about how to cover the check-out counter. Maybe he'd actually have to step up to a station himself.

"Homework tonight?" Amanda asked, sounding unenthusiastic.

I couldn't picture hitting the books in my current frame of mind. "Um, I think I could use a break. Think I'll go to bed early."

She nodded. We refilled our sodas and headed for home. It was getting dark already, and the chill had intensified. I shivered and shifted my pack on my back.

Our dorms stood adjacent, with no more than a hundred yards between the entrances. Amanda made a halfhearted offer to walk me to mine, but our routine was to go to hers together, and then I'd hurry home. There were no hiding places in the intervening distance—a couple of bushes and a few trees that were too skinny to conceal anyone—and everything was brightly lit. I wasn't worried, so I turned her down.

"Call me," Amanda said at the doors to her dorm, getting out her card to swipe through the lock.

I nodded. That was part of the routine, too—I'd always call to let her know I'd reached my room safely.

"See you tomorrow."

I watched her in, then headed for my dorm, walking briskly to fight the cold. After about twenty steps my arms broke out in goosebumps. The back of my neck prickled. I hadn't seen or heard a thing, but my heart started hammering.

I glanced around—nothing. I walked faster, listening intently. All I heard was my own footsteps, until behind me a thud and a flash of light happened simultaneously.

I yelped and spun around. Two men were grappling on the sidewalk where I'd just passed. One had white hair.

"Oh, shit!"

I pulled out my phone and punched the redial, backing away from the fight. A flash of a brownish ponytail made my heart jump in fear.

"Caeran!"

I froze in terror, watching the near-silent battle. They were fast, and weirdly graceful even as they struggled. The way they fought was almost like a dance, or some weird martial art unlike any I'd ever seen. Another flash of light dazzled me and I staggered backward.

"Campus police."

"T-this is Lenore Whiting. The guy—the white-haired guy —"

"Where are you?"

"In front of Zuni."

"Get inside."

"He's fighting—"

"Get inside, now!"

I couldn't agree. I couldn't move. I stared in horror as the white-haired guy caught Caeran in a hold that couldn't be comfortable. One of Caeran's arms was twisted up at his side, and he looked like he was having trouble breathing.

"Lenore, are you there?"

"Yeah."

"Are you inside?"

"No."

Pepper spray! I shoved the phone in my pocket and scrabbled in my pack for the spray. Caeran was straining against the other guy's hold, but his knees were bending.

I found the spray and set up to use it, but I didn't want to hit Caeran, too. The two of them were still grappling, and—weirdest yet—they were starting to glow.

Caeran's free hand shot up toward the other guy's face. A blinding flash made me gasp and flinch away. When I looked back, Caeran and the white-haired guy were both lying on the ground, face down.

I think I whimpered as I forced myself go toward them, pepper spray at arm's length. My gaze stayed on the white-haired guy, though it was Caeran I was trying to get to. He moved, making me jump and let out a squeak.

Caeran pushed himself up to his knees. I kept the pepper spray pointed at the white-haired guy, though he seemed to be out cold.

"Are you all right? Oh, God—you're bleeding!"

He blinked and put a hand to his forehead, fingers coming away bloodied. "It is nothing. Go inside."

"Caeran—"

He looked over his shoulder, grimaced, and shot to his feet, grabbing my arm. He practically carried me to the door of my dorm.

"Go inside," he repeated.

"Come with me. Let me fix that for you—"

"No need."

He started to pull away but I caught his arm. "Please don't go. Please!"

I sounded panicked, and it wasn't because I was scared of the white-haired guy. I was afraid Caeran would disappear and I'd never see him again.

He glanced backward, frowned, then relented. "All right. Quickly."

I shoved the pepper spray into my pack and got out my card. Swiped it through the lock and we were in. Caeran took hold of my elbow again and propelled me through the lobby like he knew his way around.

My cell phone rang. I dug it out of my pocket.

"Hello?"

"Lenore? This is campus police. Are you inside?"

"Yes."

"Good. Stay there, and stay on the phone."

Caeran pushed me into the elevator and punched the button for my floor. I stared at him, wondering how the hell he knew it. Maybe I was thinking too loud again.

"Tell me what you saw," said the cop on the phone.

I closed my eyes. I didn't want to make trouble for Caeran, but I'd already mentioned the fight. I decided to stick to minimal details.

"I heard a noise behind me. When I turned I saw the white-haired guy and another guy fighting."

"Two men? Anyone else?"

"I didn't see anyone."

"Can you see them now?"

"No, I'm in the elevator, going up to my room."

"Does your window look that way?"

"No, it looks east."

"That's OK. Tell me when you get to your room."

The elevator doors opened. As we got out Caeran shot me a sharp glance, but said nothing. We walked down the hall to my room. I unlocked the door and we went in.

"OK, I'm in my room," I told my phone buddy.

"Stay there until we contact you again. Do you want me to stay on the line with you?"

I looked at Caeran, who had sat on the end of my bed and dropped his face into his hands. "No, I'm all right. Thanks."

I put the phone on the desk and dumped my pack on the floor beside it. Caeran didn't move, except that I could see his breathing. I wanted to wrap my arms around him. Instead I went into the bathroom and fetched a damp washcloth and my box of bandages.

Now that the crisis was over, I noticed that Caeran's hair wasn't in a ponytail; it was braided in a queue that hung halfway down his back. He didn't have his pack, though he was wearing a jacket of the same soft buckskin.

I knelt by the bed and gently pulled his hand away from his bloodied forehead. He resisted a little, then gave in and held still while I dabbed at his cut.

Except I couldn't find the cut. I gently wiped the blood away, and all there was beneath it was a fresh, pink scar. I stared at it for a moment, unable to understand, then moved on to wipe the blood from his hand.

His fingers curled around mine, stopping me. I looked up into his eyes—those eyes unlike any others I'd seen.

"This is why I cannot be with you, Len." His voice was rough and low. "I am not human."

I laughed in surprise, so suddenly I hiccuped. "Oh—what are you, an alien?"

He shook his head slowly, no humor in his face. "My people have lived here since before yours evolved."

My heart gave a painful squeeze. "Your...people?"

"The ælven."

"Excuse me? Did you just say you were an elf?"

He frowned, letting go of my hand to make an impatient gesture. "'Elf' is a corruption—laden with misconceptions. We are *ælven*. We are immortal."

7

I stared at him. He was talking about the stuff of legends. It made sense in a weird way—or rather, it made a lot of other things make sense. The mind reading. The uncanny grace and beauty.

Madera's handmade furniture. If you're immortal, you've got plenty of time.

I swallowed. "Your family, too? Madera?"

"Yes."

I was having trouble breathing. There didn't seem to be enough room in my lungs for more than short little gasps. I pointed toward the front of the building.

"What about him?"

Caeran leaned back a little, his gaze sliding toward where I pointed. "He is of our kind, but different. He suffers a disease —"

"Other than psychopathy?" I was getting giddy.

"—a disease that interferes with his digestion. The only food that will sustain him is blood. Human blood, or ælven."

"A *vampire*?"

"The source of those myths, yes. But many of the myths are wrong."

I stared, open-mouthed, out of questions. My mind was quietly exploding.

Caeran caught my hand again. "I am sorry to have caused you so much trouble."

"No," I whispered, still reeling.

"I fear I may have—"

"Madera!"

Caeran looked startled. "What?"

"That guy—the vampire—he was in the library today. He was looking at the Spanish colonial section! He was looking for

Madera, wasn't he?"

Caeran's cheeks paled. "Possibly."

I grabbed my phone from the desk and held it out to him. "You've got to warn him."

His brows drew together. "But the police will have found the alben—the vampire—by now."

"You're saying he can't get away from them?"

"Not easily, as I left him unconscious." Caeran's wry tone tugged oddly at my heart. I loved his humor—rare as it was— even though this wasn't the time for raptures.

"You used that thing on him. The flash of light thing, same as Mirali did to me."

"Yes. The alben have less skill with it."

The phone in my hand rang, and I nearly jumped out of my skin. I answered it.

"Lenore Whiting."

"Miss Whiting, this is Officer Gordon from campus police. We responded to your call about a suspicious person."

"Yes. Did you find him?"

"No. We found a small amount of blood on the sidewalk."

I stared at Caeran. From his expression he had either heard Officer Gordon or he had read my thoughts.

"Out in front of Zuni? That's where he was fighting."

"Yes. We're still looking for him, but you should stay inside, all right? Don't leave the dorm."

"Right. Thanks."

I hung up, then held the phone out to Caeran again. "Better call."

"I do not know the number."

"I programmed it in. Just in case. It's under 'M.'"

He gave me a pained look, then took the phone. I got up and went back to the bathroom to give him some privacy. Rinsed out the wash cloth, put away the bandages. Tried to get a grip on what was happening—what I was learning. If I could believe it.

I splashed some water on my face, then rubbed it hard with

my towel, making sure I was awake and not in the middle of some fantastic dream. When I looked in the mirror my skin was red, my eyes stressed. I ran a brush through my hair, took a deep breath, and went back out.

Caeran was talking rapidly, quietly, into the phone in the strange fluid language that must be their own. Ælven language. I fought down an urge to giggle. There was nothing funny about our situation. There was a killer—a freaking vampire—loose on campus.

And if it hadn't been for Caeran, I'd have been dinner.

He ended his call and handed me back the phone. I put it on the desk and sat next to him on the bed.

"Um, thank you for saving my life."

He turned his head and a small smile touched his lips. "I had no choice. I could not let you be harmed."

Well, that made me feel good. "How did you know, though?"

He glanced down at his hands. "I heard about the first attack, and could not rest until I knew it had not been you. I came here, to the campus, and learned that you were safe, but I also found signs that the attacker was alben. Since then I have been watching over you."

"What? Since when?"

"Monday evening."

Caeran had been tailing me for three days, and I'd never noticed? But then, he was an ælven—my brain still had trouble with the word—and he had magical powers.

"What about your family? Will the vam—the—"

"Alben."

"Alben. Will he bother them?"

"The others have left. They have gone...to join Madera."

His gaze grew stern, as if he was cautioning me.

I drew a sharp breath. "Can the alben read minds?"

Caeran nodded, and my stomach sank. I tried to remember if I had thought about Madera's home in the library that afternoon. I didn't think I had, and I quickly turned my thoughts away from it now.

"H-how close does he have to be?"

"Fairly close."

"In the same room?"

"Not necessarily."

I groaned. After all my efforts to be sneaky taking his picture, the alben had probably known the minute I did it. No wonder he wanted to kill me.

"He will not harm you," Caeran said softly.

"Thanks, but I can't expect you to devote your entire life to protecting me."

He laughed. "That should not be necessary."

"Don't fight him again, please. I don't want you to be hurt."

"I will try to avoid injury, but I cannot promise not to fight him. He will continue hunting until he is stopped."

I stared miserably at the floor, knowing he was right, and suspecting that campus police were no match for the alben. Maybe with Caeran watching me he would go after easier game, which was a horribly selfish thought, one I was immediately ashamed of.

Caeran shook his head slightly. "He knows you are aware of his nature, and he is also drawn to you. It is the ælven blood —it runs strong in you."

"Ælven blood? *Me?*"

"All humans have ælven blood in their ancestry."

"What?!"

The phone rang again. Stifling a curse, I grabbed it.

"Lenore Whiting."

"Len? Are you all right? You didn't call, and then your phone was busy—"

"Oh, I'm sorry, Man." I rubbed a hand over my eyes. "I got distracted. I'm fine."

"What happened? Did you see the guy?"

"Yeah. I called the cops—that's why the phone was busy. They're looking for him. Don't leave your dorm."

I talked with Amanda a little longer, though there wasn't

that much to say. I didn't mention Caeran. Things were complicated enough.

When I told her goodbye, Caeran stood up. My heart sank, knowing before he spoke that he was going to leave.

"I must continue my own hunting." He smiled as he said it, though his eyes remained sad.

I was proud of myself for refraining from grabbing him. "Come back soon, please. I want to talk with you some more."

He didn't answer, just brushed the back of his fingers against my cheek, lighting a fire in the pit of my stomach. Without another word, he turned to go.

I love you, I thought.

His stride faltered.

You are making it hard to walk away.

I gasped, my being suddenly flooded with a delicious awareness of him, as if I could taste his soul. I shivered, thrilled to my bones.

I don't want you to walk away.

But I must.

He opened the door and went out, letting it fall shut behind him.

Caeran?

No answer. I went to the door and fought with myself for a full thirty seconds before throwing the deadbolt. Much as I wanted to follow him, Caeran did *not* want me around, and if he was going after the alben I'd only get in his way.

I shuffled over to the bed and collapsed on it, aching for Caeran's arms around me. I could still feel a whisper of the thrill his mental contact had given me. Not only could he read minds, he could make psychic conversation, and it included much more than words. His voice in my head had lit colors in my mind, filled my senses with the taste and smell and feel of him. If I hadn't already fallen for him, that would have done it.

I abandoned myself to reveling in the memory of it. For all I knew, I'd never get any more, so I wallowed while the impressions were fresh.

The next thing I knew, my alarm clock came on, blasting the cheery voice of the campus station's morning disk jockey. I slapped it to shut it off and sat up, groaning.

Thursday. I had a morning class, then work at the library. Thinking about it made me restless; I didn't want to do either. I wanted to find Caeran.

Yeah, well, good luck with that. It would only happen if he wanted to be found.

I grabbed a quick shower and turned the radio on again as I got dressed, hoping to hear that the cops had made an arrest. No such luck. The library search yesterday had made the news, but the little flurry of activity around my dorm had not, and I guessed that the police were keeping quiet about their leads.

I put my pack together for the day and dragged myself downstairs. Amanda was waiting in the lobby—someone from the dorm must have let her in. She came up to me with a worried greeting.

"Did you hear anything from the police?"

"Nope. He must have given them the slip."

I headed for the doors, not wanting to answer a lot of questions about the previous night. Amanda hustled to keep up. Bright sunshine made me squint as I left the building.

"I'm so glad you got inside before he got to you," Amanda said. "That must have been terrifying, to see him."

"Yeah. Did I show you the picture I took?"

I pulled out my phone and brought up the picture. While Amanda was staring at it, I realized I'd missed another opportunity to catch a picture of Caeran. Dammit!

Amanda insisted on walking me to my class, even though it was two buildings past hers. I thanked her and told her to be careful. She had classes all day, so we'd meet again for dinner. I was on my own until then.

I drifted my way through my literature class, knowing I was doing a bad job taking notes. The professor glowered at me as I left. I'd have to do something to keep my grade from sliding, but just now I wasn't in the mood.

I walked to the library, wondering where Caeran was. If he was watching me, great. I felt safer for it, and also for the daylight and the crowds of students on campus.

Night was the scary time. Solitary walks—even of a hundred yards—weren't safe. This vampire—this alben—might not be able to come out in daylight, if that particular myth was true. I wished I'd thought to ask Caeran.

I signed in to work, exchanging hellos with Tony and Carla, the rest of Thursday front desk crew. Dave wasn't around, for which I was grateful. Carla took off for lunch shortly after I arrived.

I collected a stack of data forms to enter into the system in between helping customers, to keep myself busy so I wouldn't dwell on things I couldn't control. Halfway through the first form I looked up as someone came up to my station.

Caeran. My heart flipped over. He leaned his elbows on the counter and bent his head toward me, so close I could smell him.

"The alben is in the building," he murmured.

"What?" I lowered my voice at Caeran's gesture. "Should I call the police?"

He shook his head. "He can evade them."

I glanced at Tony, who was watching curiously. He looked away. My heart was pounding as I looked back at Caeran.

"I can't really leave," I whispered.

"You are safer here, with others nearby. I only wanted to warn you."

"How did you know he was here?"

"I tracked him here last night."

"He spent the night in here?" I glanced at Tony, then asked my next question silently.

Caeran, can he go out in sunlight?

"Yes, but not easily," Caeran said softly.

So that one's true? Sunlight will kill him?

"It's more like a severe allergy. Do not consider daylight a guarantee."

"OK." I frowned. "What should I do?"

"What you normally do. I will be nearby."

How can I call you if I need you?

"Exactly like that. But louder." His lips curved in the lopsided smile I'd grown to cherish.

Caeran, talk to me.

The smile widened slightly, and he shook his head. I watched him stroll over to one of the couches by the front door and pick up a book.

I was intensely frustrated, and frightened halfway to freaking out. The alben was in this same freaking building, and Caeran was acting like Mr. Cool.

I turned back to my forms and tried to lose myself in data entry, but I was stressed and kept making errors. I kept looking over at Caeran, too, which didn't help. I wanted him to talk inside my head again and fill me with the bliss I'd felt last night. I wondered if this was how addicts felt about their next fix.

Making an effort to focus, I shifted the angle of my monitor so my back was toward Caeran. It didn't help much. I kept remembering him leaning on my counter, so much closer than he had stood that first day. I couldn't recall at what point I'd become addicted to the way he smelled. Probably when we were sitting together up in the Wesley Collection.

I froze, hands poised over the keyboard, my thoughts skittering along an unpleasant path of possibility. I started to look toward Caeran, then realized he couldn't deal with this one.

I picked up the phone and dialed the number for the Wesley Collection. Barb answered on the second ring.

"Hey, Barb, it's Len. Can you do me a favor?"

"I can certainly try."

"You know that book I was looking at last week? Could you pull it for me? Don't let anyone use it?"

"Someone's using it right now, I'm afraid."

My heart thudded. "Who?"

"A community borrower. Do you want the name?"

I closed my eyes. "Does he have white hair?"

"Yes, though he's certainly not old enough for it. He looks a little like your friend from last week."

"I know who it is, but yes, give me the name."

"One moment."

Caeran, are you hearing this?

I looked over at him. He looked like he was still reading, but he nodded.

"It's a Richard Gutierrez."

"OK, thanks."

"Do you want me to pull the book after he turns it in?"

"No, thanks. I'll work on something else.

I hung up and turned to my monitor to bring up the record for Richard Gutierrez. There were four of them, but only one was a community borrower. He'd had his card for three years.

I'm thinking Richard Gutierrez recently had his pocket picked.

Caeran didn't answer. I looked over and saw him nod again.

Should I call the cops now?

He shook his head slightly.

But we know exactly where he is. They can walk right in and arrest him. There's only one entrance.

Caeran lifted a hand. I waited, but he just went back to reading.

He's tracking down Madera. Shouldn't we stop him?

Caeran frowned, pressing his lips together.

This is crazy. Will you please just talk to me?

He closed his book, stood, and headed for the elevators. There was no one at the counter, so I told Tony I'd be right back and hurried after Caeran. I found him leaning against the wall in the alcove between the elevators and the restrooms, arms folded across his book.

"He has probably learned Madera's location," he told me. "We are too late to prevent that."

"So we call the police and they take him into custody."

"He would only escape them," he told me.

"Escape from jail?"

Caeran nodded. My heart sank.

"So there's no way to stop him?"1

"I can stop him. Not here, though. Too many people are near."

"What are you going to do, wait for him to leave?"

"Yes."

"Caeran..."

He looked at me, patiently waiting, and my stomach sank. I knew I wasn't going to talk him out of it.

"I wish you wouldn't," I whispered.

"There really is no choice. If I do not stop him, he will continue to kill. He will try to kill you."

"Is this always what happens when you meet one of these —alben?"

Caeran's gaze dropped. "Yes. We are enemies by nature."

"But you're the same."

"We are kin, yes." He smiled wryly. "Kinship does not necessarily mean affinity."

"Is there no way to cure the disease?"

"Our healers have tried for many centuries."

"What about science?"

"We have tried that, too, as much as we are able. It is not easy for us to pursue research."

I nodded, understanding. "No labs. No funding."

"We have learned more about the nature of the illness, but nothing that would help to cure it."

"Maybe I'll switch to pre-med."

He glanced up at me, confused, then he must have read my meaning in my thoughts. His cheeks bloomed with sudden color.

"Our troubles need not concern you."

"It's a little too late for that."

The elevator door opened and I jumped. Caeran stepped away from the wall, waited a moment for the two girls from the elevator to get out of earshot, then leaned closer to me.

"Your coworkers are wondering where you are."

He started to walk forward but I stopped him with a hand against his chest. "Wait one second."

I got my phone out of my pocket and stepped back, then snapped off a photo. Caeran looked like a startled deer, but at least I had his picture.

"Why?" he said.

"To remember you by."

"You would be better off forgetting."

"No way."

He frowned, then brushed past me on his way back to the couch. Had I pissed him off? Too bad. I wasn't sorry.

I returned to the counter. Carla was back from lunch, so it was my turn. I was getting cold vibes off of Tony, so I turned to him with a smile.

"Would you like to go first, Tony? I can wait."

He looked slightly less huffy. "No thanks. I'm meeting Chivonne."

"OK. I'll be back early, promise."

I grabbed my pack, signed out, and headed toward the entrance. Instead of going straight out I sat down two seats away from Caeran and rummaged through my pack.

"Lunch break," I said quietly. "Care to join me?"

"No thank you."

"Can I bring you something?"

"I'm not hungry."

I know you eat. I've seen you. I could bring you some chile stew from the SUB.

A corner of his mouth twitched, but he kept his eyes on his book. I sighed and stood up.

I'll be back in half an hour.

Caeran gave a single nod. Unwilling to leave, I slung my pack over my shoulder and sort of stomped out.

Amanda's schedule didn't match with mine on Thursdays, so I was on my own. Usually I took an hour for lunch, but I couldn't stand the thought of being away from Caeran that long.

A shorter lunch meant I could take off work half an hour earlier, unless things were really busy.

I walked over to the SUB and headed for the pizza kiosk. When I came within sight of it I hesitated, remembering my first encounter with the alben. Just thinking about it set my heart racing with fear.

He's in the library, I reminded myself. *He won't come outside because he's allergic to the sun.*

Shaking off the dread, I walked up and ordered my usual pepperoni slice and soda. I went back outside with them, not willing to push my luck so far as to sit at the same table. Instead I sat on the edge of one of the big planters full of tired-looking petunias. They were valiantly blooming, though the snow and frost would get them soon.

The sun was warm, but a cool breeze countered it. My arms sprouted goosebumps. I pulled my sweater out of my pack and shrugged into it, then finished my pizza, thinking about Caeran.

Nice to have him watching over me. Not good that he was aiming to fight the alben. He hadn't said it outright, but he'd implied that he intended to kill this enemy. I didn't like the idea of Caeran killing to protect me, though I understood why he thought that was the only choice.

I'd made a promise, though, to inform the campus police if I saw the suspect again. I was failing in that promise by going along with Caeran.

I bit my lip. Maybe I should call them even if he didn't like it. There was just one problem with that, though—what if they mistook Caeran for the suspect?

No, I couldn't take a chance on that happening. I had to leave the cops out of it.

I sipped on my soda, surprised at the hollow gurgle I got through the straw. I'd drunk the whole thing without realizing it.

I took out my phone to check the time, and got distracted by Caeran's picture. His expression reminded me of when I'd first seen him: uncertain, worried. Gorgeous despite all that.

I had to figure out a way to keep him in my life. He wanted me, too, I was pretty sure. He was being all noble and self-sacrificing, which I guess was nice except that he was sacrificing my feelings, too.

I looked at the time. Twenty after. I needed something to do for ten minutes. Settled for checking my email, for which I had to go back inside to pick up the SUB's wireless. There was a hello-where-should-we-get-dinner from Amanda, and nothing else of interest. I suggested Greek, then logged out and headed back to the library.

As I walked in the doors I looked toward the couch where Caeran had been sitting. He wasn't there. I was about to panic when I saw him coming out of the elevator. I had a few minutes, still, so I waited by the couch. Caeran smiled slightly as he joined me, enough to make my heart start tap-dancing.

"Where did you go?" I asked.

"To verify that he is still...reading."

"Oh." I lowered my voice. "Maybe he hasn't found it yet after all."

Caeran tilted his head, as if considering this possibility. His gaze flicked in the direction of the Wesley Collection.

Still time to call the police.

He shook his head. "It would only make things more difficult. Better to wait until he leaves here."

And let him find out where Madera is?

"I know it seems odd, but if I succeed, he will get nowhere near Madera."

I stared at him, out of arguments, down to just drinking in his presence. I was greedy; I wanted as much as I could get every time I saw him, because it could always be the last time.

He gazed back at me, then gently took my hands and squeezed them. At his touch I wanted only to please him, only to belong to him. I saw a swallow move his throat. He leaned close to whisper in my ear.

"You will be late."

"Caeran—"

He stepped back, shaking his head slightly as he let go of my hands. He held my gaze for a moment, then resumed his place on the couch and picked up his book.

Damn it.

I trudged past the front desk, waving halfheartedly at Tony, and continued to the staff lounge where I signed in exactly thirty-six minutes after I'd signed out. I went to my station, glanced toward Caeran who was busy blending in, and dove into my stack of data entry.

The afternoon dragged. I had three more hours—or two and a half—to get through. Between keeping an eye on Caeran and worrying about the alben upstairs, I was in an anxious mood. I finished my stack of data entry forms, went back and got another, and watched the afternoon light through the glass wall gradually go golden.

Just before four o'clock business picked up, and I had a line for a few minutes. It made me cranky, because I'd wanted to leave early. I tried to get through the customers as fast as possible, not really paying attention to who they were. When I saw a guy's gray sweatshirt in front of me I didn't look up at first, greeting him automatically as I finished entering the previous transaction.

"How can I..."

I froze as my gaze met his. Black eyes, all the way black from the pupil through the iris. He had the hood of the sweatshirt pulled up over his hair, but a few white wisps clung to his forehead. The killer.

8

The alben leaned toward me. "Do you have a car?"

My thoughts flicked toward Caeran, then as quickly away. I wanted to scream for help but the killer would hear.

Car. I pictured the Saturn, then pulled my keys out of my pocket and held them out to him. He smiled, eyes narrowing.

"Oh, no," he said softly. "You are coming along."

"I can't leave work."

"Make an excuse."

I hesitated, trying to think of a way out. Suddenly my brain felt like it was on fire. I gasped, and it stopped just as fast before I could scream.

Come along, unless you want to feel that again.

I cringed. His voice told me a lot about him, things I didn't want to know. He was hungry. He was impatient. At the core, he was totally self-driven and cared nothing about anyone else. Instinct screamed at me to get away.

The burning started again, just a tickle. I grabbed my pack and dashed for the staff lounge, and it stopped.

My breath came in short, sharp gasps as I hastily signed out. Half an hour early—maybe someone would clue into that. I hoped so. Where was asshole Dave when I needed him?

Lip balm, I thought as loudly as I could while I dug in my pack with shaking hands. *Where's my lip balm?* My hand closed around a large cylinder and I pulled it out without looking, trying not to think. I shoved it in my pocket, found my lip balm and used it, then shrugged into my pack.

He was waiting by the lounge door, and fell into step with me. I walked toward the front entrance, which faced south. He pulled his hood forward and took out a pair of sunglasses. While he was putting them on, I glanced at the couch. It was empty.

I looked away, thinking about my car. I hadn't gassed up, so it wouldn't get far. It had less than half a tank.

We passed through the doors into the late afternoon sun. I glanced at the killer. He had his hands dug into the kangaroo pocket of his sweatshirt, the hood as far forward as it would go. He looked like the Unabomber.

I should have let him incapacitate me; Tony and the others would have taken care of me. Didn't think of it soon enough.

Or maybe he would have just knocked them out, too, and grabbed me. I shivered.

Just survive, I thought over and over, not letting other thoughts into my head. I walked slowly, hoping that would keep me alive. Maybe someone would spot the killer, make a call. Maybe we'd pass a campus cop.

Why was I alone? Where was—*just survive*.

My car was parked in the lot behind my dorm. I walked up and unlocked the passenger door.

"Get in," he said, standing by the open door.   He watched as I walked around and got in the driver's seat. I looked around, hoping to spot a cop or—someone. The parking lot was deserted.

Only after I'd closed the door did the killer get in. I cracked my window open, needing air, and sat still. My heart was racing and I felt a little woozy.

"Take me to the home of Miguel de Madera."

I swallowed, feeling the blood drain from my face. "What?"

"I know you have been there."

"It's a long way."

"Drive."

I buckled my seat belt and started the car. This was not good. I did not like being in a car with this guy, even though I was in control of the vehicle. Didn't the self-defense courses say never let them get you in a car?

He hadn't fastened his seat belt. Maybe I could roll the car and kill him. Trouble was, I'd probably kill me, too.

That might possibly be my best option, I thought grimly. I

backed out of the parking space.

As I pulled onto the boulevard he fastened his belt. I bit my lip and avoided looking at the gas stations we passed, keeping my thoughts on the freeway instead.

What did he want with Madera? Whatever it was—not good. Not good at all. I suspected that his wish to get to Madera's was the only reason I was still alive. It followed that I'd be dispensable once we got there.

Just survive.

I loved the idea, but it was getting harder to visualize. The help I'd hoped for had not materialized, and the farther we got from campus the faster my hopes faded. I was on my own.

So. Review of options: no. Don't think, just drive. A chance will arise.

I frowned. That sounded like wishful thinking.

A shiver of dread went through me. To keep from panicking, I started running through songs in my head, starting with every Gilbert and Sullivan patter song I could think of. Let him sort through that.

Traffic was light despite the nearness of rush hour. The miles flew past. Maybe I'd get stopped for speeding.

That hope faded as I passed the Bernalillo exit. Sometimes there were speed traps on I-25, but not usually on a week day. We had three or four hours of driving ahead. Less than an hour until sunset.

It would be good to get out of the car before then. Somehow.

I glanced at the gas gauge despite trying not to think about it. I shifted my attention to the speedometer instead. In a fit of spite I accelerated to eighty-five miles an hour, fifteen over the limit. My passenger didn't seem to notice. It didn't make me the fastest jerk on the road, and I chickened out on being truly reckless. Somehow I still hoped for escape.

That hope twisted in my stomach and I flinched away from the reasons why. Grabbed for The Mikado instead. *The flowers that bloom in the spring, tra la...*

I cruised past the three Santa Fe exits, keeping my eyes on the road and my brain engaged with music. We were now past my normal stomping grounds. The farther we got, the more tense I was starting to feel.

Partway through Glorieta Pass the car coughed. I glanced at the instrument panel. The little gas tank light had come on. The car coughed again.

"What is it?" demanded the killer beside me.

"We're out of gas."

I didn't look at him, but I could feel his rage. I gripped the wheel, bracing for an attack, but it didn't come.

"Take this exit." He pointed toward the ramp we were approaching.

"There's no—"

"Take it!"

A slam of pain accompanied his shout. I winced, and almost flinched out of my lane.

I took the exit, cruising to a halt at the stop sign on top of the ramp. He peered at the sign that called out Glorieta to the right, Pecos to the left. Glorieta was a tiny village—really just a bedroom community. No services.

"There is gas in Pecos?"

"Uh—yeah."

"Go left."

I turned the wheel and nearly stalled the car, but managed to coax it across the bridge and onto the back road to Pecos. Downhill, mostly. I coasted, instinctively saving the gas for the uphill stretches. We passed a historic marker and an old adobe building with crumbling walls. We were on level ground now, at the bottom of the canyon. I drove until the gas was gone and the car finally died. As we lost momentum I pulled onto the shoulder. The car drifted to a stop.

It was cold in the canyon, and darker. The hills and mesas hid the setting sun. I dropped my hands into my lap and sat still, waiting for the storm.

"How far to the gas?"

"I don't know. A few miles, maybe."

"Do you have a gas can?"

"No."

He turned toward me in his seat. I stared out the windshield.

"So this is why you are so fond of music."

His voice was acid. It drove my pulse faster, though I tried not to show it. My hand inched closer to my pocket.

Lip balm. Too dry.

I swallowed. Maybe I was about to die. Didn't want to think about that.

"Yes, maybe you are."

I could feel the anger in his voice, like a wave of heat washing over me. I cringed, then reached for the door—except my hand didn't move. I was paralyzed.

"Or perhaps not die, not yet. But you will pay for your trick."

He shifted closer. Inside I winced, since my body couldn't. His breath—dank, unpleasant—reached me as he leaned toward me.

The back seat exploded.

= 9 =

I thought we'd been rear-ended, but the next second I realized we weren't alone in the car. Caeran had come through from the trunk and launched toward the alben.

I cried out in fright, by which I learned I was no longer frozen. I scrambled out of the car, stumbling into the road. Luckily there was no traffic.

The car was jouncing with the struggle going on inside it. A flash of light made me flinch back. The air had that prickly feeling as if lightning was about to strike.

I stepped in front of the car, both to get out of the road and to try to see what was happening through the windshield. Another flash of light was followed by a burst of flame. I shrieked, terrified the Saturn would catch fire and explode. I could see thrashing forms inside, both in the front of the car now.

I wanted to do something to help Caeran but I didn't know how. I took the pepper spray out of my pocket and turned it so I was ready to discharge it. My hands were shaking and my breath was ragged.

Another flash of light, this time accompanied by a dull thud. I could see the alben's white hair; his hood had slipped off. He had Caeran pressed against the passenger door. I moved around to look more closely and through the side window saw his hands around Caeran's throat.

"No!" I yelled.

Fear and caution both left me, replaced by fury. I grabbed the door handle and yanked it open.

Both of them tumbled out. The alben still had hold of Caeran, but his grip had loosened. Caeran broke it with a kick to the alben's gut, and rolled away. I stepped in and emptied my pepper spray at the alben's head.

I'd half feared the spray wouldn't affect him, but his scream of pain was most gratifying. I coughed and stepped back, eyes stinging. Caeran got to his feet and moved to stand over the alben, holding out his hands.

The alben's cries subsided. He went still.

I stared at Caeran, whose hands were glowing. A pale beam of light poured from them down toward the alben. Instead of illuminating him, it pooled over and around him, thick and slow like honey, obscuring him.

After a while, Caeran lowered his hands. The glow remained around the alben briefly, then began to fade.

I stepped up beside Caeran. "Is he dead?"

"No." He glanced toward a house just down the road, and added in a low voice, "Not here."

I hadn't noticed the house. I wondered idly if the alben had. They might have gas right there, a can in their garage. Ironic.

I turned to Caeran. He was gazing into the woods, frowning thoughtfully.

"Th-thank you," I said.

Suddenly I was shaking uncontrollably. Cold, and probably shock.

Caeran drew me into his arms, wrapping me in his warmth. I shuddered with relief, and struggled not to dissolve completely.

"I'm s-so glad you were there! I was so afraid."

"I am sorry I could not let you know."

"How did you keep him from sensing you?"

"We have ways of masking our khi."

I sniffled and looked up at him. "Khi? Is that like chi?"

He nodded. "Same concept."

"Let me guess. You had it first."

His smile bloomed, filling my heart. "Yes."

He smoothed my hair back from my face. I wasn't shaking any more. I held still, hoping for a kiss, but instead he gently let me go and stepped away.

He crouched beside the alben and rolled him over. The

alben's face was blotched and red from the pepper spray. Caeran slid an arm under his shoulders.

The alben lunged.

I screamed as the killer sank his teeth into Caeran's shoulder. Furious, I used the only weapon I had—the empty pepper spray can. I bashed it into the alben's head as hard as I could, and raised my arm to hit again.

The alben looked up and snarled at me, blood on his teeth and lips, the whites of his eyes red as well. I flinched back, and the next instant he was gone, sprinting for the woods.

"Oh, God! Caeran!"

He was on his feet before I could try to help him. Blood ran down his shirt. His eyes blazed as he turned toward the woods.

"Caeran!"

"Get in the car and lock the doors." He took one step forward and vanished.

"CAERAN!"

Gone. Shivering again, I ran to the car. Shoved the passenger door closed and hurried around to the driver's side.

The dome light illuminated the wreckage: the back seat on the passenger side was down; the front seat lay back across it, maybe broken; and everything inside was singed. The stink of burned fabric made me grimace, but I got in and obediently locked up.

I cracked my window to let in some fresh air. I pulled out my cell phone, thinking I should call for help, but there was no coverage in the canyon. I turned it off so the battery wouldn't run down. Having nothing more to do, I broke down in sobs.

I cried out of dread for Caeran, terror of the alben, and frustration. Cried until I was all cried out, then fumbled in the back seat for my box of tissues. The top few were scorched, but I found clean ones beneath them and mopped my face.

I was cold, and automatically tried to start the car so I could run the heater. Reminded of the lack of gas, I shed a few more frustrated tears, then calmed down.

If—*when*—Caeran came back, I didn't want him to find me

blubbering. Or if the alben showed up, I'd need to defend myself.

I dug my foot-long flashlight from under the driver's seat. It made a good club. I sat with it in my hands, shivering now and then, staring out the window toward the woods.

A few cars drove past. Each time, the sudden brightness of their headlights made me flinch. After what seemed like an hour, I saw movement in the woods. I gripped my flashlight, holding my breath.

The movement resolved into a figure walking toward me. No white hair; it was Caeran. I sighed with relief.

He tried the passenger door. I hastily unlocked it. Caeran opened it and looked in at the seat.

"Here," I said, leaning across to pull the recline lever. The seat didn't spring back up as it should have, but with Caeran's help I got it upright and it seemed like it would stay. He sat down, pulled the door shut, and sighed wearily.

"Did you...find him?"

"No." Caeran grimaced. "He is more resilient than I expected."

Frowning, he turned and peered toward the trunk. I shone the flashlight into it through the opening behind the folded seat. I gasped as I caught sight of something, then realized it was Caeran's pack.

Caeran reached a long arm back to fish the pack out, set it at his feet and faced forward again, then leaned his head back and closed his eyes. He looked tired, and that worried me.

"How's your shoulder?"

He glanced at it, then touched it, smearing blood. It was still oozing. I grabbed a handful of tissues and pressed them to the wound. Caeran took over, and I got another tissue to wipe the blood off his fingers.

"Why didn't it heal?"

Something flicked across his face, an emotion I couldn't read. "It is deep."

"You should get it looked at."

He met my gaze, then looked out the windshield. He seemed to be thinking, so I waited. I was happy just to watch him, just to be with him. Finally he sighed and turned his head.

"Will you take me to Madera?"

I hesitated, caught off guard by the request. "Won't the alben follow us?"

"He knows how to get there. He may be on his way already."

"If course I'll take you, if that's what you want."

"I think it would be safest for you there, with all of us to protect you."

My heart skipped. "Don't worry about me."

"I have no choice."

A whisper of a smile accompanied his words, and my heart beat even faster. It thrilled me to think that he cared for me, though his determination to leave it at that drove me crazy.

"Caeran..."

I reached out a hand and touched his cheek. So enchanting, so breathtaking. He seemed always to be haunted by sadness, and that made me want to comfort him.

He covered my hand with his own, then gently pulled it away and pressed a kiss into my palm. My whole body approved of that. I swallowed, tingling.

"We need to find fuel, yes?" he said.

"Oh. Yeah. Um, maybe I could ask at that house."

"I will come with you."

"You look kind of scary at the moment."

His eyes hardened. "I will come with you."

"OK."

We got out and I locked the car, shoving the keys in my pocket. It was dark now, and getting colder. All I had was my sweater. I shivered.

The lights shining though the windows of the house looked warm and enticing. Aromatic wood smoke added to the impression; cedar, I thought. It made me want to go inside and huddle by the fire.

Caeran stood behind me as I knocked on the door. Living out here, these folks probably didn't get many visitors, and probably liked it that way. There was a long pause, but finally the door opened a crack and an older Hispanic man looked out.

"Hi," I said. "Sorry to bother you. My car ran out of gas and I was wondering if you happened to have any. We just need enough to get to Pecos."

He looked from me to Caeran and frowned. "No habla anglais."

Dammit. He probably did speak English, just didn't want to be bothered with us. I struggled to conjure up my high school Spanish.

"Um...Yo necesidad gasoline...un poco..."

"Funcionamos de la gasolina. Podemos pagarle," Caeran said over my shoulder. His voice was musical, the words flowing and liquid, almost as beautiful as his own language.

The old man blinked, then his eyes widened as he caught sight of the blood on Caeran's shirt. "¿Esta en apuro?"

"No, señor. Habia una lucha, pero ha hecho." Caeran dug in his pocket and produced a twenty dollar bill, which he held out to the man. "Para la gasolina."

The man stared at the money, then called over his shoulder in rapid Spanish. I glanced at Caeran, hoping he'd understood and that the man hadn't been telling his companion to call the cops. He stayed in the doorway, watching us. Somewhere in the house a door slammed.

Guess we weren't going to get invited in to sit by the fire. I pulled the sleeves of my sweater down over my hands. I could understand the man's suspicion. We looked pretty disreputable.

A minute later a teenage boy joined the old man, carrying a gas can that sloshed appealingly. Caeran traded his twenty for it and made a slight bow.

"Muchas gracias, señor."

The old man watched us away. I glanced at the forest as we returned to the car, but it was too dark for me to see anything. Caeran would know if the alben came back.

I opened the tank, then took the gas can from Caeran. It was only half full; the old man had got the better end of the deal. It was enough to get us to Pecos, though. I sniffed the can to make sure it wasn't water. Coughed on the fumes, and poured most of the gas into the tank.

I knew you were supposed to save a little to prime the engine. The carburetor? Except I wasn't sure how to find the carburetor. I decided to just try starting the car first.

I closed up the can and went to put it in the trunk. Caeran blocked me from touching the car, holding his hand out for the keys. I picked out the Saturn key and gave it to him, then stepped back.

No surprises in the trunk. A cold breeze made me shiver. I put the gas can inside, shut the lid, and took back my keys, anxious to get in the car and get warm.

Caeran peered through his window as I unlocked the doors. No one was hiding in the back seat. We got in and I pumped the gas pedal a few times, then turned the key. The car started.

"Yay!"

I yanked my seat belt across. The sooner we got moving, the sooner the engine would warm up.

Pecos was less than ten miles away. My stomach grumbled as we passed a burger place, but I didn't want to stop the car and risk not being able to start it again. I pulled into the gas station and cheered again, silently this time.

Caeran put a hand on my arm, stopping me from getting out. I waited, watching him. His gaze was distant, as if he was straining to hear something. Finally he let me go and nodded.

"Bathroom break if you need it," I said. "I'm going to get something to eat and drink, too, unless you'd rather go back for hot food."

He shook his head. He got out of the car and stood watching as I pumped gas. I used my sleeve to protect myself from the icy pump handle. When I was done, Caeran followed me into the store.

My own personal bodyguard. It would have annoyed me, except that I didn't want to have to face the alben alone again, thanks. I was grateful for Caeran's vigilance.

I washed up, letting the hot water run over my hands for a long time. Caeran was waiting for me out in the store. A burly guy who looked like he'd rather be fishing watched both of us suspiciously from behind the front counter.

I grabbed an orange, a cardboard turkey sandwich, chips, a soda and a candy bar. Dumped them all on the checkout counter and went back for a six-pack of bottled water, a pair of gloves and a sweatshirt to augment my wardrobe. The credit card would groan, but I didn't care.

I picked out a second sweat for Caeran, holding it up to him to make sure it was big enough. They didn't have any plain ones; the least offensive one said "New Mexico" above some petroglyph designs. Caeran frowned.

"That is not—"

"Yes it is necessary. You look like an extra from a monster movie. Come on, I'll pay for it and then you can change in the bathroom."

He accompanied me to the counter but before I could get out my card he plunked down four more twenties, which brightened the clerk's mood considerably. I wondered how big a bankroll Caeran had. I'd been thinking he was poor, because of camping in the bosque, but I now knew the reason for that wasn't financial.

I pulled my new sweatshirt on over my sweater while the clerk put the food and my gloves in a bag. Caeran picked up his sweat, but instead of heading for the bathroom he grabbed the water and went to the door. I accepted the bag and the change, thanked the clerk, and followed Caeran out to the car.

"Caeran—"

"I will put it on."

I sighed and got in, dumping the change into the bag and extracting my soda and the sandwich before putting it behind my seat. Caeran pulled off his bloodied shirt.

There was no one else at the pumps, so I was the only one who got to enjoy the view. His skin was perfect except for the wound on his shoulder, which was still oozing slightly. I frowned in concern.

"It still hasn't healed."

He glanced at it. "It is better."

"We should put a bandage over it."

He took a tissue and folded it in quarters, then pressed it to the wound, where the blood made it stick. I had a moment to admire his torso—as gorgeous as the rest of him—before he pulled on the sweatshirt. He balled up his bloodstained shirt and tossed it into the back seat, an act that was refreshingly uncontrolled.

"Do you want to call Madera? Let him know we're coming?"

Caeran hesitated, then nodded. I gave him my cell phone, and while he made the call I unwrapped the sandwich. His voice mesmerized me, even though I couldn't understand the words. Kind of nice that he didn't bother to hide his language from me any more. I loved listening to the music of it. Unfortunately, the conversation was brief. Before I'd swallowed two bites, Caeran closed the phone and gave it back to me.

I offered him the other half of the sandwich. "It isn't great, but it's sustenance."

He looked about to say no, then changed his mind. "Thank you."

"Thank *you*, you're the one who paid for it."

He took a bite and chewed it. "You are right, it isn't great."

"Chips will help."

I opened the chip bag and put it between us, grabbing a handful for myself. The salt improved the sandwich. I finished my half and took a swig of soda, then got out my new gloves and handed the shopping bag to Caeran.

"There's an orange in there, if you want it."

I drove back to I-25 and turned toward Las Vegas. Caeran ate slowly, taking a single chip now and then. He finished the sandwich and fished out the orange, which I was glad to see. He never seemed to eat enough, and with his injury he was probably dehydrated.

He fed me a couple of sections of the orange. I savored them, coming from his hand. When the fruit was gone, he opened a bottle of water and drank a third of it in one swig.

"So how did you get in the trunk?" I asked.

"I heard the alben's plans, and came ahead."

"But you didn't have a key."

He held up a hand, palm toward the glove box. I saw a faint glow, then the box door dropped open.

"OK." I looked back at the road, wondering what other surprises he had in store.

Caeran quietly closed the glove box and took another sip of water. A couple of minutes passed in silence.

"Which one of you did the fire trick?"

"The alben. I am sorry—I will pay to repair your car."

I gave a laugh. "Don't even worry about it. I have insurance."

"And how will you explain the damage?"

"Hm. Fumes from the gas can and a cigarette?"

"You do not smoke."

"I didn't say it was *my* cigarette."

He shook his head and smiled—really smiled—for the first time since the fight. Relief poured through me, surprising me. I hadn't realized I was so tense.

The miles stretched on into the night. Traffic was light, mostly truckers. Their headlights dazzled me; I looked away. I drove in silence for a while, hoping Caeran would sleep, but he didn't and the questions piled up in my brain. Finally I gave in.

"So, the myth about vampire bites—is that one true?"

Caeran's brow creased. "Partly."

"Which part?"

"Mortals are not susceptible to the disease."

My gut tightened. "But you are."

He shrugged, then winced. "It is a disease. Sometimes

multiple exposures do not cause infection."

The other side of the equation remained unspoken.

I gripped the steering wheel harder, suddenly frightened. Caeran was in danger of losing his family, of becoming his own enemy. I dreaded the possibility.

He looked out of his window, slowly drinking his water. I left him alone, not wanting to pester him with questions that might hurt.

It started to rain, points of light hanging on the windshield, dancing with each passing vehicle. I turned on the wipers.

In Las Vegas I stopped at the usual convenience store and topped off the tank. It wasn't really necessary but I needed a break, and I figured Caeran might, too.

The clerk, a plump Hispanic woman, looked at Caeran as if she remembered him. I felt a sudden dread that the alben had been here, that he might still be here. I looked around, panicked, and the clerk's gaze shifted to me.

Caeran grabbed my elbow and propelled me along one of the aisles, away from the counter. He stopped at the far end in front of a rack of salted nuts.

"He is not here," he said softly. "We are far ahead of him."

"How can you be sure?" I whispered back. "Maybe he hijacked someone else."

Caeran frowned, then glanced at the clerk, who was helping another customer. "She saw my kindred recently as they passed through on their way north. That is why she is watching me."

"Oh." I relaxed a little, swallowing. "Funny that they stopped here."

"I recommended it to them."

I met his gaze, saw his slight smile, and couldn't help smiling back. "I see."

"Do not fear. The alben will not trouble you again."

We visited the restrooms, then I picked up a bottle of juice. Caeran chose a bag of almonds, and I magnanimously paid for it along with my juice and the gas. Feeble gesture, but I wanted him to know I wasn't planning to mooch just because he seemed to be flush.

The rain had lightened up a bit. We hurried back to the car. As before, Caeran made me wait until he had checked it before getting in. I cranked the heater as I pulled out and turned onto the Mora road.

So what was next? We'd go to Madera's and hole up. So much for my Friday classes. Would next week be a loss, too? That could seriously mess up my grades. I'd have to get in touch with my professors, make arrangements to work outside of class, if possible. I could do some of that online, but I suspected Madera didn't have Internet access. Possibly no one in Guadalupita did.

Commute to Las Vegas for Internet? Or to Mora, if I was lucky.

Beside me, Caeran shifted in his seat, frowning. Was he listening to my rambling thoughts? I didn't love the idea, but I figured I'd better get used to it if I wanted to spend time with him.

"How long do you think we'll need to stay at Madera's?" I asked.

"Until we catch the alben."

"'We?'"

"My kindred and I."

I didn't like the sound of that. Caeran's face wore the grim, no compromise expression I'd seen before.

"Any chance he'll give up and go away?"

Caeran hesitated, then shook his head. "Now that he has found us...you see, our blood is their favorite food. Humans are easier to hunt, but ælven blood makes them much stronger. And there are other reasons..."

"Like what?"

His face hardened more. "Procreation. They will take any opportunity to conceive with us."

I grimaced. "I got the impression they weren't that picky."

"They abuse humans also, but any offspring from such

couplings are mortal."

"Oh. So they don't count." I tried to keep the edge out of my voice, but his casual dismissal of mortals annoyed me.

Caeran sighed. "Conception is much more difficult for us than for you, and our instinct to continue our species is strong."

"I suppose your people don't, um, couple with the alben willingly?"

"No."

His voice was filled with anger. I didn't want to hear about whatever he was remembering.

I took a swig of my juice. "Do they always live alone?"

"Alone or in small groups. Too many hunting at once attracts unwanted attention."

I nodded, and glanced at him. He was still frowning. I'd done it again—made him unhappy with my questions. I should just shut the hell up.

The rain turned to snow. I put down my juice and concentrated on driving. The Saturn had front wheel drive, which was good, but I didn't have snow tires, and no chains in the trunk. It was early in the season but I knew that the northern mountains could still get whomped.

By the time we reached Mora the snow was sticking to the road. There was no traffic; we were alone in the storm. I wondered what the snow plow service was like up here.

I slowed down and leaned forward, peering through the flying snow to see the stripes on the road. Tense; I hated driving in snow. I kept an eye on the odometer, unsure if I'd recognize Guadalupita in the storm, never mind the turnoff to Madera's.

A solitary streetlight came into view; mercury vapor staining the falling snow ruddy orange. It shone on the post office, and I could see the bar beyond, windows dark. I drove on, looking for Madera's driveway. When the carved owl loomed up, bright in my headlights, I braked to a crawl for the turn.

The snow was getting deeper. Possibly we'd get snowed in. That made me I realize I had nothing with me for an overnight

—hadn't even thought to pick up a toothbrush at the store. Damn.

Caeran straightened in his seat, leaning forward with a look of concentration on his face. He was staring out the windshield, but not at the snow. He reminded me of a hunting dog, listening to things I couldn't hear.

A light glowed dimly up ahead. The sense of relief it gave me was ridiculous. It wasn't an end to our problems, but at least it was the end of the road. Madera's house seemed like an oasis now, the old hacienda's many fireplaces calling to me.

The light resolved into the porch light by the front door, beaming out from beneath the *portal*. Softer light glowed from the windows of the front room. I rolled to a stop, parking nose in though I doubted there'd be other cars needing room. Turning off the engine, I sighed, glad to be done with the driving.

Caeran turned his head. The dash lights glowed softly, lighting the edges of his features, making him beautiful in a new, mysterious way.

"Thank you," he said after a moment, "for bringing me here. I am again in your debt."

"Oh..." I shook my head, unable to articulate my fleeting, embarrassing thoughts. It was a pleasure being with him; I'd do anything he asked just for the sake of his company.

He glanced away, reaching for his pack. "We should go in."

I fished my own pack out of the back seat and followed him, sad that our time alone was over. Funny, since we mostly hadn't talked. I would never get enough of his company, though, even in silence.

The door swung open as Caeran reached it. Madera welcomed him in with a gesture, and gave me a nod that seemed like an afterthought. He spoke to Caeran in their language. Caeran stopped him with a raised hand, glancing at me.

"She knows."

Madera looked alarmed for an instant, then his dark lashes hid his eyes as he turned to face me. "You have earned Caeran's trust. You are welcome here."

"Thank you," I said, wondering why it felt like a ceremonial response.

Madera stepped toward the right-hand door, looking at Caeran. "Let me tend your wound."

I followed them into the front room, where four others were sitting by the kiva fireplace. Four other ælven, I reminded myself. Three men and a woman. They stared at me, the stranger.

Caeran paused. "Len, may I make you known to my kindred? These are Savhoran, Lomen, and Tiruli. Nathrin you will remember."

"Yes," I said, smiling at Nathrin. "How is Mirali?"

He nodded. "She is better, thank you."

They were all clearly stamped with Caeran's genes. The woman was taller and more slender than Mirali. Silence stretched, and I felt compelled to fill it.

"Um, it's nice to meet you all."

Madera stood waiting by the far door. Caeran went to join him, and I hurried after.

"You could stay and warm yourself by the fire," Caeran said quietly.

"I'm coming with you."

I wasn't about to sit down with a group of strangers who looked at me like I was an escapee from the zoo. Caeran made no more objection, and while Madera frowned at me slightly, he didn't say anything.

He led us onto the enclosed *portal*. I looked out through the glass walls and saw snow falling gently into the courtyard — and the fountain calmly flowing. Madera opened the second door on the right and went in with Caeran. I followed.

It was larger than the room I'd slept in on our previous visit, and looked halfway between a treatment room and a guest room. There was a bed against the back wall, but more prominent was a massage table under a cotton cloth printed with the tree of life. Madera took this off, leaving the table covered only by a plain contour sheet. He set the cloth aside and went to a small kiva fireplace in the corner. It seemed like all he did was wave his hand, and flames sprang up around the wood that was laid there. Gas fireplace? I suspected not.

Caeran sat on the table and pulled off his sweatshirt. It was stuck to his wound and I winced as he worked it free. Blood had dried all over that side of his chest, smeared from his shirt. The wound was an ugly dark gash on his left shoulder, now oozing again, fresh blood glinting in the firelight.

He had taken it for me, this wound. At least partly for me.

Madera stood before a tall piece of furniture against the wall—a beautifully carved cupboard, obviously his work—that stood high enough to serve as a counter. He came to Caeran with a bowl of steaming water (though I saw no kettle on the counter) and a small stack of soft cloths. The steam had a fragrant smell, like fresh herbs. Madera soaked a cloth in the water and pressed it against Caeran's wound, then moistened another and began washing away the dried blood.

I wanted to help, but there wasn't much I could do, so I just concentrated on positive thoughts. I pictured the wound already healed, and Caeran walking free in the sunlight, untouched by the darkness that threatened.

Caeran looked up, startled. He and Madera both turned their heads to stare at me.

"What?"

A smile curved Madera's lips. "Nothing. Carry on."

He replaced the cloth over the wound with a fresh one, again soaking it in the herb-water. This time he gently rubbed the wound. Caeran winced. I took his hand and he looked at me, smiling.

Madera removed the cloth and peered closely at Caeran's shoulder, then spoke in their language. Caeran listened, nodding once. Madera took the bowl and the soiled cloths away to the counter.

"He is going to treat the wound," Caeran told me. "You will not want to watch."

I frowned. "What's he going to do?"

"Cauterize it," Madera said over his shoulder. "It is the best means of preventing infection."

Ouch. I swallowed.

"I'll stay."

"Len—"

"If you tell me honestly that you want me to leave, I will."

I held Caeran's gaze. He looked worried, but said nothing. After a moment he glanced away.

Madera handed him a glass of cloudy liquid. "Drink this. It will dull the pain."

I tried for a joke. "Maybe I should have some."

"It would kill you." Madera turned to gaze at me. "I have treated your kind long enough to know the differences. This herb is a narcotic to us. It is poison to you."

I swallowed. "OK. Good to know."

Caeran drank the solution. I watched Madera working at his counter, thinking that his unique knowledge might hold keys to some of humanity's greatest medical problems. All hidden here, in the middle of nowhere, New Mexico, in the mind of one being who was not human.

Madera lit candles, making the counter look more like an altar than a workspace. Maybe it was. What did I know about his methods? He'd spent centuries perfecting them, no doubt. His people trusted him, so I really had no choice but to trust him, too.

He spent a few minutes puttering at the counter. The only sound in the room was the crackling of the fire. I watched Caeran. When his eyelids started to droop, I took the empty glass from his hand and set it aside.

Madera returned, putting a hand on Caeran's good shoulder. "Lie back, now."

He lifted Caeran's legs onto the table and settled him on his back, then returned to the counter. A new smell rose in the room, one I couldn't identify right away. I looked at Caeran and found him gazing at me, softly smiling.

"You are very stubborn," he murmured.

"One of my more charming points, don't you think?"

I was being flippant to cover my nervousness. Pain was not something I enjoyed, mine or anyone else's. I hoped Madera would work quickly. I glanced at him just as he turned, and I realized what the new smell was: hot metal.

= 10 =

The silver rod Madera held was small, not much bigger than a swizzle stick. The sphere at the end of it glowed orange-red.

I grabbed Caeran's hand and held his gaze. He didn't resist. Maybe he'd already seen the thing, or seen it in my thoughts. I wrenched my mind away from it, and out of desperation, sang.

> *"Sorry her lot who loves too well,*
> *Heavy the heart that hopes but vainly..."*

Gilbert and frickin Sullivan again. And could I have picked a more depressing song? Never mind, keep singing.

A coloratura I was not, but I'd sung Josephine in high school, and I managed not to sound too much like a dying cat. I kept my eyes locked on Caeran's until he closed them. I imagined I could feel the heat as Madera came to his other side.

The healer laid a free hand on Caeran's chest. A hiss and the taste of searing flesh as I drew breath to sing the next line.

The skin around Caeran's eyes tightened in pain. I wrapped my free hand around his and kept singing, ignoring everything else.

> *"Sad is the hour when sets the sun,*
> *Dark is the night to Earth's poor daughters..."*

I poured myself into the melody, which was beautiful and one I'd always loved. The words were angst-ridden; I'd loved them too when I was younger, but now they seemed too wildly despairing. I didn't want Caeran to think that was how I really felt. It was just the music that mattered.

As I reached the final high note, Madera stepped back. I

didn't sing the last two words.

Caeran's face was pale, his hand clammy in mine. Sweat beaded on his furrowed brow. I brushed it away.

He opened his eyes and shivered. "Is it ov-ver?"

"Yes," Madera said.

The healer held his hand in the air over the wound, now red and puckered. A soft glow shone in the space between. Caeran closed his eyes and shuddered again. I started toward the bed to get a blanket, but he wouldn't let go of my hand. The tree-of-life cloth was in reach, so I grabbed that instead and spread it over his bare chest.

"Interesting choice of music," Madera said.

"It was the first thing I could think of," I said defensively.

Caeran laughed. "It was p-perfect."

Madera raised an eyebrow. "An expression of pain for the easing of pain? I confess, it never occurred to me."

"It worked," Caeran said.

His eyes were on me, and I sensed he really meant it. He wasn't just being kind. Poor Josephine's anguish had eased him.

I smiled. "Glad it helped."

"You know that song well. It came from deep in your heart."

"I used to sing it a lot."

His eyes flickered, the gold in them catching the firelight. "Why?"

"Oh, you know." I shrugged. "I was a teenager. They always feel like the world is ending."

Some kids dyed their hair black and punctured themselves in strange places. I sang light opera.

Madera lifted his hand and the glow beneath it faded. He peered at Caeran's face, then returned to the counter and came back with a gauze pad and a roll of cloth.

"You can be of help, Lenore."

He set the bandaging down and stepped to the head of the bed, then put his hands under Caeran's neck and good shoulder, lifting him a few inches. Caeran's head rolled.

"Dizzy," he complained.

"It is the herb." Madera glanced at me. "Can you hold him here?"

"Sure."

I slid my arm under Caeran's shoulders, supporting his head, and put my other arm around and under his ribs, out of Madera's way. I was close enough to smell Caeran's scent through the herbs and the lingering scorch. He gazed at me and I gazed back, held by those beautiful eyes.

Madera finished the bandaging all too quickly. He stepped back and I had no choice but to lay Caeran down again. Madera laid his hand on Caeran's brow.

"Rest now."

Caeran sighed and closed his eyes. The last of the tension drained from his face.

"Sleep well," I said softly, and saw Madera glance at me. "Or do you people sleep?"

Madera's lips twitched. "Not as you do. We rest, but we have greater control over our states of consciousness."

"Oh. Well then, rest well, Caeran."

His lips smiled slightly, then went slack. I got the blanket and covered him with it, then wandered over to watch Madera at the counter. He collected the cloths, the bowl, and the swizzle stick onto a tray. I fetched the glass and put it beside the bowl.

"Can I help with anything?"

He paused briefly, considering. "Stay with him, if you will. I will bring fresh clothing for him."

He picked up Caeran's sweatshirt and the tray, and left the room. I watched the candle flames steady themselves after the door closed, then drifted back to the table where Caeran lay and stood watching him.

I wouldn't mind nursing him back to health, if it came to that. Reading to him, or singing. I'd pick more appropriate songs next time.

Caeran's lips widened in a smile. "But I liked that song."

"Oh, sorry! I didn't mean to disturb you."

His eyes half-opened and found my face. He smiled again, and my insides went watery.

"I am glad you are still here," he said.

"I forgot you could hear me. I'm probably driving everyone crazy."

"No. Madera has shielded this room."

"Wish he could do that to my head." An image of a tinfoil helmet flitted through my mind.

Caeran chuckled. "I could teach you to guard your thoughts. We all learn to do it."

"But I'm not one of you."

"You can learn this. You improvised quite well, in the car."

With the alben. Fear stabbed at me with the memory. I pushed it aside, not wanting to think about the alben right now. Hoping he was far away.

Caeran's gaze sharpened. "He will not touch you. You are safe here."

I managed a smile. "Don't worry about him. Think about better things. I will, too."

He relaxed, eyelids drooping. "Sing to me again."

I thought for a moment and came up with "Kalimando," a song from Cirque du Soleil's *Mystere*. Very lullabyish. I sang it, unable to provide the harmony but holding it in my head, hoping Caeran could hear it that way. I pictured the acrobats, too—I'd seen the show and this was my favorite number— athletes suspended by pairs of bungee cords, flying in unison, dancing in the air, their costumes glimmering, ethereal.

By the time I finished the song, Caeran's eyes had closed and a soft smile curved his lips. I thought he was gone—resting or whatever—until he spoke.

"What language is that?"

"None. It's nonsense words."

"Lovely anyway." His eyes opened and turned to me. "Lovely."

I felt my face heating. "You're supposed to be resting."

"This is very restful. You have a beautiful voice, and your

soul lights up your singing. So fair, in so many ways." He blinked. "Forgive me—I ramble."

"Ramble away, if you're going to talk like that. I can use all the compliments I can get."

He smiled, then it faded. "I wish..."

I waited, not daring to prompt him. He closed his eyes, frowning a little, and I wondered if his shoulder was hurting. He murmured something I didn't catch.

"What?" I whispered.

Not vainly.

I held still, stunned by the sudden contact, the delicious warmth of his mind. I sensed dull pain lurking somewhere distant, but far more present was a depth of gratitude and affection. Just as suddenly, as if a window had closed, the sensations ceased.

I stood unmoving, trying not to think, just reveling in what I'd felt the moment before. If all I could have were occasional moments like this, I'd take it.

The door opened behind me, startling me. I turned and saw Madera, a small pile of clothing in his hands. I stepped out of his way as he set the clothes on the bed and came to look at Caeran.

He held one hand above Caeran's brow, the other over his shoulder. I saw the glow rise in both places. Was this part of the healing? Or something else? After a moment, Madera stepped back, then caught my eye and nodded toward the door.

Reluctantly, I picked up my pack and followed him out. Caeran needed to rest, and if I stayed I'd probably keep distracting him, no matter how hard I tried not to think.

Madera softly closed the door, then turned to me. "What you saw was khi. It is the source of healing, but that is only one of its aspects."

"Khi," I said, stumbling on the word, which sounded like a soft hiss when Madera said it. Caeran had mentioned khi, once. Forever ago. "I see. Thank you."

"Very few mortals are able to detect khi. I believe Caeran's assessment of you is correct."

"Assessment?"

"That you have a high level of ælven blood."

"Oh."

I thought about my parents, both terrific people, neither of them remotely like Caeran and his kindred. Madera seemed amused.

"Perhaps you are hungry. May I offer you refreshment?"

"Something hot to drink would be nice. Thanks."

With a gesture he invited me to walk with him, following the enclosed *portal* around the courtyard rather than going inside. We overshot the kitchen by a bit, but I didn't mind, since it meant we didn't have to pass through the living room where the others were gathered. The fountain made me feel peaceful, and now that I wasn't driving in it, the snow was beautiful.

Madera opened a door onto the small hallway I'd seen on my last visit, and we passed through it to the kitchen. A fire burned in a kiva fireplace I hadn't noticed before, making the room cozy, filling it with the smell of fragrant cedar. Madera filled a kettle and lit his stove, then joined me at the table.

"Thank you for bringing Caeran here." He seemed less formal, more friendly than I recalled.

"Glad to. So...is he pretty much safe? Since you treated the wound?"

Madera spread his fingers. "I cannot be certain. I have done all I can."

I nodded. That was the answer I'd expected. Wait and see.

"Have you had to treat a lot of—wounds like that?"

"More than I would like. Not so many in recent decades."

I looked at him, a thought occurring to me. "Did you build this house?"

He smiled. "Yes. This was the first room." He gestured the length of the kitchen, and I could see how it might have begun as a one-room adobe house. A long time ago.

The book Caeran had wanted from the library was about the Spanish colonists. Several stray bits of information clicked into place.

"When did you come here?"

"To this valley? After the Pueblo Revolt. I was in Santa Fe before then."

"So that's...1680. But I don't think there were any settlements here at that time."

"Correct. I saw the coming disaster with the Pueblos. I knew the colonists who survived it would flee, but I did not wish to leave with them. I chose New Spain as my home for specific reasons. Fortunately, the natives thought well of me and raised no objection when I left before the slaughter began. I came here, far from any of their cities."

"You must have been alone here for a long time."

"Not quite two centuries."

I shook my head, unable to imagine it. "Weren't you lonely?"

"I was not entirely alone. I received visits from passing hunters, and before long they knew they could come to me for healing. It gave them a reason to let me live in peace."

"But you never saw any of your own people."

He gave me a wry look. "I preferred it so."

I wanted to know why, but didn't want to be rude, so I didn't ask. Instead I chose a less personal question.

"Are your current guests the first ælven who have come here?"

"Not the first. Twice before I have had visitors of my kind."

"So, they knew you were here."

"They knew I had set off to come to the colonies. The rest took research, as you have seen."

A memory of the alben standing at my counter, his face shadowed by the hood of his sweatshirt, made me frown. "Did Caeran tell you the alben was looking for you too?"

"Yes, when he warned me you were coming. We have taken precautions."

"Why would he be looking for you? Not for healing."

"No."

The kettle boiled, emitting a sweet, low tone unlike the shrill whistles I was used to. Madera got up to fill his teapot with hot water, then returned to the table.

"He might seek me thinking I am an easy target. Do you remember when you first saw him?"

"Yes. It was in the Student Union Building at UNM." My pulse quickened as I recalled how the alben had caught my eye —how similar to Caeran he looked—and then the way he had noticed me.

Madera straightened in his chair, looking alarmed. I glanced up at him. Had he seen the alben in my thoughts?

"Did you ever see him more closely?" he asked.

"Yeah. I took a picture of him, too. Want to see it?"

"Please."

I dug my cell phone out of my pack, realizing as I did so that I didn't have my charger. Again. I'd just have to keep the phone turned off unless I needed it. I flipped it open and brought up the picture I'd snapped of the alben in the library, then handed it to Madera.

"It isn't very clear, I'm afraid."

He peered at the image, frowning, then abruptly shut the phone and gave it back. "Clear enough. Thank you."

"Someone you know?"

Madera nodded, looking unhappy. He got up and fussed with the tea, taking out cups and plates from a cupboard. I powered down my phone, but not before looking at my picture of Caeran. He looked vulnerable, startled, but still gorgeous. I'd erase that other one, when I was sure it was no longer needed.

I stowed the phone as Madera came back with a tray bearing teapot and cups, honey, bread, cheese, and a plate of apple slices. The tea he poured smelled like butterscotch, and tasted a little like toast. It was delicious and a comforting warmth in my belly.

I hadn't thought I was hungry but the apples and cheese were too tempting. I proceeded to snarf down a lot of them while Madera sipped tea and watched me. Finally, in an attempt not to be rude, I thought of another question to ask him.

"You have electricity, but I haven't seen any television sets."

He smiled slightly. "No. I have no wish to have your world and all its troubles brought into my home. Forgive me if that sounds harsh."

"I don't blame you. Lots of people feel the same." I finished my tea and he refilled my cup. "Thanks. But you aren't averse to modern comforts like electricity and gas."

"No. They are convenient. I resisted the telephone for a long time, though. My clients were ecstatic when I finally purchased a cell phone."

I smiled. "Do you have a lot of clients?"

"A fair number. Some come from other communities, as far as Taos and Red River. Some from even farther, if they have serious problems and don't wish to see a conventional doctor."

"Do you have to be certified by the state or something?"

"No. Curanderos are not recognized as medical practitioners, and I do not charge for my services."

I blinked in surprise. "Not at all? Forgive me, but...you must have some way to pay your expenses."

"I accept gifts from my clients. Occasionally they give me cash, but more often food, goods, or liquor."

"And that supports you, and pays the taxes on this place?"

He smiled. "No. I have reserves. One accumulates things of value when one lives a very long time."

I was getting close to being too nosy. I ate another slice of apple. "I thought maybe you sold the furniture you make. You could, you know. Santa Fe would eat it up."

"That would involve interacting with people a great deal more than I prefer, though it is certainly a good notion. If I ever have need of funds, I might consider it. I would employ an intermediary, of course."

I raised an eyebrow. "Of course."

Madera's eyes narrowed in amusement. "You have come here under extraordinary circumstances. I seldom have so many visitors at once. Were you to ask any of my neighbors, they would tell you I am a recluse."

"Then I'm doubly honored to be your guest." I watched him freshen both our teacups. "Your name isn't really Madera, is it?"

"I have gone by that name for centuries."

That sounded like a rebuff. I drank my tea, trying to think of a safer subject.

"But you are right," he added in a softer voice. "My true name is Madóran."

I met his gaze. For the first time I realized that he was just as gorgeous as Caeran, in a slightly different way. The lines of his face were longer, the planes sharper, his crystal blue eyes more intent. I'd been so fixated on Caeran I hadn't even thought about the others, but they were all stunning.

"Your names are all so lyrical," I said.

"Our culture reveres beauty, in all its forms."

"I can see that."

I glanced out of the window toward the courtyard. The snow was deepening on the edges of the fountain, though the water still danced.

"Do you heat the fountain with khi, or electricity?"

Madóran grinned. "Electricity is easier. Khi would require constant attention."

"Ah. But it's still magical."

I looked out toward the fountain again. Like everything else about Madóran's home, it was quietly beautiful.

Madóran, too. All of the ælven were stunning, but the others didn't take my breath away like Caeran did. Here, in the calm of the kitchen, I could acknowledge that I was more than infatuated with Caeran. He'd saved my life a couple of times, now. I owed him everything, and I was willing to pay up.

Madóran rose. "If you do not mind my leaving you briefly, I will ready a room for you."

"Thanks. And thanks for the supper. It was just what I needed."

He smiled, then left the kitchen by the door we'd come

through. I poured the rest of the tea into my cup and picked up the last slice of apple. Crisp, with a perfect balance of sweet and tart. At this point I'd be surprised to learn that Madóran had not grown it. He had a lot of resources.

I, on the other hand, did not even have a spare pair of panties.

I'd had a vague plan of driving back to Las Vegas for supplies, but it looked like the snow was going to prevent that. I wished for a TV, if only to consult the Weather Channel. I knew there was no chance of Internet.

I moved over to the fireplace and sat on the low flagstone-topped banco beside it, basking in the warmth. The fire was down to coals, so I added a piece of wood from a nearby bin and watched the flames spring up around it.

I loved fires. When I had a house, it would have fireplaces all over, like this place.

It was nice, being here, but I had to figure out what to do next. I could rinse out my undies each night until I had a chance to shop, or until it was safe to go home. I wondered how long that would be. I'd have to call the library in the morning, let them know I wouldn't be there. Dave would be pissed, and Amanda would be disappointed.

Amanda! I was supposed to meet her for dinner. She'd be freaking out!

I went back to the table and got out my phone, powered it up and dialed Man's number. I only hoped she hadn't called the cops.

"Len! Where have you been? I've been trying to call you for hours!"

"Sorry. It's been a nutty day."

"Where are you? In your room?"

"Ah—no. I had to drive up north. It's snowing here, so I probably won't be back tomorrow."

"Snowing? Len, where are you?"

"I'm at a friend's house. There was sort of an emergency."

"Are you OK?"

"Yeah. It's a long story and my phone's running down, so I really can't go into it, but don't worry. I'm fine."

"I thought the campus killer had got you!"

He tried.

"Listen, in case I can't reach Dave tomorrow, will you tell him I won't be in?"

"OK. When will you be back?"

"I'm not sure. I'll call you."

"Is something going on?"

I took a steadying breath. "Sort of. Can't talk about it right now."

"Is it that gorgeous guy?"

"That's part of it."

"Len! You ran away with him!"

"Not quite."

The door opened and Madóran came in. He saw me on the phone and frowned.

"Listen, Man, I've got to go. I'll touch base with you in the next day or so. Don't worry."

"Yeah, right. You'll be busy jumping all over that guy's bones."

"It isn't like that. I'll call you. Bye."

I powered down the phone. Madóran came to the fireplace and stood gazing at me.

"I must ask you not to discuss us with your friends."

"I haven't. I was just letting them know I was all right."

He held my gaze for a long moment, as if weighing the truth of my words, then nodded. "Your room is ready."

I followed him back to the enclosed *portal* and around to the north wing. He led me to the same room I'd slept in on Saturday. This time there was a fire in the tiny kiva fireplace. There was also a pile of clothing, much like what Madóran had brought for Caeran, on the dresser. I set my pack down next to it.

"Our females do not have much clothing to spare. These are from my wardrobe, in case you should wish to change."

I looked up at him. "Thank you! That's very thoughtful."

"Please do not leave the house unescorted." He paused, the frown returning to his brow as he gazed into some unseen distance. "The alben may be in the area by now, and will be looking for a vulnerable target."

"Fine with me. I'll just hole up. Maybe get caught up on my homework."

"If you wish for something to read, I have a small library. Some of my guests are residing there now, but tomorrow there will be opportunity for you to see it."

I nodded. "Thanks. So...do you have a plan for dealing with the alben?"

He frowned again, as if the question pained him. "We are discussing what to do."

"If I can help at all..."

We both knew that was unlikely. Madóran smiled, though.

"Thank you. I wish to talk with you further, perhaps tomorrow."

"OK," I said warily.

"About our people. There are things you should understand. You are weary, though. Tomorrow is soon enough." He went to the door. "Rest well."

"Good night."

He shut the door behind him, leaving me with an altered impression of him. On my first visit he had seemed stern, disapproving. Now I sensed more complex attitudes toward me. The disapproval was still there, but muted, tempered with resignation and also with a degree of amusement and even liking.

I liked him too, I thought, though I felt reservations as well. Despite his graciousness, I suspected he viewed me as an inferior creature, to be tolerated and controlled. To him I would never be an equal. He had untold centuries of experience, and I would probably not even live for one century.

I sighed, and picked up the top piece from the stack of clothing he'd left for me. It was a full-length caftan sort of thing.

The fabric felt like cotton, soft and heavy. There were also a shirt and loose trousers of the same fabric, dyed a light gold.

I slung the caftan over my arm and headed for the bathroom. I wanted a shower to wash the fear and the burnt-car stink away. I lingered a long time under the hot water, scrubbing my scalp with a lavender-scented soap that I suspected my host had made. He probably grew the lavender, too.

Madóran was taller than me; the caftan was too long by almost a foot. I grabbed a handful of it and hiked it up so I could walk back to my room, my clothes tucked under my arm along with my freshly rinsed panties wrapped inside a hand towel.

The flagstones of the *portal* were ice-cold, but despite that I paused at the door of the treatment room. It was closed, and I figured Caeran was still resting inside. I wanted to open the door, just to look at him, but I knew I shouldn't disturb him. He'd had a hell of a day.

I closed my eyes, laying my free hand against the door and silently wishing him well. If anything I could give would help him heal, I'd give it.

Dragging myself away, I continued along the *portal* to my room. I glanced out at the fountain as I reached the door. What I saw made me stop in surprise.

Madóran stood in the courtyard facing the fountain, his back to me, arms half-raised and his palms to the sky. Snowflakes fell softly into his hands and caught in his loose hair, puffs of white against the black. He was wearing another caftan, and apparently he'd walked all around the fountain, because it was circled by footprints.

Was he praying? Communing with nature? I felt as though I shouldn't be watching, but kept staring at him until I started to shiver in my wet hair and bare feet. He hadn't moved.

Giving up, I ducked into my room and quietly closed the door. Dumped my dirty clothes on the floor and hurried over to the fire with the towel containing my panties, which I spread out on the banco to one side of the fireplace. I huddled on the other side in the warm glow, combing my hair with my fingers as it dried, wondering about Madóran.

He'd said he was a recluse. He now had seven house guests that I knew of, maybe more. The hacienda was big, but not so big it could absorb that many people without things getting a bit cozy. Madóran had said there were guests sleeping—or resting, whatever—in the library. Maybe he'd had to share his own bedroom as well. Was he standing out in the snowy courtyard because it was the only place he could be alone?

I frowned. That might be one reason, but I didn't think it was the only one. He'd looked like he was doing a ritual, almost. Something to do with healing Caeran, maybe?

Or with repelling the alben.

I shivered and bent closer to the fire. A small, pretty copper bin stood nearby, holding a few pieces of firewood. I added one to the coals and stayed beside the fireplace until my hair was dry and I'd stopped shivering. Stayed there a while longer, musing over everything that had happened that day, until my eyelids got heavy.

The bed felt fantastic, and the caftan made a fine nightgown. I lay daydreaming about Caeran, but when I slid into sleep my dreams were far less pleasant. They involved blood and fear, anger and speed. Me running, a lot.

I woke up feeling tired. The air in the room was cold; the fire had died down. I stayed under the covers, unwilling to leave the warmth, unwilling to face the day. Only a sense of guilt finally dragged me up; I had to call Dave and tell him I wouldn't be in to work. Should call my professors, too. I'd do that, as soon as I got something hot inside me.

I hopped out of bed and scurried to the fireplace. My panties had dried, so I pulled them on and grabbed the other clean clothes from the dresser. I had to roll the legs of the trousers up. The shirt hung long on me, more like a tunic, but it was surprisingly warm. I put on my dirty socks and my sneakers, which completely ruined the back-to-nature effect of the outfit, and went out to raid the kitchen.

Sunlight gleamed from the snow in the courtyard, a white

so bright it hurt to look at it. The snow must have fallen all night; it was at least six inches deep. No sign of Madóran's footprints around the fountain. Dozens of birds were drinking and bathing there—bluebirds, juncos, and jays—reveling in what was probably the only unfrozen water for miles around.

The air in the *portal* was chilly. I hurried around the back way to the kitchen and was glad to find it unoccupied. It was not neglected, though: once again the place smelled like baking bread, and a platter of bread, butter, jam and sliced oranges sat on the counter next to a teapot under a quilted cozy.

I smiled, pleased at the sight of the oranges. Madóran couldn't have grown those.

I fixed myself a plate of food and a cup of tea, and sat on the banco by the fireplace, drawn to the cheery fire rather than the table. The bird show going on outside wasn't enough to make up for the colder air coming off the window.

As I ate, I wondered how Caeran was doing. He had healed so fast from the first cut I'd seen, maybe he was already over yesterday's wound despite its having been worse. I half hoped he would come to the kitchen, but when the door did open it was Mirali.

She smiled, fetched herself a cup of tea, and came over to the fire. "May I join you?"

"Sure."

I made room for her on the banco. She was dressed in a caftan, but it must have been her own because it didn't drag on the floor, and she wasn't that much taller than me. She looked a lot stronger than she had a few days earlier.

"You're looking well," I told her.

"Thank you. I do feel much better. I was not able to thank you properly before—"

I waved my hand. "De nada. I was glad to help."

"And now you have helped us again."

Feeling embarrassed, I took a bite of bread and jam so I wouldn't have to answer. Mirali sipped her tea, watching me.

"Madóran has told us that you are aware of our nature."

I nodded, still chewing. The conversation was going in an awkward direction.

"I am glad, for it will make it easier for you to understand why Caeran has kept apart from you."

The bread in my mouth suddenly felt dry, like a mouthful of sawdust. I took a sip of tea, trying to swallow.

"He has not had a lover in a very long time. His last was a mortal, and it broke his heart." She glanced at me as if to gauge my reaction, then went on. "Flora was mad for him, and he for her. They married, and at first they were blissfully happy. Caeran left us to live with her in Paris."

Paris. Wow. I had trouble picturing Caeran there.

"As she grew older, people began to look upon them with disapproval. They moved to London, claiming that he was her nephew, but the talk continued and they were shunned from polite society. At last Flora fled from the house, abandoning Caeran and all she owned save for the few things she carried with her. He believed she was trying to spare him further unhappiness, but though I did not know her well, I think she was eaten up by the fact that he did not age as she did."

I had managed to swallow my food by now. I took another sip of tea to wash it down, and put the rest of the bread on my plate.

"It took him three years to find her," Mirali said. "She had gone to Birmingham. When the money she took with her ran out, she sold her few possessions to pay for food and lodging. Caeran found her wedding ring in a London shop and traced it back to her. By then she had run out of funds and been put into the poor house. She contracted tuberculosis there, and died shortly after Caeran located her."

I waited for Mirali to spell out the moral of this tragic tale. A kernel of resentment burned in my chest, though I knew she was only trying to protect Caeran.

"This is not the sort of life that would benefit either of you," she said gently. "Again and again, we have watched our kindred go through such troubles. It is always the same."

"We don't have poor houses any more."

"You have places nearly as bad."

"But the attitudes you describe are outdated. We don't criticize people's choices that way nowadays. I know a couple of women who married men fifteen, twenty years younger than they were."

Mirali gazed at me, her green eyes filled with concern. They were darker than Caeran's, not lit with gold like his.

"And when it becomes forty years? Sixty years?"

I swallowed. "I always planned on being a dirty old lady."

"I am thinking of your happiness, Len, not just Caeran's."

She had a point. The feeling that I was unworthy of Caeran haunted me, though I knew he would never say so. If I was sure of anything, it was that he *did* care about me. But how much more unworthy would I feel as my youth faded?

Mirali put another log on the fire, her movements easy and graceful. "We live apart from you because trying to live among you never ends well. Long ago we concluded that we are each best off with our own kind. Caeran was hurt by Flora's loss, but it could have gone even worse for him. We often have been persecuted by your people. Accused of witchcraft or devil-worship, imprisoned and tormented—"

"That wouldn't happen now."

She raised an eyebrow. "No? We have seen times of reason and unreason come and go."

"This is a time of reason, at least in this country."

"And will that last through your lifetime?"

I blinked. Who knew? I was used to thinking things would stay the same, but I knew that anything could happen. There could be a war, a plague, some natural disaster. Worse, some nutbag could start a movement that would threaten people who lived outside the mainstream. McCarthy's witch hunts had gone on less than a century before. Would Caeran be in danger if he lived among humans when something like that happened?

"It is you I am trying to protect, as much as Caeran," Mirali said.

"Yeah, well. Thanks for the advice."

I stared down at my empty cup, feeling miserable. After a moment Mirali rose and took her cup over to the sink. I heard water running, then she came back and stood beside me. I didn't look up.

"I wish you well," she said softly, then left. As she opened the door to the entryway I heard a muted murmur of voices.

They were having a powwow, trying to figure out what to do about the alben. Me too, maybe.

Well, I had my own problems to take care of. I carried my dishes to the sink and dumped the remains of my breakfast in the trash, having lost my appetite. I washed the plate and cup, then headed back to my room via the *portal*.

= 11 =

The sun was so bright I wished for my shades, but they were in the car. When I entered my room I could hardly see, it was so dark by comparison. I left the door open, grabbed my cell phone from the dresser, and sat cross-legged on the bed.

It was later than I'd realized, almost ten. Dave would be at the library. I gritted my teeth and dialed his number.

"Wharton."

"Hi, Dave, it's Len. I won't be in today."

"You sick?" He sounded annoyed.

"No, snowbound."

"Say what?"

"I'm in Mora County. I'm snowed in. Sorry."

"Great. What are you doing in Mora?"

"It's a long story and my phone's running down. I'll explain when I see you."

I'd have to come up with a feasible explanation, but I had a couple of days for that. Dave grudgingly agreed and I hung up.

Explanation. Family emergency? That might work. It was sort of true. It just wasn't my family that had the emergency.

Next I rang all my profs, trying out my story and explaining that I might miss a week or more of classes. Their reactions ranged from cranky to understanding. I promised to find an Internet connection as soon as I could, and they agreed to email me the assignments. I didn't have all my textbooks with me, but at least I could try to keep up.

By the time I was done, my phone was nearly dead. I thought about calling Amanda, but that would probably kill the battery. I decided to save it, just in case some emergency came up. I powered it down, then fetched my pack and took inventory of my resources.

English Lit textbook. Algebra textbook. Spiral notebooks

for both courses. Handouts from American History and French classes, all the way back to the syllabus for the latter. Last week's campus paper. A science fiction novel I was halfway through. My wallet, keys, a tube of lip balm, half a roll of Life Savers, a packet of tissues, assorted pens and pencils, and one condom.

Looking at the array spread out over the rumpled bedspread, I felt depressed. I should hit the books, but I had all weekend so instead I kept out the novel and shoveled the rest back into my pack.

I succeeded in losing myself in the book, but I finished it halfway through the afternoon. As I sat up, yawning, I realized I was hungry. Time for a raid on the kitchen. Maybe I'd run into Madóran and could ask to see his library.

My door was still open. I hadn't noticed anyone going past, but then I'd been pretty absorbed in the book. No one was on the *portal* now. As I stepped out, I saw that the daylight had been dimmed and softened by an overcast of cloud. I frowned, wondering if we'd get hit with more snow.

In the kitchen a platter of sliced meat and cheese sat next to the ubiquitous loaf of fresh bread. As I put together an improvised sandwich, I wondered if Madóran had a bread machine stashed somewhere. He did have a refrigerator—I found some mustard in there—so he wasn't entirely opposed to appliances. There had to be a water heater somewhere too, come to think of it.

No sign of a dishwasher, though. I did remember seeing a washer and dryer. Mental note: wash my clothes.

I carried my sandwich and a glass of water out to the *portal*, where there were some chairs here and there facing the courtyard. I was beginning to feel a little claustrophobic, but the birds kept me entertained while I ate. There were some species I couldn't identify—one a big woodpeckery-looking thing that flashed rusty undersides of its wings when it flew off.

Where were all the ælven? Were they avoiding me? Still discussing strategy? Out hunting the alben?

I wished I could do something to contribute, but couldn't

think of a single thing that I could do better than they. Probably they were stronger, faster, smarter than me in every way. This thought reminded me of Mirali's lecture, and I grimaced. I was *not* going to get any more depressed over my inadequacy, thank you.

I got up to take my glass back to the kitchen. All silent. I grabbed one more slice of meat, stuffed it in my face, and went off to check the laundry room. I opened the washer to make sure it was empty, then turned to go collect my clothes from my room. Madóran stood in the doorway.

I jumped, and let out a small yelp. "You startled me!"

He tilted his head. "May I help you find something?"

"I found it." I gestured to the machines. "OK if I wash my clothes?"

Madóran's face relaxed. "Of course. Would you mind first showing the others your picture of the alben?"

"Oh. Sure. I'll have to get my phone, it's in my room."

He stepped back from the door, then followed me. I grabbed my phone and went with him to the big front room. All the ælven were there, including two men I hadn't met, both stamped from Caeran's mold.

Caeran himself was perched on the banco by the fireplace. He smiled slightly as I caught sight of him. The others looked surprised, and some displeased, at my appearance.

"Lenore has captured an image of Gehmanin," said Madóran. He gestured to me.

Gehmanin, eh? A mouthful.

I flipped open my phone and brought up the picture of the alben, wishing it was a better shot, and handed the phone to Madóran. He carried it around, showing it to the others. While he was doing that, I drifted over toward Caeran.

"Hi. Feeling better?"

He nodded. "Better, yes."

He still looked tired. I wanted to wrap him in blankets, feed him hot cocoa. Other things, too, but I knew better than to think about them in this room full of mind readers.

My phone emitted a chirp, and I turned to look. Madóran had made it about two thirds of the way around the room.

"The battery's running low," I said. "I don't have my charger with me."

Madóran looked at the phone frowning doubtfully. "We could try my charger."

"Sure. Or do you have email?" He gave me a blank stare; I waved a hand. "Never mind."

He continued showing the picture around, the rest of the ælven hurrying to gather close. I stayed by Caeran.

"You've been talking all day."

He nodded. "Some complications have arisen."

Like Madóran being acquainted with the alben? From the way it bothered him, I guessed that they'd been well acquainted, maybe even close. That sucked for Madóran.

"I hope you are not too bored," Caeran said, a hint of anxiousness in his voice that I probably wouldn't have noticed before my little talk with Mirali.

"Nah." I smiled to reassure him. "I've been reading. I've got homework, too, so don't worry about me getting into trouble."

His answering smile was wan. It made me want to gather him up in a hug, but I shouldn't even be thinking about that. I turned back to Madóran, who stood surrounded by ælven. As I looked, the phone in his hand went dark.

The ælven stepped back. Madóran returned my phone to me.

"Thank you. When next we pause, I will bring you my charger."

Nodding, I stuck the phone in my pocket. I considered asking about the library, but got the feeling this wasn't a good time. Instead I gave Caeran one last smile, then headed back to my room. As the door of the front room closed behind me, I imagined I could feel the intensity in there increase.

In an attempt at virtuousness, I got out my English Lit textbook and read through my next assignment. Had trouble getting into it, though the poetry was beautiful. My thoughts kept drifting back to the ælven, wondering when they would finish their discussion, and what would happen then.

The third time I realized I'd lost track of my reading, I gave up and shut the book. Studying just wasn't happening.

I got up and wandered out onto the *portal*. The light from the courtyard had gone blue. The cloud cover was thicker, and there were only a few birds in the fountain. I couldn't check the time on my dead phone, and I hadn't seen any clocks around the hacienda, but I figured it was late afternoon or early evening. The ælven would break for supper soon, I hoped.

I went and collected my dirty clothes and the caftan that Madóran had lent me, and carried them to the laundry room. They didn't take up much of the washer. The only thing I could think of to add was Caeran's bloodstained shirt that was still out in my car.

I fetched my keys from my room and went out through the entryway and the small door in the zaguan. Clouds hung low overhead, darker than even a few minutes earlier. Shivering, I hurried toward the car, picking out the door key. A movement to one side caught my eye.

Someone running toward me across the field, out of the south. It took me a second to register the white hair, the flapping hood.

I screamed and ran for the hacienda. The alben caught me on the *portal* before I got to the door. My keys went flying.

His fingers dug into my arms as he dragged me backward. I shrieked obscenities at him and kicked uselessly, falling to my knees. He yanked my arms so hard I gasped, then the door of the hacienda banged open.

= 12 =

I barely glimpsed the three ælven who came out. The alben released me and I slipped, banging my hip on the step as I fell. The ælven were past me in an instant, their feet soundless as they crossed the hollow boards and pursued the alben into the snowy field.

My hip hurt, my arms hurt, and I was terrified. Tears ran cold down my cheeks as I rolled onto my backside and stared toward the field. They had all vanished.

I indulged in a moment of blubbering, then got unsteadily to my feet and started looking for my keys in the snow. Voices and footsteps came out of the house.

Arms wrapped around me, vise-like, pulling me upright. I squeaked, fear overwhelming reason for a moment until I realized it was Caeran holding me, after which I dissolved into tears.

He stroked my hair, murmuring in my ear. I couldn't understand what he was saying and didn't care. It was the tone, the softness in his voice, that soothed me. I struggled to stop crying. He was guiding me back to the hacienda.

"M-my keys. I dropped them."

"I will find them," someone said nearby.

I looked up and saw it was Nathrin. I tried to smile, saying, "Thanks."

Caeran urged me gently toward the door. I went with him, ignoring the stares of the others. They'd all come outside, even Mirali.

Caeran took me into the front room and parked me on the banco by the fire. I winced as my hip made contact with the flagstone. I'd have an interesting bruise, for sure. I hoped that was all.

I shivered despite the warmth of the fire. Freak-out still had me in its grip. Caeran sat next to me and put his arms around me again.

"I am sorry, Len," he murmured.

"Wh-why? Not your fault."

"I promised you he would never touch you again."

I shook my head, trying to make my teeth stop chattering. "I'm the one who went out."

"Yes," said a stern voice above us, "and you should not have done so. Did I not warn you not to leave the house alone?"

I looked up at Madóran. "My bad. I w-was just going to my car. Didn't think..."

Caeran squeezed my shoulders. "Never mind."

"You must not set foot outside unescorted," Madóran said in a milder tone.

"Yeah, I get it."

He laid a hand on my forehead. I closed my eyes as incredible heat poured into me, banishing the shivers, turning my limbs to liquid. Madóran's hands moved gently over my arms and my hip, soothing the pain away. My sobs subsided. I felt like I was sitting in a golden pool. When the warm hands went away, I opened my eyes.

Madóran was kneeling on the floor in front of me, watching me with a tiny frown. I took a deep breath and swallowed.

"Thank you."

He nodded once, then stood and went to speak to some of the others who were returning from outside. Caeran's kin shot disapproving glances toward me.

"I should go away," I said, rubbing at my eyes. They were probably red.

Caeran's answer was to tighten his hold on me. I looked at him and his eyes caught me, mesmerizing me just as powerfully as the first time. Everything else slid away, insignificant, until someone came too near to be ignored.

It was Nathrin. He held out my keychain, and dropped it in my palm when I lifted my hand.

"Thank you," I said, sniffing.

He actually smiled, then raised an eyebrow at Caeran before turning away. I tried for a joke.

"I sure know how to bring a stop to a party, huh?"

Caeran laid his cheek against mine. "It is not your fault, and it was hardly a party."

"They disapprove of me," I whispered.

"Ignore them."

His lips brushed my hair with the words, sending a shiver through me that had nothing to do with cold or fear. It felt wonderful sitting with Caeran's arms around me, but I knew it couldn't last. Shouldn't last.

"I really ought to go wash my face," I said, making a halfhearted attempt to pull away.

"You look fine." Caeran smoothed my hair back.

"I'm a mess. It's sweet of you, but let's be real."

I made a more determined move to stand up, and Caeran let me go. Then I made the mistake of looking back at him. His eyes were filled with worry and a hint of pain. That mustn't be the beginning of worse feelings—I couldn't let it.

I managed a feeble smile. "Thanks. I feel a lot better. Maybe I'll take a hot shower."

Another of the ælven came in—the other woman, not Mirali. All the others stopped talking, and Madóran took a step toward her.

"Any sign?"

She shook her head. "They are still pursuing him." She gave me a long, hard look, then moved to the other end of the room.

Great. Yep, it's all my fault.

I headed for the entryway, wanting to get out of there as fast as possible. Tried not to glance back at Caeran. Failed. Gave him a wave, then ducked out.

An ælven was standing by the front door, on guard, it looked like. He frowned at me, and I hustled across to the kitchen.

I'd forgotten most of their names. It didn't help that they all looked so alike.

In the kitchen I made myself drink a glass of water and eat a handful of nuts from a bowl on the counter. My stomach protested, but didn't rebel. I filled the glass again and took it with me to the inner *portal*.

The courtyard was steeped in shadow, almost dark. I felt oddly exposed, as if I'd lost my coat and was open to the cold night. The air in the enclosed *portal* was chilly, but it wasn't a coat that I was missing. It was Caeran.

Not wanting to think in that direction, I hurried to my room and pulled the door shut, dousing myself in darkness. I fumbled for a light switch. No luck. I groped my way to the bed and managed to turn on the bedside lamp without knocking it over.

Very carefully, I set my glass on the table, then sat on the bed and gave in to a fit of the shivers. My arms were still sore where the alben had grabbed me—I could feel the bruises developing. The hot shower was sounding better and better, but I didn't have any clean clothes to change into. My laundry was still sitting in the washer. I felt tears threatening, only because I was frustrated and overwhelmed.

Hoping that doing something would help me pull myself together, I went over to the fireplace. The ashes of last night's fire were cold, and there wasn't any way to empty them. The only tool was a fireplace poker. I used it to push most of the ash to the side, then stacked fresh wood against the back wall of the kiva in a half-tipi shape.

There was no kindling, no paper, no matches. How did Madóran build the fires—did he carry all that stuff with him from room to room?

Actually, he probably didn't have to build a lot of fires most of the time. Remembering that I was only one of many guests, I decided to do the best I could on my own.

I raided my spiral notebooks for paper and stuffed it underneath the firewood. A search of all the drawers in the room turned up no matches. Fighting tears of frustration and stress, I decided to wash my face and then go look for matches in the kitchen.

The *portal* was still dark. It had been lit the night before; there must be a switch or something somewhere—maybe by the door to the front room. I went that way to look and heard muffled voices from beyond the door. It sounded like they were arguing.

Not my problem. I was a temporary guest. I'd be leaving—soon, I hoped—and they wouldn't have to worry about me any more. And no, this was *not* my fault. I did not bring the alben down on these people. He would have found them without me.

I saw a pale rectangle on the wall by the door and put my hand on it. Not an ordinary light switch, just a plate, but when I touched it flames flickered to life in lanterns all along the ceiling of the *portal.* I caught my breath at the beauty of the light racing around the passages, then headed to the bathroom.

On a small shelf embedded in the wall I found a comb. I used it to tidy my hair, then scrubbed my face with hot water and Madóran's lavender soap, and combed my hair again.

My reflection looked a bit wild-eyed, but I felt a lot better. Next order of business: matches, and maybe a cup of tea.

I expected to find the kitchen unoccupied, but when I went in, Madóran was standing at the counter, chopping carrots. A large pot was burbling on the back burner, and the smell of cooking onions made my stomach rumble.

"Can I help?" I asked.

Madóran glanced up at me. "Do you like to cook?"

I shrugged. "I'm not a gourmet, but I can chop veggies."

He offered me a knife, a cutting board, and a bowl of potatoes. It was strange standing next to him at the counter, doing something so mundane, but it was also comforting.

"Is the meeting over?" I asked.

"No, they are still discussing what to do. I had little to add, and thought I could be of more use preparing supper."

A slight note of strain in his voice made me look at him. There was tension in his face. He knew the alben, I recalled.

"Have the ones who went after him...?"

"No. They have not returned."

"I hope they're all right."

Madóran scooped a pile of sliced carrots into the soup pot, then began chopping roasted green chile. I blinked as the fumes stung my eyes. He must be teaching all Caeran's family how to eat spicy food.

Don't think about Caeran. Think about anything else.

"My laundry." I put down the knife. "I forgot to run it."

"I started it. You might check to see if it is done."

Nodding, I headed for the laundry room and quickly shifted the small load to the dryer, putting it on gentle in case Madóran's caftan might shrink. Weird to think of Madóran using these modern machines, but I was sure glad he had them.

When I got back to the kitchen, the rest of my potatoes had vanished along with the chile. Madóran was leaning over the pot, stirring and frowning.

"What else can I do?" I asked.

"Fill the kettle."

I did that, and set it on the front burner, then watched Madóran shake some herbs into the stew pot from various jars. He seemed satisfied at last, and beckoned me over to the table. He was looking at my arms, and I glanced down, wondering if I'd gotten soot on the sleeves.

"You are still feeling some pain."

"Oh—that. Yeah, he grabbed me pretty hard."

Madóran reached out and stroked my arms, brushing the soreness away. I repressed a shiver, still amazed by what he could do.

"Thank you. That's a lot better."

He smiled slightly. "It is the least I can do after scolding you."

"I deserved it. I can't believe I was so stupid."

"A mistake any of us might have made."

His gaze was gentle, even kindly. So different from the way the others looked at me. I was grateful, and surprised.

"I thought you disapproved of me."

He glanced down. "I did, at first, but you have shown unexpected depths. Also, I can see that it is too late."

I frowned, unsure what he meant. Was he talking about Caeran?

"It's not too late," I said defensively.

Madóran raised an eyebrow. "Perhaps I was mistaken," he said, and stood up.

The kettle had begun to sing its low, melodious note. It sounded mournful, or maybe that was just my mood. Madóran made tea, bringing the pot and two cups to the table along with a bowl of fruit that I was proud to be able to identify as figs. He pushed them toward me, and I picked one up.

"Don't tell me you grew these."

"There is a fig tree in the plazuela." He gestured toward the courtyard. "Did you not see it?"

"I wouldn't know a fig tree if it bit me."

"It has no leaves at the moment."

I tilted my head. "You must love this place."

He paused, gazing at me. "I do. I have been here long enough to grow attached."

Yeah, two or three centuries would do that, I guessed. I bit into my fig. It was soft and sweet, mild compared to the dried figs and cookie fillings I was used to.

"And I always intended to stay. I meant to love it, so that —"

He stopped abruptly, frowning. Lifted the lid of the teapot to see if the tea was strong enough. The fragrant steam rose between us, obscuring his face for a moment.

"This is ready."

He poured for me, then for himself. I sipped and sighed, grateful for the warmth. The window was chilly, and I still felt a little fragile.

"You were trying to forget your former home?" I asked.

That was nosy of me. Maybe Madóran didn't want to talk about his past, least of all with a pesky mortal. I took another swallow of tea, trying to think of a different subject.

"Yes," he said after a moment. His voice was filled with sadness. "There are many things I would like to forget. Those of course are the things I cannot help but remember."

"Sorry."

He shook his head, smiling slightly. "I lived in Italy, and before that in Greece. I have been a healer for many centuries. It has been my lifelong study."

"Healing your own kind?"

"And humans. More and more, humans. Once you did not outnumber us so vastly, but we breed very rarely."

I nodded. Caeran had said that.

"How many of you are there?"

"Fewer than a thousand."

I was shocked. "In the whole world?"

He nodded. "I cannot be certain of the number. When I came here, I severed all contact with the others. I intended to remain apart from them."

Why? I hastily took another fig, trying to shift my thoughts.

"Because of Gehmanin," Madóran said.

"I didn't mean—"

"I know, but let me say this to you. It is not safe for me to discuss it with the others." He gazed at me, blue eyes sharp and earnest. "Will you accept my confidence?"

I swallowed. It was the least I could do.

"Sure."

Madóran stared at the teacup between his hands. "Gehmanin was my lover, long ago."

I must have gasped, because he glanced up, smiling wryly. "*Long* ago. We have both had other loves since."

Whoa. I took another swallow of tea, trying to grasp what I was hearing. Gehmanin, who was now an alben, had once been...and that meant...

"He would have returned to me had I asked it. He wanted me to ask it, but I never would."

Unable to think of a single thing to say, I just listened.

"We first met on Samos. He was a favored member of Polycrates's court. Well, we both were, but he far more than I. He let himself be idolized; he basked in it. I considered his behavior too public, too involved with mortals for safety. We argued, and I came to see that we would never reconcile that difference. So I...left."

His voice rang with heartache. Even now, centuries later, he regretted this loss. How could these people endure such pain?

"I traveled to Rome, and threw myself into study. Watched the empire thrive, and then begin to decay. I could see its end approaching, so I moved again, this time to Egypt, there to pursue my learning in a different context."

"Were you alone all that time?"

"You mean without companions of my own kind. Yes, I was alone in that sense. I had friends among the mortals—even lovers, occasionally—but my own folk were elsewhere. Most went deep into the forests of Europe, hiding from the waves of invaders. Many of them live there still, though the forests are much smaller now."

He poured more tea for us both. I watched his hands—graceful, steady, no wasted movement. How I wished I could come close to that.

"All the time I was studying the arts of healing, I was also searching for understanding. The alben's suffering is very old, you see. It came with us from our homeland, which has long since sunk beneath the sea—"

"Atlantis?"

He shook his head. "Atlantis is a myth, cobbled from fragments of various histories, including ours. Our home was more distant, far away in the center of the ocean. It was there that the alben's sickness first arose, and our ancestors fought the first wars over it."

"Is anyone—are any of you—still alive from that time?"

"None that I know of."

"But you're immortal."

He smiled sadly. "Even immortals grow weary of this world." He took a fig, turning it in his fingers as he admired it. "And immortal does not mean indestructible. We can be killed."

He ate the fig, looking thoughtful as he chewed. I sipped my tea, wondering why he wanted to tell me all this.

"It was in Egypt that Gehmanin found me," Madóran continued. "He begged me to see him, and I agreed. I should have refused, but I was weak.

"In one evening, he reminded me of all the reasons we should not be together, even as he argued that we should. He wanted to go to the Egyptian court and claim kinship with their gods. Certain of our gifts would stand as proof of such claims, or so he maintained. Gehmanin wanted the adoration of mortals. He could never see that it was a dangerous trap."

"I suppose you could have gotten away with it."

"Perhaps, but the chances of discovery and disaster were too great for my liking. Moreover, I thought it unethical. Gehmanin and I never did agree on ethics." He smiled, glancing up at me.

"After the Dark Ages, I returned to Rome. From time to time I saw other ælven. Their visits to human cities were always temporary; they preferred the solitude of their hidden enclaves. I could not convince them that we must find ways of living in harmony with humans, especially since they—the ælven—were at war."

War. Ugly word.

"With the alben?"

Madóran nodded. "That war—the first war—never really ended. The alben fled to Europe, and we followed when our homeland drowned. The struggle has continued."

"How did you keep from getting dragged into it?"

"By living among humans. Even so, there were times when my kindred would beg me to join them—to mend their wounds, and heal those who sickened with the alben's curse. Those latter I did try to help, but I never found a cure."

Fear crawled down my spine as I remembered that Caeran was threatened by this curse, as Madóran called it. My throat went dry, and I sucked down more tea.

"Gehmanin sought me out again, and I refused to see him. He sent messages with my friends from the woodland clans. I realized he would never give up, so I cut my ties and came to the New World."

"That must have been terrifying." I remembered studying the Spanish Colonial era. Much of it wasn't pretty.

"It was needful. I did not regret it. Despite the wars that have troubled this land, I have found peace here."

"Until now."

He sighed, and sipped his tea. "All things come to an eventual end."

"I'm sorry."

"*You* did not bring Gehmanin here."

"I sort of helped, though."

"No. Do not think I mean to belittle you when I say that your absence would have made no difference. Gehmanin would have found me in any case."

"Do you think he wants you to heal him?"

Madóran closed his eyes briefly. "No doubt. In many ways. I can do nothing, though."

"And the others..."

"They mean to kill him."

He stared at the cup between his hands, eyes going hard. I wanted to help, to offer comfort, but I couldn't think of anything to say. Gehmanin was a stranger to me, one I knew only as a brutal killer who wanted to consume my life. I couldn't pretend that I disagreed with the other ælven.

"Nor do I know what I want," Madóran said softly. "I can find no reconciliation."

"You still care for him."

"But his actions are wrong. The more so, now."

I frowned, staring at the satiny wood of the table. "It's so unfair. You should have access to the best medical research facilities. There's got to be a way to find a cure."

Madóran looked bemused. "Sadly, I dare not seek out the means of conducting such research."

"You need an ally." A flicker of excitement kindled in my chest. "You need an ally, and I need to choose a major. Why don't I make it pre-med?"

He blinked. "What?"

"I haven't chosen a career path. Medical would be fine. I'd be more interested in research than practicing, but that's what you need anyway."

Madóran stared at me, seeming confused. Maybe he hadn't kept up with the human educational system.

"It would only take me a few years to get through med school. That's nothing to you, right? And then I can get a research job somewhere, with access to a lab."

Madóran's frown told me he still didn't understand. I was getting more excited the more I thought about it.

"I can work on your problem! Help find a cure for the alben. Maybe figure out what makes you immortal, too."

"Lenore—"

"Just say you think it's a good idea, and I'll go away and not bother you for a few years."

He smiled, shaking his head. "It is a generous thought, but your lifetime is brief. You should spend it pursuing your dreams, not our troubles."

"I *want* to do this. This inspires me like nothing else has. I was thinking about business school, because at least you can get a job. But this is way better."

"And how would you explain the nature of your research?"

I waved a hand. "We'll do that on the side. My official research will be on human health issues, and if you feel any obligation, you can help me with that. For as long as you've been studying us, you probably know things about humans that no one else does."

The disbelief in his eyes faded, replaced by a spark of interest. "You are envisioning a huge commitment. What if you discover that this work is not to your liking?"

I shrugged. "If I flunk out, I'll have to try something else. But I won't flunk out. I'll have every reason not to."

A slow smile spread over Madóran's face. "A cause."

"Yes! You help us, we help you. It might even convince your people to change their attitude toward humans."

His glance flicked aside. I could see that he doubted that one, and I didn't blame him. People—humans—could be pretty rotten a lot of the time.

A timer went off. Madóran got up and opened the oven, sending the smell of baking bread through the kitchen. I offered to help, and Madóran cheerfully ordered me around the kitchen to fetch dishes, butter, silverware. He sliced the bread and gave me a heel, still steaming. I put some butter on and watched it melt into the bread, then munched it down.

"Mmm! You know, you could be a professional baker."

He chuckled. "Too social for me."

"Oh, yeah. And you probably don't need the money."

The food was ready. Where were people going to eat it, I wondered? There was a table in the front room, but it wouldn't seat more than eight, squeezing. The kitchen table was only big enough for four.

"We will manage. Help yourself while I go tell the others supper is ready."

"Hey, Madóran?"

He paused at the door, looking back.

"Thanks," I said. The word was inadequate to cover all my gratitude, for the healing, the trust, the inspiration. And the fantastic bread.

He smiled and went out.

Left alone, my nervousness crept back. I didn't want to be here when all the ælven came through. I filled a bowl with soup, grabbed another piece of bread, and headed back toward my room.

The *portal* was warmer now, probably from all the gas lights. The glow they cast was golden, cozy. I decided to park in one of the chairs there to eat. Picking one next to an end table where I could set my plate, I settled in to enjoy my meal.

I could hear the murmur of voices, see the shadows of my fellow guests passing through the entryway to the kitchen. Ignoring them, I curled my feet under me in my chair, trying to be invisible.

The soup was savory and delicious, with chicken and beans and shreds of greens, and just enough chile for a slow burn. I gobbled it down, then ate my bread slowly.

I heard the door to the south wing, the kitchen wing, open. Like a guilty school kid, I put my feet on the floor and sat up straight in my chair, watching the newcomer approach through two layers of glass, an unfocused shadow. My heart started racing and I knew before I could see his face that it was Caeran.

He carried a supper plate, and smiled when he saw me. I smiled back, then tore a piece off my bread and popped it in my mouth. My heart was racing; I was thrilled that he had joined me, though I knew I should stay away from him.

He set his plate on my table and drew another of the chairs closer. "I do not blame you for hiding."

I swallowed. "How's the argument going?"

His smile faded. "Some wish to set a trap for the alben, luring him back here to capture him. Others wish to hunt him down."

"Those three haven't come back yet, have they?"

Caeran shook his head as he ate a spoonful of soup.

"So maybe it'll be a moot question. If they catch him."

Unless he catches them. But three against one? I doubted he had much chance. Poor Madóran.

I wrenched my thoughts away from that, picked up the last bit of bread from my plate and stared out at the courtyard. It was dark compared with the lighted *portal*, though I could see the glint of starlight on the fountain's restless water.

"What do *you* want to do?" I asked. "Trap him or hunt him?"

"I want to fulfill my promise to you. Keep you safe."

"You're evading the question."

Caeran put his plate down. "I would rather hunt him."

He didn't sound enthusiastic, which made me think he was choosing the lesser of two evils. I could understand that; neither solution would be pleasant. Proximity to the alben under any circumstances had proved to be unpleasant.

"How's your shoulder?" I asked.

Caeran put a hand to it absently. "I hardly notice."

"Madóran's good."

"Yes."

"And you heal so fast. I'm really envious of that one."

Caeran gave a fleeting smile. It made me want to throw my arms around him. Instead I looked back at the fountain, and thought through the words to the Major General's song from *Pirates of Penzance*.

Caeran turned to look at me; I could feel his gaze. My cheeks started tingling, and I lost track of the lyrics.

"Is something wrong?" he asked.

I met his gaze, though it made me unsteady. "I just don't want to bother you with all my silly thoughts."

"So you give me a silly song instead."

"You said you'd teach me how to guard my thoughts."

"Yes. It is simple. You begin by summoning your inner light, here." He placed a hand on his solar plexus. "Let it flow all through you, then spill out to surround you."

"The white light thing? Really? You guys started that?"

He looked amused. "I suppose we did."

"OK, I'll try it."

I closed my eyes and followed his directions. I'd done some visualizations with light in a yoga class. It was easy, though I wasn't sure it felt real. I could picture myself surrounded by light, but had trouble believing it would protect my thoughts.

I had to protect them, though. I didn't like keeping secrets from Caeran, but the secret I was protecting wasn't mine; Madóran had entrusted me with it, and I didn't want to fail that trust.

White light, white light.

I focused on that until I felt I'd reached a level of stability, then opened my eyes. Caeran was watching me. He nodded.

"That is good. You have done this before."

"A little. Do I have to keep concentrating?"

"A corner of your mind must tend the shield. It becomes second nature with practice."   "Thanks."

He smiled, and I came close to throwing the whole shield idea away. If I couldn't trust Caeran...

I looked out at the fountain again, because looking at him weakened my willpower, and it wasn't that strong to begin with. I *liked* looking at Caeran. I wanted to do more than that, but I didn't want to create trouble or pain for either of us. Or for Madóran.

"Can I help?" Caeran asked softly.

"Help?"

"With whatever is troubling you."

"I don't think so."

"You must not blame yourself—"

"I know. I'm not."

Needing to move, I picked up my plate and stood, gesturing at Caeran's, which still held half a piece of bread. "Are you finished with that? Want more soup?"

"Let me take them," he said, standing up. "You were hiding."

He was right, but I shook my head. "I want to look in the kitchen for some matches."

"Matches?"

"To light a fire in my room. It's cold."

A glint of humor came into his eyes. "I doubt you will find any."

"He's got to have matches for the stove. I'll be right back."

I held my hand out for Caeran's plate. He gave it to me, keeping the bread. I hurried to the kitchen.

Trying to keep a distance from Caeran wasn't any fun. Too bad I couldn't leave; that would be the easiest way. I could bury myself in my homework, maybe. The thought didn't thrill me.

In the kitchen, two of the ælven were sitting at the table, eating soup. I smiled a hello, then ignored them, busying myself with washing Caeran's and my dishes. The ælven were silent, and I could feel them watching me. I concentrated on keeping my white light charged.

When I'd finished the dishes, I opened the drawer nearest the stove. Cooking utensils. The drawer below it was full of dish towels and a couple of potholders. No matches. I didn't want to toss the whole kitchen in front of the others, so I went back out to the *portal*, where Caeran was nibbling his bread.

"You were right. I couldn't find any matches."

He grinned and jumped up from his chair. "Take me to your room and I will light the fire for you."

Oh, what a straight line! Virtuously ignoring it, I led him to my bedroom. He went right to the fireplace and peered at the wood I'd laid.

"Paper?"

"There wasn't any kindling."

"Ah."

He glanced at me, eyes gleaming. I sat on the end of the bed and crossed my arms, wondering if he planned to do the boy scout thing. It was tedious—I'd tried it at summer camp.

He held out a hand, palm toward the fireplace. In three seconds, the wood burst into flame.

"Holy—cow!"

Caeran beamed at me as the paper burned in a whoosh. I nodded.

"OK, I get it. No matches. Dang, you sure know a lot of cool tricks!"

"Tricks?"

"Things like this." I gestured to the fire, then moved to the banco, holding out my hands to the warmth. "Things I wish I could do."

He was close, sitting across from me, the opening of the fireplace between us. Firelight played on his features and lit glints in his hair, making me want to stare at him. I sucked a deep breath and looked back at the fire.

"Len?"

"Hm?"

"Have I done something wrong?"

Oh, shit. White light, white light.

"No."

He was silent for a long moment, then said, "Was it me you were hiding from?"

I closed my eyes. "Sort of."

"Should I go, then?" he whispered.

I could not bring myself to say "yes," no matter how much I tried to tell myself it would be for the best. The fire's heat beat on my eyelids and my cheeks. My hands started trembling. I pushed them toward the fire, but Caeran's hands closed around them, drawing them back. Opening my eyes, I saw that I was closer to the flames than I'd thought. He'd saved me from burning myself.

His hands were warmer than the fire, almost as warm as Madóran's. He wore his concerned look, golden-green eyes worried as they watched me. I couldn't look away.

I swallowed. "I don't want to cause you any pain."

His expression lightened as if with new understanding. He looked down, his thumb caressing the back of my hand.

"There is pain before us either way. The pain of separation

now, or at the end of your life."

OK. Yes, that was true.

"Which would be easier for you?" I whispered.

He paused before answering. The fire snapped.

"I would gladly endure your death for a lifetime of your company."

My heart gave a giant squeeze inside my chest, and I knew without a doubt that this was what I wanted. Sorry, Mirali. Sorry, everyone else. Ultimately, this choice was mine and Caeran's.

"Though," Caeran added, looking up at me, "it would be hard for me if you left before then."

I drew a shaky breath. "I'm not Flora."

He smiled like the sunrise. "I know. You understand much better than she ever could."

I wasn't sure he was right about that, but I let it pass. "I won't make you leave your people, anyway."

"Will you come and live with us?"

"Uh...well, I want to finish college."

He nodded. "Of course."

"And then, I sort of had a career in mind. See, I was talking with Madóran—"

"Madóran?" Caeran frowned.

I explained the research idea. He listened, looking skeptical at first, but I got caught up in my excitement again and by the time I'd envisioned curing cancer, AIDS, and the alben's curse, he was smiling.

"This is your heart's work," he said.

"Yes."

"How can I help?"

"Um. You could help me study, I guess."

"Shall I enroll in your school?"

"Wow. Um, I think they'd want some ID."

"I can arrange for that."

It stunned me to imagine going to school with Caeran. Sharing an apartment, maybe. Oh, my, yes. I would like that.

I'd forgotten to keep up the white light. I forgot everything but Caeran when I looked into his eyes. He smiled, leaning closer, and my heart tried to fly to him.

A door slammed in the distance; the front door, I thought. Caeran looked that way, then stood up, releasing my hands. He glanced back at me.

"They have returned."

= 14 =

He was out the door before I could answer. I followed him along the *portal* to the entryway. Cold air blasted me as he opened the door. There was snow on the entry floor; also blood. Three ælven men were in the entryway, two carrying the third, who was bleeding from a terrible wound in his throat.

Madóran pushed through the others watching from the front room's doorway. Caeran stepped back and I hopped out of his way as he held the door to the inner *portal* open.

"This way," he said.

"Yes." Madóran stepped out, beckoning to the two holding the wounded man. "Bring him here."

Caeran and I both followed them to the treatment room, Caeran's room. Madóran took charge, ordering the two to lay their friend on the massage table. When his gaze fell on me I spoke up before he could banish me.

"How can I help?"

He glanced at the wounded man, who looked more pale than Caeran had at his worst, then back at me. "You are willing?"

I nodded. If I was going into medical, I'd have to get used to this sort of thing.

"Pour water into a bowl and bring me cloths."

I stepped to the work counter. The pitcher stood on it, and I found a bowl and a stack of cloths inside.

"Are either of you hurt?" Madóran said behind me.

Two voices murmured "No."

"Caeran, take them to the kitchen and give them something to eat."

I glanced up as they left. One of the two ælven looked back at me and frowned. Caeran pulled the door closed, smiling brief encouragement to me. My heart leapt, then I turned to the work at hand.

The water in the pitcher was cold. I poured some into the bowl and brought it to the table where the wounded ælven lay. Madóran had a hand on his forehead, and held the other hand over the bowl. Instantly it grew warm in my hands. I jumped, but managed not to drop it.

Madóran dipped a cloth into the bowl and began cleaning the ragged wound. Blood pulsed from it slowly. I winced. It looked like a wild animal had attacked the poor guy. Had Gehmanin done this?

"Yes," Madóran said softly. "I can feel his khi."

Oh, ugh!

He cleaned the wound, then asked me to help him strip off the wounded man's shirt. I set aside the bowl and carefully removed the shirt while Madóran lifted the patient's torso from the table. The man moaned, and Madóran spoke to him in their language. I heard him say "Savhoran" and remembered that was the name of one of Caeran's family.

There were other wounds on Savhoran's chest—scrapes and cuts—but none as bad as the neck wound. He'd been in a vicious fight, it looked like. I wondered if Gehmanin was still at large.

"Can you lay a fire?" Madóran asked.

"Sure."

I went to the fireplace and piled some wood, not bothering to worry about kindling. Madóran glanced at me as I returned to the table, then lit the fire from where he stood, holding a hand out as Caeran had done. It took a few seconds longer, I assumed because of the distance.

Madóran had gone through all the cloths. I carried the soiled ones away and brought back another stack, then poured more water into the bowl. Madóran finished cleaning the other wounds, then held both hands over Savhoran's neck and closed his eyes.

I held still, watching the glow develop around Madóran's hands and spread up his arms. His whole head and shoulders were surrounded with a golden light that was breathtaking.

If only I could learn to do that. I had a feeling it was beyond me, though.

Madóran withdrew his hands and opened his eyes, frowning as he gazed at Savhoran. I wondered if he was going to cauterize the wound, as he'd done with Caeran.

"He is too weak to bear it, I believe," Madóran said quietly. "He has lost a good deal of blood."

"What if we got him to drink something? Rehydrate him?"

He gazed at me thoughtfully. "That might help. He needs it in any case. Would you go to the kitchen and fetch a bowl of broth? Not from the stove—there is plain broth in a pot in the refrigerator. Do not bother to heat it."

"OK." I headed for the door. "Anything else?"

Madóran nodded toward the pitcher. "More water."

I grabbed the pitcher and hustled to the kitchen, glad to have something to do. Caeran and the two who'd brought Savhoran in were sitting at the table, and several other ælven were in the room, leaning against the counters or perched on the banco by the fire. I put up my white light shields and focused on getting out the broth, ladling some into a bowl, and filling the pitcher.

"How is he?" asked a tight, female voice.

I looked up at—Tiruli, that was her name—who was standing by the table. Everyone in the room was watching me.

"He's badly hurt. He lost a lot of blood."

She winced, and the pain in her face tipped me off. She must be Savhoran's lover.

"*I* should be helping him," she said in a desperate voice. One of the others put a hand on her arm and spoke to her, too quietly for me to hear.

The best thing I could do for everyone's sake was to get back to the treatment room. I dared a glance at Caeran and found him smiling softly at me. I put the pitcher and bowl on a tray, added a spoon, a glass, and a couple of napkins from the stack on the counter, and hurried back to Madóran.

He had his hands over Savhoran's neck again, and was frowning in concentration. I set the tray down on the counter and closed the door, moving as quietly as I could. Madóran was a statue. I stood and watched, trying to send healing thoughts.

After a few minutes he moved, breaking the stillness. The glow faded from around him as he looked at me, then lifted Savhoran up.

"Bring the broth."

I fetched the bowl and held it while Madóran got the patient upright. Savhoran slumped, and I thought he must be unconscious, but Madóran put a hand on his brow and murmured to him, and he opened his eyes.

Madóran took the bowl. "Steady him."

Gingerly, I put a hand against Savhoran's back, between his shoulders. His skin was ice cold and I abandoned shyness as I wrapped my arm around his shoulders and pressed against him, sharing my body heat. He looked ready to pass out. Blood trickled from his neck wound down his bare chest.

The broth was steaming now. Madóran held a spoonful up to Savhoran's lips and murmured to him again. The words sounded like water rippling down a stream. I had to learn this language.

With Madóran's coaxing, Savhoran drank several spoonfuls of the broth. He then started shivering, and I looked at Madóran for guidance. He should be getting warmer, not colder.

"He is in shock. Would you bring a blanket from the bed?"

I fetched two and wrapped one around Savhoran's shoulders, the other around his legs. Madóran managed to get him to drink about half the bowl of broth before he went limp. I grabbed him to keep him from falling, and with Madóran's help gently lowered him onto his back, then rearranged the blankets to cover him.

Madóran put a hand on Savhoran's brow and another over the neck wound. He stood that way for several minutes, frowning. At last he looked up.

"He is weak, but to delay might endanger him further. I

will treat the wound now."

I nodded and helped clear the area. Madóran directed me to press a folded cloth against the wound while he prepared his tools. I did so, watching for signs that Savhoran was returning to consciousness. Madóran hadn't given him any of the drug he'd given Caeran, unless he'd slipped it into the broth.

This was going to be bad. No drugs, and the wound was worse.

The smell of hot metal rose in the room. I closed my eyes, calling up the white light again, as much to shield me from distress as to protect my thoughts.

"Sing to him, Lenore."

"He's unconscious—"

"That does not matter. Take his hand and sing to him. It will help."

Keeping one hand pressed against the wound, I slid the other under the blanket and took hold of Savhoran's cold fingers. What to sing? Not "Sorry Her Lot"—that was really inappropriate this time.

I fixed on "Ubi caritas et amor," a Gregorian chant I'd learned in high school chorus that had sent me on a prolonged chant phase. I began to sing it softly, over and over. The words were Christian, which maybe wasn't terribly appropriate either, but the melody was what mattered; melody and vowels. I'd heard that "Ah" was a sacred sound in many cultures—part of the reason for "Amen"—and this chant had plenty of "Ahs."

Savhoran's fingers clenched on mine and he made a small sound as Madóran began cauterizing the wound. I squeezed back and kept singing, switching chants now and then. Couldn't tell if Savhoran was conscious, and didn't dare open my eyes to check. I kept thinking of white light, sending some of it to him, trying to ignore the smells and sounds of what Madóran was doing.

It seemed to go on forever. I coughed once, and wished for a glass of water, but I went on singing. After going through all my favorite chants, I came back to "Ubi caritas," and had just finished the second verse when I felt a lightening, as if the sun had risen in the room.

I looked up and saw Madóran gazing down at Savhoran, his hand on the patient's brow. Oh, thank god, it was over.

I sang the "Amen" of the chant, then fell silent. Madóran stood motionless, wreathed in golden light. Savhoran's fingers relaxed in my hand.

For a long time we were still. My hand was going to sleep, but I didn't want to disturb Savhoran by moving it. At last Madóran stepped back, and I withdrew at the same time.

He was frowning, dissatisfied. I adjusted the blankets and waited for instructions. Madóran turned away, going to the counter and collecting his tools. I gathered up all the used cloths and Savhoran's shirt while Madóran filled a tray. I poured water into the glass I'd brought and left it within Savhoran's reach.

He hadn't moved, and his forehead was contorted with pain. I felt helpless, and wished I knew better what to do for him.

Madóran opened the door, and I followed him out, bringing the laundry. He paused to close the door, then stood with his hand on it for a moment. He looked worried.

"What is it?" I whispered.

He looked at me. "I may have been too late."

It frightened me even though I didn't fully understand what would happen if he was right. I swallowed.

"You did everything you could."

He nodded. "But that does not make failure easier."

"Maybe you didn't fail."

"Time will tell."

He turned away, heading down the *portal*. I followed him to the laundry room, where I put the cloths and shirt into the washer. Remembering my own laundry, I rinsed my hands in the work sink. Madóran made room for me.

"Did you get a chance to eat?" I asked.

"Yes, earlier."

"Anything else I can do?"

He glanced up at me. "No. Thank you, Lenore. You have been a great help."

This was gratifying, though I suspected he could have done without me. I started to pull my things out of the dryer.

"I would not have done as well without you. You have an instinct for healing."

Blushing, I mumbled a thank-you, and with my arms full of laundry, headed back to my room. I yawned, and wondered what time it was. Dead phone and no clocks in the place that I knew of. It didn't matter, I guessed.

Putting away the clothes took all of three minutes. I was tired, but I didn't want to turn in yet.

The fire had died down to coals, so I scooped them together with the poker and added a couple of pieces of wood, then coaxed a flame out of them by blowing on the coals. I sat there warming my hands until I was sure it wouldn't go out.

There were only three pieces of wood left in the bin. Have to get more tomorrow. The woodpile was outside the house—I'd seen it as I was driving in, a huge wall of cut firewood stacked along the driveway as it continued into the property. I would have to ask for an escort while I fetched wood.

I glanced toward the open door. I wanted to see Caeran, to reassure myself that I hadn't imagined his interest. Silly, I knew, but I was bedazzled and insecure.

He was probably in the front room with the others. I hadn't seen any of them walking around, so I assumed the great debate was back in session. I went out and along the *portal* to the north door into the room, and listened.

Voices. Not as strident as before. I opened the door a crack and peeked through.

Everyone but Savhoran was there. Madóran leaned against the wall beside the door into the entryway. Caeran sat with Tiruli by the fire, holding her hand.

My hackles rose. I told myself he was just comforting her. She did look pretty glum; staring at the floor instead of paying attention to the discussion.

One of the men was talking, his back to me. I looked away from Caeran and started listening to what the speaker was saying.

"We cannot afford to wait. We know how to lure him here; let us do it."

"It would place her in deadly danger," said Nathrin. Mirali, beside him, shot him a glance that I couldn't read.

"We can protect her," said the first guy.

He was one of the ones I hadn't met until recently, and I had completely spaced his name. Annoyed with myself, I looked at each face in the room in turn and tried to remember the name that went with it. Nathrin and Mirali were easy. Tiruli next to Caeran, and the guy sitting on her other side was Lomen. Faranin I remembered because it reminded me of Faramir. The guy with his back to me was Bir—Bir—something.

Caeran was frowning. "It is not our decision. She is not some lesser creature to be used as we will. The choice must be hers."

"If you asked her, she might be inclined to agree," said Bir-whatever.

Caeran's eyes narrowed, and I began to have a bad feeling that they were talking about me. Madóran's head came up, and he looked straight at me.

Oops. White light, white light.

"There is another possibility," Madóran said. He was looking at the speaker now, not me. He ignored me as he went on. "Gehmanin came here seeking me. Let me serve as the lure."

"No!" cried the others. Mirali looked alarmed and half rose from her chair. Several of them started talking at once, all protesting Madóran's suggestion.

"Your skills are too valuable to be risked," Nathrin said above the others. "I am sure any of us would place ourselves in danger rather than it be you."

Madóran smiled wryly. "My skills have not been available to you for centuries. It would hardly be a loss to you."

"Madóran, no," said Mirali in a worried voice. "We are so

grateful to have found you."

Caeran spoke up. "Let it be me. He will want to finish our dispute."

Madóran shook his head. "You have not recovered your strength."

"I am well enough."

"Gehmanin is not to be underestimated!" Madóran's eyes flashed as his gaze swept around the gathered ælven. "You must all see that. If he was able to isolate and defeat Savhoran—"

"He was not defeated!" said Faranin. "We intervened—"

"And he may yet die, or worse!"

I heard a note of anguish in Madóran's voice that made my heart ache. He had done all he could for Savhoran, and it might not be enough.

The shock of his shouting had silenced the others. Fear hung heavy in the room; dread of a solitary monster who had once been one of them.

I opened the door and stepped in. All eyes turned to me, and two or three of the ælven scowled. Ignoring that, I looked at Madóran.

"I thought I should ask if there's anything I can do to help."

"Thank you, Lenore, but this is not your battle. You must stay here in safety."

The first speaker, Bir-something, turned to me. "Actually, there is a way you can help. We have been discussing how to lure the alben close to the house again, so that we may capture him. You could help us by showing yourself outside."

My stomach clenched, a reaction I wasn't expecting. Sweat broke out in my palms. The memory of my last trip outside set me trembling.

"I can do that," I said.

Caeran shook his head, frowning. "Len, no."

"We will be in wait, of course," said Bir-something to me, smiling now. "You will not be harmed."

"She was promised that before!" Caeran stood, dropping Tiruli's hand and striding toward me. "I will not risk failing her again."

"You could accompany her. That would improve her safety, and perhaps entice Gehmanin to come forward."

I frowned. "Wait—no—"

"I will not let you go out alone," Caeran said.

I bristled, but this was not the time for a discussion of my rights. I knew he meant well, and inside I was secretly pleased by his protectiveness.

"Look, how do we even know he'll come back here? Maybe you scared him off."

"He will return," Madóran said. I met his gaze, and realized he was thinking of the past.

Quickly dropping that thought, I re-envisioned my shield, then turned to the instigator. Bironan—that was his name.

"What do you plan to do when he shows up?"

He stared back at me, surprised. Apparently they hadn't thought that far.

"If you're outside he'll know, won't he? He'll be able to sense you."

"We can mask our khi. If we wait along the north side of the house..."

"He will sense you," Madóran said. "He is older than any of you, unless I am mistaken. Do not underestimate him."

"And anyway, what if he's watching from the north?" I added.

Bironan frowned. Caeran came up beside me, his arm brushing mine and making my skin tingle.

"He may be outside even now," he said.

"So there's no way to set up any surprises for him." I looked from Bironan to Madóran for confirmation. Madóran gave a grim nod. "Then whoever is going to be the cavalry will have to wait at the door, and come out as soon as he shows. When do you want to stage this?"

"By day," Bironan said. "He will be at a disadvantage."

"He might not approach in daylight," Madóran said. "Before dawn or at dusk would be better."

"Before dawn, then. If he does not come, we try again at dusk."

Ugh. I hoped he would show up the first time. I wasn't looking forward to this.

Caeran slid his arm around my waist. I could feel the disapproval in the room. I looked at him, and he smiled.

"At dawn, we venture out to your car."

"Or to the woodpile. I'm almost out of firewood."

"The woodpile," Madóran said, suddenly intense. "He will be less likely to suspect an ambush there, and we can come at him from two directions."

"How?" I asked. "I thought there was only one door."

Madóran gestured to the windows, which were all tall, floor to ceiling. "These are as good as doors. The library has some as well."

Bironan nodded. "Nathrin and Lomen can stand ready here. Faranin and I will wait in the library."

Madóran turned to me. "You will both carry wood bins. If need be, you can use them to block him."

I nodded, knowing that at best that would buy me a few seconds. I wasn't about to underestimate Gehmanin, not after what I'd already seen of him.

It was a plan. Madóran and Bironan started discussing details. I'd had enough, and since I was feeling a bit paranoid in the midst of all these semi-hostile ælven, I whispered to Caeran.

"I'm going to my room. You're welcome to join me."

I felt the color creeping into my cheeks as I said it. He answered softly.

"I will, in a little while."

He squeezed my waist, then let me go. Slightly dizzy, I headed toward the inner *portal*, and sighed with relief as I closed the door behind me.

A soft, blue light illuminated the courtyard. Moonlight, I realized. It had been dark earlier, but now the snow was all aglow, and the fountain danced glinting in the night. It was breathtaking. I stopped to watch for a while.

This was a magical place. Madóran had breathed beauty into every part of it. The more I knew of him, the more I admired and liked him. It didn't hurt that he seemed a lot more tolerant of me than most of the others. Maybe that came from taking care of humans for a few centuries. He was used to us.

The research partnership I'd proposed to him might shift everything for the ælven. Perhaps that was an ambitious hope; Madóran might just be humoring me, but I truly believed our working together could benefit both humans and ælven enormously. If I was up to the task.

It felt good to have a mission. My life had changed drastically in the last twenty-four hours. When I got back to school I'd have to reevaluate my course load and start shifting my emphasis to pre-med.

I went to my room and sat by the fire, leaving the door open. The warmth was soothing, helping me relax. I suddenly realized I was dog tired. It must be pretty late.

Have to learn to pay more attention to the moon. Could tell time that way, maybe.

Maybe time didn't matter so much.

It probably didn't, to the ælven. They probably thought humans were obsessive, breaking the day into hours and minutes and seconds. We were like ants; busy all the time. The number of hours and seconds we had were limited, so it mattered to us to keep track of them.

What was it like to be immortal? It had always sounded like a fairy tale, but I was beginning to think it might be daunting, and a lot less fun than silly humans supposed.

Madóran was probably older than the others, if what he'd said about Gehmanin was true. And he seemed to feel more pain from life's misfortunes, not less. He must have failed to save hundreds, thousands of patients over time, and yet his grief that he could do no more for Savhoran was acute.

Savhoran. I should check on him, make sure the fire hadn't gone out. I got up and went to his room, quietly opening the door.

A sudden movement startled me and I gasped. There was someone in the room. For a heart-stopping second I thought it was the alben, then Caeran turned to me from the bed against the wall.

His eyes were wide. He glanced at Savhoran, still lying on the table, and gestured for me to be quiet. I nodded and came in, carefully picked a piece of wood out of the bin, and added it to the fire.

Savhoran stirred and muttered. I stepped to the table to look at him, though I wasn't sure what I could do to help him.

His brow was dappled in sweat. I fetched a cloth from the cupboard and poured some cool water on it, then bathed his face. Caeran watched me, silent.

Maybe I shouldn't have added wood to the fire. Savhoran was in a high fever, it looked like. I wasn't sure, but I thought you were supposed to keep people warm when they were in a fever. Who knew if that applied to ælven, though.

Madóran. I hoped he'd come to check on Savhoran soon. Laying the folded cloth across Savhoran's forehead, I stepped back and looked at Caeran.

He came to me, taking my arm and steering me toward the *portal*. When we were out in the cooler air, he carefully closed the door.

"Madóran asked me to stay in this room tonight, to watch over Savhoran."

"Oh. Yeah, that's probably a good idea." I sighed. "It's been a long day. I should probably get some sleep if we're getting up at yuck o'clock."

Caeran looked puzzled for a moment, then smiled. "May I visit with you briefly?"

"Sure."

He offered his arm. I took it, feeling strange about this sudden stateliness. He escorted me to my room and we sat by the fire. I added a piece of wood and sat watching it catch, enjoying the crackle and the fresh heat.

Twice in the last two days I'd been attacked by Gehmanin.

Tomorrow might make it three for three. I rubbed my upper arms, trying to get rid of goosebumps that had nothing to do with the temperature.

A crazy impulse to seduce Caeran right then, just in case one or both of us died tomorrow, came into my brain and made my nipples tighten. I swallowed, hiding the thought under a blanket of white light.

"Have I upset you?" he asked.

"No! No...sorry, there are just some thoughts I don't want to share."

He pressed his lips together, then spoke carefully. "If it is one thought you wish to protect, you need not hide them all."

He looked at me and the yearning was in his face. Instantly my heart filled with an answering ache. I saw another meaning in his words; he wanted to touch my thoughts as he'd done before. I felt giddy just at the thought of it. Oh, how I wanted that! But I'd promised Madóran to keep his confidence.

"How do I protect one thought?"

"Take the thought and surround it with light. Layers upon layers, until it is a glowing globe. Then set that globe aside in safety."

Sounded too simple, but what the hell. I closed my eyes and renewed my shield, then thought about my conversation with Madóran in the kitchen and swathed it in light. With each indrawn breath I added another layer of light, and the memory became an image: a globe of light, with me and Madóran inside it, talking—or rather Madóran talking and me listening. The image began to fade as I wound more and more layers of light around the globe. Finally all I could see was the light.

Now to set it aside. I had no clue how to do that. Where to store a thought safely? My brain produced the image of a safe deposit box. The glowing globe obligingly shrank down until it would fit in the box. I closed the lid over it, slid the box into its drawer, and locked it with my key.

Maybe that would work, or maybe it was futile, but at least I'd tried. No way was I going to give up a chance to be close to

Caeran.

I opened my eyes. Caeran was leaning against the adobe wall of the fireplace, watching me. He smiled.

"Your khi is very bright for a mortal's. Have I told you that?"

"Not in so many words."

I reached for him, and he drew back, glancing down at my borrowed shirt. I looked and saw that it was smeared with blood. No wonder the ælven had grimaced at my appearance.

"I could take it off," I said.

He smiled. "You'd be cold."

"You could warm me up."

His expression grew wistful. "You did a great thing, assisting Madóran. Any of the others would have been placing themselves at risk, to be in contact with Savhoran's blood."

I hadn't thought of that. Caeran was already at risk, but no need to make it worse. I got up and went to the dresser where I'd just put away my clean clothes, took out my t-shirt, and changed into it, dropping Madóran's shirt on the floor.

I returned to my seat by the fire. "Better?"

Caeran reached out and caressed my cheek. I leaned into it, hungry for more, for as much of him as I could get.

His arms slid around me, drawing me close. I felt the heat of the fire on my side, but it was a shadow compared to the blaze in my heart.

Oh, yes. I felt my brain shutting down as pleasure sensors leapt to life. Warm breath on my neck. Strong arms wrapping me tight, and strong shoulders beneath my arms. The silky touch of his hair on my cheek. The clean, salty smell of him—I would never get tired of that smell.

My left side was roasting. I didn't care. Caeran must have noticed, though, because he shifted us to the bed. I practically floated, shamelessly willing to go with him anywhere.

"Len," he breathed into my ear.

"Yes." It was my answer for anything he cared to ask.

His lips closed on my throat. I buried my face in his hair,

and ran the fingers of one hand up through the soft tresses. He shifted and suddenly we were kissing, long and slow. My insides melted and slid down into a molten puddle between my hips.

This was what I'd been wanting. Totally selfish. Yes, yes, yes.

He paused and drew back, searching my face. The firelight caught the gold in his eyes like an opal's flash.

I wish I could stay with you.

And there he was, glowing in my mind, delicious beyond description. I closed my eyes, my head slumping back as I drank in the sensation of him.

Stay a little while.

Will you forgive me if I do not? I want our time together to be unhurried.

I knew an impulse to scream with frustration. Caeran's arms tightened around me. I thumped my forehead into his shoulder.

Why wait? We'll have my whole life to be leisurely.

My heart, I know. I promise you the wait will not be long. Tomorrow we will have the night to ourselves.

Assuming we survive the morning.

We will survive.

Slowly, gently, he pulled away. I felt him sliding out of my mind, the ache of loneliness filling the void he left. He softened it with kisses all over my face. I shuddered, clinging to him.

"Soon," he whispered. "Tomorrow."

"I'm holding you to that."

He smiled, kissed me once more, and left. I collapsed backward onto the bed, still tingling, still ready.

Oh, man. Twenty-four hours. I did *not* want to wait.

= 15 =

Think of it as a reward, I told myself. Help capture the bad guy and the handsome prince is yours.

I snorted, then got up and chucked the last two pieces of wood on the fire and set the empty wood bin by my door. Pretty feeble defensive shield, but it was better than nothing. I flinched away from imagining having to hold off Gehmanin with it. I didn't want to go to sleep thinking of him.

Instead I went back and sat by the fire, reliving the past few moments with Caeran. Soon I had trouble keeping my eyes open. I pulled off my borrowed trousers and dropped them with the shirt, then crawled into bed. Too tired to rinse out my panties.

Have to go commando tomorrow. I grinned into my pillow, imagining Caeran's reaction to that as I fell asleep.

A bang startled me awake. I jumped to my hands and knees on the bed, staring wildly toward the door, heart pounding.

Caeran peered in, looking apologetic. The bang had been the door hitting the wood bin. A dim glow from the courtyard behind him told me the sky was lightening.

"It is time," he said gently.

I rubbed a hand across one eye. "OK. Give me a minute."

I dragged myself out of bed, my limbs feeling leaden as the adrenaline jolt subsided. Changed into my jeans and pulled on my socks—have to wash them today, for sure—and my shoes. Out of habit, I stuffed my keys and wallet in my pockets. If I was lucky I might get to drive into Las Vegas today.

It was chilly in the room; the fire was long gone and the morning was cold. I wished for my coat and thought about putting on the caftan, but it might hinder me if I had to run so I skipped it.

My hair was a mess. I combed my fingers through it, straightening it as best I could. Maybe Gehmanin would think Caeran and I had been having wild hot sex all night. I wished we had.

No more delaying. I picked up the wood bin, took a deep breath, and joined Caeran on the *portal*.

Caeran was holding another empty bin. The others were all there, even Mirali and a strained-but-determined looking Tiruli. Seeing her reminded me of Savhoran, and I worked my way over to Madóran to ask how he was doing.

"Somewhat better," was his guarded reply.

My appearance was the signal for everyone else to take their places. They split into two groups, one heading for the front room, the other going west along the *portal* and disappearing into a room that must be the library. I never had gotten a chance to look at Madóran's books.

Had I really only been here two days? It seemed like forever.

Madóran hung back with me and Caeran. The curandero wore the stern expression I'd seen when I first met him.

"Stay together. If you separate, it will be easier for him to overcome you."

I nodded, and Caeran thanked him. Madóran put a hand each on our shoulders, then headed for the library.

I looked at Caeran. "Here we go."

He smiled and leaned forward to kiss my cheek. *All will be well.*

We walked down the *portal* together and into the entryway. My arms had turned to gooseflesh from the cold and dread.

"Let me go out first," Caeran said.

He opened the door and looked out, scanning the ground in front of the house. After a moment he turned to me and nodded.

He is there. To the northeast. Do not look that way.

I came out, gripping the metal handles of my wood bin. Caeran led the way toward the woodpile. I kept my gaze straight ahead but watched for any movement from my right.

We were almost to the woodpile when pain stabbed my head. I dropped my bin and fell to my knees, clutching my temples.

I heard sounds of running and struggle, but it was all muffled. Paralyzed by pain, I couldn't do a thing.

Shouting. More running. Suddenly the pain ceased. I looked up in time to see three ælven pass me and round the end of the woodpile, joining the others who were fast disappearing to the north.

Caeran lay beside me in the snow. For a heart-stopping moment I thought he was dead, then he groaned.

"Caeran!" I caught his face in my hands. "Are you hurt?"

He blinked up at me, squinting in pain. "Len."

There was no blood that I could see, though Caeran looked deathly pale. I dragged him into my arms, weeping. "What did he do to you?"

"The same thing he did to you," said Madóran behind me.

I turned my head to look at him. A breeze blew his dark hair across his face. He looked angry.

He knelt beside me and placed a hand on Caeran's brow. Caeran winced slightly, then relaxed. I held onto him, shivering.

"He used khi as a weapon," Madóran said. "That is forbidden among our people."

"He d-did that to me before," I told him. "On campus."

Madóran glanced at me. "You did not mention it."

"I guess not. A lot's happened since then."

He looked back at Caeran, the anger leaving his face. After a moment he stood.

"He will be all right. Come, we must go inside."

Caeran's arms wrapped around me. I had no inclination to move, though I knew Madóran was right. I let go of Caeran, staggered to my feet, and offered to help him up.

He joined me and immediately caught me in a tight hug. He was looking better. He urged me toward the house.

"Wait." I grabbed my wood bin, took it to the pile, and

started throwing wood into it. "Least we can do is get some damn firewood," I said through shuddering jaws.

After a moment Caeran joined me, quickly filling his bin. Madóran came to help, and when it was full he took my bin from me, insisting on carrying it inside.

We went into the front room, where I parked by the fire and shivered. Madóran stood peering out the nearest window, frowning, still holding the bin of firewood. He turned to Caeran.

"Keep watch. I will return shortly."

He was gone even as Caeran nodded. Caeran added wood to the fire, pressed my hands and kissed my forehead, then took up watch at the window.

I was warming up, but the fear was kicking in, so I shivered even harder. I hoped the ælven hunters were staying in groups. Maybe Gehmanin would have trouble overpowering three or four at once. Nothing less seemed to stop him.

I felt sorry for Madóran, but the bastard needed to die.

I moved closer to the fire, rubbing my arms as they warmed up. So much for my half-formed hope of driving to Las Vegas today. There was no way they'd let me go, even with Caeran. Even if we crammed the car full of ælven, there'd be a real danger that Gehmanin would attack us. I knew it wasn't even worth asking.

Madóran returned with a tray of hot tea, bread, butter, and jam. He exchanged a glance with Caeran, who shook his head. Madóran poured tea into a mug and handed it to me.

"We need a different strategy. Gehmanin will not walk into an ambush again."

"Why not?" I said. "If he can zap everybody with khi—"

"But he cannot. You did not know this, Len, but he had to focus in order to stop you with khi. He immobilized you fairly quickly, and that allowed him to direct his efforts toward Caeran. If there had been more of us—"

"He would not have approached at all," Caeran said, coming to claim a mug of tea. "You are right, we need a different tack."

They talked unenthusiastically about possible variations on the ambush while I stretched out on the banco and baked. My head was throbbing. I was feeling seriously bummed.

Before long the ælven returned, all in a clump. They'd stayed together, which was good. No one had been hurt this time. They clustered around the fire, a handful of auburn-haired hunters, disappointed that they'd lost Gehmanin.

"He went into the village," Bironan said, frowning in annoyance. "We could not follow without drawing too much attention."

Madóran nodded, as if he'd expected to hear something like this. "He will use every possible advantage, without concern for ethics or the safety of others."

I frowned. Those "others" were human beings. My people. Was Gehmanin terrorizing someone in Guadalupita even now?

I remembered how he'd holed up in the library for a day. He must have gone to ground somewhere, but there weren't any big institutional buildings in the village. The closest thing was the Post Office.

The hair on the back of my neck prickled. I sat up.

"I think I know where he might be."

Madóran looked up from pouring tea for the new arrivals. The others looked at me, too—some with skepticism, others with respect.

"He's got to get under cover during daylight, right?" I said. "He couldn't stay in the woods because you all were after him. So he's in some building. I think it might be the Post Office."

Nathrin shook his head. "He could as easily have gone into a house. He might be feeding even now."

Madóran frowned. "I do not think he would risk that. The discovery of a dead or dying human in this small village would draw attention he does not want."

"He could be holding hostages," Bironan said. "There would be no discovery until after he was gone."

"But he has no immediate plans to leave." Madóran emptied the last of the tea into a cup and handed it to Mirali.

"Until he has what he wants, he will be careful to cause no disruption."

"That's why I think he's in a public building, hiding out in a closet or something," I said. "The only one Guadalupita has is the Post Office."

"And the bar," Caeran added.

I looked at him. "The bar! I'd forgotten about it. Holy c— cow, he could be spending every day in there!"

"They would not be open at this hour," Madóran said.

"He could break in," said Bironan.

"Or if he's been hanging out there, he might be able to talk his way in for a cup of coffee," I said. "It makes sense. It's the perfect place for him to spend the day. As long as he bought enough booze, they'd be happy to have him."

Nathrin looked from Bironan to Madóran. "So, do we seek him there?"

Caeran shook his head. "A fight in the village would not be wise for any of us."

"True," Madóran agreed. "I have come to like this home, and have no wish to leave it."

Everyone was silent. Reminded of how much I owed Madóran, how generous he had been to all of us, I tried to think of an alternative to the ælven hunting down and killing Gehmanin.

"What if we sent him a message?"

Now almost all of them looked skeptical, except Caeran and Madóran. Madóran raised an eyebrow.

"To what end?"

I answered uncertainly. "Well, we could tell him to leave. That you wouldn't hunt him if he just left you alone and found some other territory."

"No," Caeran said. His sternness surprised me. He looked at me, eyes hard. "He has shown himself to have no ethics. There would be no way to guarantee that he would honor such a demand. Short of all of us staying together, never leaving this house except in groups, we would always be in danger."

Well, that wouldn't work. I had my short little life to get on with, and Madóran would probably like to have his house back one of these days.

"What does he have to gain by staying here?" I said, annoyed. "He's got to know he hasn't got a chance against you guys."

"Perhaps he is seeking healing," said Nathrin slowly. He looked at Madóran. "We sought you out for that reason. He might have done the same."

I bit my lip, and kept my gaze on the floor. Madóran would have to decide how much to tell the others.

"Yes, perhaps so," he said after a long pause. "Alas, I cannot help him."

"He may not know that."

"Then I must tell him. I will go to the village."

"No!" cried the others.

"I am known there. He would not dare attack me in front of so many."

In the chaos that erupted, my gaze locked with Caeran's. We both knew that the alben would dare just about anything.

"What about a parley?" I shouted over the noise. The others fell quiet, staring at me. I hurried on. "Send him a message that he can come here at dusk, and you'll talk with him, and he won't be harmed unless he tries to harm one of us. One of you."

"He will not honor bargains," Caeran said.

"He might honor this one, if it's to his advantage. Never mind his ethics, would he trust you to keep your word?"

"Yes," Lomen said, looking at me seriously. "It is part of the creed we live by, to be true to our word."

"OK. So he'll believe you. He'll come here, and Madóran can explain that he can't help, and then…" I hadn't thought that far.

"Then he will leave," said Bironan, "and we will be bound to allow him, and we will have gained nothing."

"No," Madóran said quietly, "he may agree to leave us in

peace. Let us try this. I will talk to him."

He looked troubled, and I remembered him saying that Gehmanin would never give up. Madóran had crossed an ocean under extremely dangerous conditions to get away from him.

Shove that thought in the safe-deposit box. Wrap the whole thing in light.

I felt frustrated. My idea wasn't very good, but no one had suggested anything better. At worst, the net gain would be zero.

"How do we send him the message?" Nathrin asked.

Madóran stood, picking up the tray with the teapot. "I will telephone the bar. If he is not there, we must adjust our plan."

I followed him out, and in the kitchen I grabbed the kettle and filled it. Madóran stood watching me.

"I'll fix more tea. Where's your phone?"

He didn't answer. I turned and saw him staring into distance, frowning in grief, the tray forgotten in his hands.

"I'm sorry," I said, gently taking the tray from him. "Forget this, it was a crummy idea."

He shook his head. "No, we must try. If I talk to him, he may accept—he may choose easier targets."

"But he'll never quit," I whispered. "He'll come back."

Madóran closed his eyes. I put the tray on the counter and, shyly, touched his shoulder.

"You are right," he said, his voice rough. "The only thing that will free me is his death. But I cannot kill him."

"The others will."

"I wish..." he looked up, his cheeks wet with tears. He gave a hopeless laugh. "I wish you had completed your studies, and we could offer him the hope of a cure."

"Would that hope mean anything to him?"

"Yes, if it were real. But it is only a dream."

"Maybe not. Can he be patient for a while? Would he agree to go away and come back in, say, ten years?"

Madóran stared at me, looking astounded. "I do not know," he said slowly.

"Well, it's worth a try, right? So where's your phone?"

Wiping his face, he walked over to a nicho set into the wall, where a cell phone sat plugged into a charger at the feet of a wooden statuette—a santo, I realized. Too roughly carved to be Madóran's work. The birds in the figure's hands marked him as St. Francis. A gift from a grateful patient?

Madóran dialed, then spoke into the phone in Spanish. I caught the word "blanco." He waited, then tensed and began speaking quietly in ælven. At last he paused briefly, said one more word, then hung up. He stood perfectly still for a moment, not even breathing that I could see, then looked up at me.

"He has agreed."

"Hah!" I clapped my hands.

"Agreed to come here at dusk, as we discussed. I will propose the plan to him then."

I blinked. "Why didn't you just propose it over the phone?"

Madóran smiled wryly. "I know him. He will pay more attention if I address him in person. It is what he wants, after all."

"You're not going to be alone with him!"

"No. I want everyone present. I intend to make him swear to leave all of you alone."

"You think he'll keep that promise?"

"A pledge he makes to me, in person, I believe he will keep."

The entryway door opened and Caeran came in. He looked from me to Madóran, and I wondered if he was maybe just a little jealous. I went to him.

"Gehmanin was at the bar. Madóran talked to him. He's coming here at dusk."

Caeran's eyes narrowed. "So."

"Will you tell the others?" Madóran asked him. "I need some time alone."

The kettle began to sing. I hurried over to it, splashed some hot water into the teapot and swished it around.

"Very well," Caeran said.

"I would like everyone to gather in the hall before dusk. We must all be together when Gehmanin comes."

"All right."

I emptied the water from the teapot, put in the strainer, and measured out tea as I'd seen Madóran do earlier. He turned and watched me pour boiling water into the pot.

"Go on, grab your alone time. We'll be all right."

Madóran set his phone in the nicho and left by the west door. I glanced up at Caeran.

"Progress, I think."

He smiled, though he still looked worried. He came over and slid his arms around my waist. A warm glow started in my stomach and crept up my chest.

"Um. I should keep an eye on the tea."

"It needs a few minutes."

He kissed me. I forgot about the tea, Madóran, the alben, everything. Only Caeran filled my awareness. I wrapped my arms around his neck and pressed against him, wanting more, wanting everything, here, now.

After a while he drew back. Smiling softly, he brushed a hand across my hair.

"The tea should be ready."

I took a long breath. "Tease."

Slightly dizzy, I turned back to the counter and lifted the strainer from the teapot. Looked like tea, smelled like tea. I put the pot on the tray, refilled the milk pitcher, and carried it to the front room, Caeran opening doors ahead of me.

A couple of people had left. The rest looked up as we came in. I poured tea while Caeran passed along Madóran's request. The discussion picked up where it had left off, and Caeran had the unenviable task of defending Madóran's plan, with which he didn't fully agree.

Wanting to recharge my phone, I grabbed my firewood bin from the corner and slipped out, hurrying along the *portal* to my room. I put the bin by the fireplace, unearthed the phone from my pack, then as an afterthought picked up my clothes from yesterday and headed for the kitchen via the laundry room.

This doing laundry every day sucked. I had to get some more clothes.

Tomorrow. If Madóran's plan worked, I could go to Las Vegas tomorrow. Or back to Albuquerque, maybe.

That seemed strange—I felt weirdly distant from home and school. But I had to go back to school. More than ever, now.

I headed for my room, but stopped when I opened the door to the *portal*. Madóran was standing by the fountain again. This time his arms were at his sides, and he must have been there a while, because the birds were playing in the water as if he didn't exist. Sunlight sparkled on the ripples and filled the courtyard with blinding brightness, making it a well of light.

I tried to step through the door slowly, but wasn't slow enough. The sudden thrumming of dozens of wings penetrated the glass wall as the birds swirled up and away. Madóran turned to look at me.

"Sorry," I mouthed.

He smiled, shook his head slightly, and beckoned to me. It felt odd, going out into the area where I assumed he'd been praying or meditating or something like that. The snow grumbled under my sneakers as I joined him by the fountain.

"I didn't mean to disturb you," I said.

"Nor have you. I was just thinking of you, in fact."

"Me?"

"Yes. It is generous of you to pledge yourself to researching a cure for the alben's curse, but I am not sure it would be right of me to promise Gehmanin that you will do this."

I clamped down on a flare of impatience. My stubborn streak was handy at times, but also could get me in trouble.

"I *will* do this. Never mind Gehmanin, this is the most exciting job I can imagine! I can't wait to get started."

He gazed at me thoughtfully. "You do have an aptitude for healing."

"And I'm grateful to you for helping me find it." On impulse, I added, "May I be your apprentice?"

Madóran's brows rose. "Curanderismo is a different path

than western medicine."

I nodded. "Especially your brand. I'd still like to learn from you."

"We shall see." He seemed pleased by the request.

"Can I help with anything now? Fixing lunch?"

He glanced toward the kitchen as if he'd forgotten about the food thing. "Ah, yes. You can indeed help, but I wish to look in on Savhoran first."

"May I come with you?"

His face darkened with concern as he nodded. He turned to the fountain again and closed his eyes. I held still, watching the water, keeping my thoughts as quiet as possible. My skin tingled a little, and I could almost imagine a glow surrounding the fountain, but it might have just been the sunlight.

After a moment Madóran headed for the north door into the *portal*, and I followed. Savhoran's room was warm, with a fire softly crackling. I went to it and added another piece of wood while Madóran looked at Savhoran.

He was restless, still fevered. I watched Madóran change the dressings on his throat, wincing at the sight of the cauterized wound. It was angry red, and seeping a little in a couple of places. Madóran gently covered it with fresh gauze, then held his hands above it.

I did some yoga breathing and pictured white light around them both. Madóran looked up and beckoned me to the table. He moved his hands to a couple of inches above Savhoran's temples, then gestured to me. I placed my hands in the air where he'd shown me, and Madóran returned his hands to the throat.

A deep hum—not a sound, but a sensation—filled me as I stood there. I concentrated on visualizing light. My hands grew warm.

Let it happen. Just let it all happen. Observe.

"Blue," Madóran whispered.

"What?"

"You are thinking white. Make it blue."

OK. Blue it is. I pictured the sky after sunset, the glowing blue that was one of my favorite colors. I closed my eyes and tried to hold the color in my thoughts, going back to the glowing sky whenever my mind strayed.

"A little lighter."

Obediently I pictured the sky closer to dawn. Not yet pink, but more on the light side than the dark.

The occasional crackle of the fire was the only sound in the room besides our breathing. I tried to sync my breaths with Madóran's, but his were awfully slow. I needed more practice.

Blue. Just blue.

I counted my heartbeats to time my breathing, and also to avoid mental meandering. Repetition was good for focus. I lost all sense of time passing: inhale, two, three, four, hold, two, three, four, exhale...

Something shifted and I opened my eyes. Madóran had stepped back.

"Enough for now," he said.

Savhoran was lying still, no longer fretful. His face looked peaceful. I exhaled, relieved, and tiptoed out of the room after Madóran.

"Why blue?" I asked as we headed for the kitchen.

"Have you ever seen a glacier?"

"On TV. Not in person."

"Did you see images of crevices and deep holes?"

"Yeah."

Madóran opened the kitchen door and paused to look back at me. "What color were they?"

"Kind of turquoise."

He nodded. "Blue is the heart of ice. A good counter to burns."

"Oh. OK."

Under Madóran's direction, I chopped and measured and fetched things for another stew. He put some of the beans to soak in a huge pot, then started making bread.

"How soon do we run out of food?" I asked as I attacked an

onion.

He paused to look at me, eyes narrowing in amusement. "I can call to the village for supplies. My credit is good."

"Wouldn't that be putting someone in danger, having them come here?"

"Not in daylight. Not today. Gehmanin will do nothing rash before dusk."

"Grocery run today then? You've got six eggs left."

"I will call after everyone is fed."

This took a while. At home my cooking tended to start with a box or a can. Madóran's way was undeniably tastier, and probably healthier and less expensive, but it was slow. I watched, trying to learn. He began to explain what he was doing, telling me why the onions went in first, then the garlic, then spices.

"Each flavor is layered upon the others," he said, stirring the pot and waving the aroma toward his face. I leaned closer to smell, got a snootful of red chile, and sneezed.

"Good chile," I said, wiping my watering eyes. "Don't tell me—you grew it."

He smiled. "No. I have a client who comes up from Chimayo. He pays me in chile."

"Well, it's good stuff." I grabbed a napkin from the stack on the counter and wiped my face.

Madóran picked up another napkin and poured a small mound of the red chile powder into it, then twisted it up into a makeshift pouch. "Take some home with you."

"Thanks."

I could feel myself blushing as I accepted the gift. Madóran was so generous, on top of being patient. I'd have to learn to cook from scratch, if only to do justice to his kindness.

He smiled, then went back to stirring the stew. "Now we add broth. Will you hand me a ladle from that drawer?"

I stuffed the chile into my pocket and grabbed the ladle. More layers went in: cabbage, zucchini, and finally the beans. By the time Madóran sent me to the front room to inform the crew that lunch was served, it was mid-afternoon.

Caeran, Nathrin and Mirali were the only ones there. Mirali offered to go round up the others while the two guys followed me to the kitchen. Caeran and I took our lunch out onto the *portal* again and sat together watching the birds.

"Discussion over?" I asked.

"We have reached the point where we must agree to disagree."

"How can you stand arguing so much?"

"It is what we do instead of fighting."

I chewed a bite of bread while that sank in. His people had been around a very long time. It made sense that they had worked out compromises, ways of living that didn't involve conking each other on the head. Especially since they didn't have a lot of heads to spare.

All at once I felt part of a very young and primitive tribe. Why did Caeran even bother with me?

He reached over and laid his hand on mine, sending a shiver through me. My appetite vanished.

"I don't suppose you'd consider..."

No, but I would like to stay with you until dusk.

Sold. What do we do, play pinochle?

Would you sing to me again?

Oh, lordy. *I'm not that good.*

He smiled, eyes shining. *I love your voice.*

Bironan and Lomen came out of the kitchen, glanced at us as they walked past, and continued around the *portal* toward the library. When they'd gone, I looked at Caeran.

"Not here."

He raised his chin and his eyes went distant, then he picked up our plates and grabbed my hand. We went to the kitchen, where Nathrin and Mirali were talking with Madóran and Faranin at the table. Depositing our plates by the sink, Caeran led me on through the entryway into the front room. For the first time I could remember, it was empty.

Caeran dropped my hand and went to a bookcase in the far

corner. A black guitar case that I hadn't noticed before leaned against it. Caeran brought it to the fire.

"Can you play?"

I glared at him. "You peeked."

He laughed, shaking his head. "I only suspected. You sing so well, I thought you must have a general gift for music."

"Even if I did, which I don't, that wouldn't mean I could automatically play any instrument. That's the sort of thing you people do."

Caeran laid the guitar case on the floor and unlatched it. "Only because we have had longer to acquire a multitude of skills. You are thinking of Madóran."

"Of course I'm thinking of Madóran. He's freaking amazing. And how about you—can you play? Better than I can, I bet."

"No. I have never been especially skilled at music. I play the flute a little, that is all."

He lifted the lid, revealing a guitar that looked surprisingly plain. I'd expected beautiful wood, filigree work and inlay, maybe Madóran's carving. Instead it just looked old.

I lifted it out, looking for a maker's mark or some other clue to its origin. There was nothing. Sitting on a hassock, I settled it in my lap and ran my thumb across the strings. It was in perfect tune, so Madóran must play or at least take good care of it. The tone was warm and mellow.

Caeran sat on the banco, watching me expectantly. I glanced at him.

"I'm not very good."

He just smiled.

I strummed a couple of chords, feeling self-conscious. I hadn't played much in the last couple of years. My guitar was at home, at my folks' house. I knew a few bits of fingerstyle that I'd picked up from listening to CDs, but nothing really showy. Most of what I knew were folk songs that my mom sang to us when we were kids.

There was the song about a logger who stirred his coffee

with his thumb. I wasn't sure I could remember all the words, though, and it was a silly song anyway.

I sang "Shenandoah," because I could remember it, and because it was easy. It also fit my mood—the yearning. A note I'd been fond of in my miserable teens. It still resonated for me, so that singing it was actually comforting. I zoned off into the music, forgetting everything, even Caeran.

As quietly as I played and sang, it wasn't quiet enough. When I reached the end of the song and looked up, there were others in the room: Madóran and the three I'd seen with him in the kitchen, watching me along with Caeran.

"More, please," Caeran said.

"Um..."

"Please," said Bironan, surprising me. Usually he looked annoyed, but now his face was softer than I'd ever seen it.

I launched into "The Water is Wide," followed by "The Minstrel Boy." That one got the ælven exchanging glances; apparently the war and slavery talk disturbed them. My ignorant, savage tribe was still hashing out those problems.

What was I doing here? I didn't belong with these people. I *loved* being around them, but I could never fit in with them, really.

My fingers fidgeted on the strings, restless, seeking the comfort of a familiar pattern. Strumming through a sequence of chords, I looked for a song that would suit my mood but not offend my listeners. Too many of the stories were about violence and loss. Even the lumberjack song ended sadly.

A knock at the front door made me freeze for a moment. Madóran left the room. The other ælven seemed unconcerned, and after a moment I heard Madóran and someone else talking in Spanish. I caught "huevos" and "leche" and knew it was the grocery delivery.

Turning back to the music, I switched to newer songs—still old, but some of the songs from the sixties and seventies had more of a spirit of hope. I stumbled through Taylor's "You've Got A Friend," followed it with the Beatles's "I Will," then fell silent.

"Thank you, Lenore," Madóran said.

I looked up and saw that all the others had gathered, everyone except Savhoran. The were all looking at me, their faces sentimental. Caeran gazed at me, openly adoring, as if he thought I'd been singing that last song just for him.

Well, I had. Too self-conscious to sing any more, I laid the guitar back in its case.

"It's a beautiful instrument. Thanks for letting me play it."

"You are welcome to play it whenever you wish." Madóran looked around the room at the others. "It is time."

Glancing at the windows, I saw that the daylight had gone golden outside, and the shadow of the hacienda was slanting long across the field. The front *portal* had been dark since noon, with the sun passing west toward the back of the house.

My stomach twisted into a knot. Caeran moved closer and took my hand.

"Do we wait here?" Faranin asked.

Madóran gazed out the windows. "When the sun sets, we will go outside. Gather your cloaks."

The ælven dispersed. Caeran and I stayed where we were, neither of us having a cloak to fetch. I thought about going and grabbing the blanket off my bed, but I didn't want to move.

"What do we do if this doesn't work?" I asked in a small voice.

Caeran was silent for a moment. "If he refuses, we will kill him."

"But you can't—Madóran promised he would be safe, coming here."

"Not here, not now. But we will find him and kill him."

I swallowed, thinking of Savhoran, thinking of Caeran's wound. Gehmanin wasn't so easy to kill.

"You'd think he'd have left, knowing that."

"He is stubborn."

I moved to sit beside Caeran and wrapped my arms around him, laying my head on his shoulder. He winced, and I looked up at him.

"Shouldn't that have healed by now?"

A slight frown creased his brow. "It is not an ordinary wound."

Terror whispered across my shoulders. I held Caeran tighter, trying to be careful of his wound. I *couldn't* lose him. Not possible, and especially not in such a way.

His arms closed around me, warm and comforting. I shut out the fear, the dark thoughts, and tried to just bask in the incredible glory of him.

Caeran? Talk to me?

Saying what?

I closed my eyes, letting his presence fill me. *Anything.*

He didn't give me words. I didn't need them now. As he held me, I felt complete bliss. Keeping this was worth anything I had to face.

We both heard the door open, and looked up, but didn't separate. Madóran came in, a dark gold cloak around his shoulders. He carried a pile of cloth which he shook out into two more cloaks, one green, one brown.

"You may need these."

Reluctantly, we disentangled ourselves and went to accept the cloaks. I felt relief as the brown cloak settled around my shoulders, brushing the floor. Safer somehow.

"Thank you, Madóran," Caeran said.

Our host nodded. I heard the others gathering in the entryway, and Madóran led us to join them. Caeran caught my hand.

We filed outside, onto the front *portal*, facing east. The clear sky above the horizon glowed pink, and the quality of the daylight was muted. No more shadows. The sun had set.

I held the edges of my cloak together in front of me, one arm sticking out as I clung to Caeran's hand. He stepped closer. We stood waiting, watching the light fade. The pink was gone from the sky when the ælven began to stir and whisper.

They'd seen him. I peered toward the horizon, straining to

catch any sign of movement. After a minute I saw him walking across the field.

Adrenaline punched me and I tensed. Caeran's hand tightened around mine.

He will not touch you.

I nodded, fighting down the instinct to run. To a hunter like that, it would only be an invitation.

The alben crossed the driveway, glancing at my car as he passed it. His lip curved in disdain as if he didn't like how it smelled.

You're the one who torched it, asshole.

I didn't want to think his name. He didn't deserve a name. He didn't hear me either, apparently, or if he did he chose to ignore me.

He stopped at the edge of the *portal* and looked up at Madóran. "You wished to talk?"

"Swear you will make no move to harm any of these folk," Madóran said, taking in the gathered ælven and me with a gesture.

The alben glanced at us, his gaze lingering on me for a second, then nodded. "I swear."

"And we in turn swear to let you leave in peace."

The alben tilted his head, looking amused. "So, now that we have finished swearing, what do you wish to discuss?"

"Your departure," said Madóran. "We wish you to leave this land."

The alben looked around as if admiring Madóran's property. "But I only just arrived, and I rather like it."

"You will leave here, leave the country, and not return for ten years."

The alben laughed. "Ten years?"

"In ten years time, I may have the beginnings of a cure for your ailment."

The laughter ceased abruptly. The alben's eyes sharpened as he stared at Madóran. "So it is true? You continued to seek a cure?"

Madóran nodded. A look of painful hope came into the alben's face.

"I knew you would! You never give up, even when hope is beyond reach."

"Especially then."

The alben laughed again, and excitement sparked in his eyes. "So you will help me!"

"I cannot help you now, Gehmanin."

"But if you have found a cure—"

"I have not. Only a new avenue to pursue. It will take at least ten years for me to know whether a cure is *possible*."

The alben frowned, hope fading. "And in the meantime you banish me?"

"Yes." Madóran's voice took on its stern tone. "If anyone here or any of my neighbors comes to harm, I will cease to look for a cure."

"You cannot hold their misadventures against me!"

"Not if you are outside the country, true. I suggest you leave at once."

The alben's nostrils flared, and his eyes blazed fury until he lidded them, looking down at the ground. His shoulders moved with his sharp breathing. I shifted closer to Caeran, frightened of the hunter. Gradually the alben calmed, until he raised his head once more and spoke in softer tones.

"A word, Madóran?"

Caeran stiffened. I heard a whispered, "No!" from down the *portal*.

Madóran raised a hand, gesturing for peace. He stepped toward the alben, who smiled now, and held out a hand as if to shake hands. Madóran clasped his arm as I'd seen the ælven do. The alben's smile widened.

Suddenly he spun and jerked Madóran's arm, slinging him over his shoulder. He was off and running across the field before the ælven could cry out.

16

"God *dammit!*" I yelled, wrenching my hand from Caeran's and digging in my pocket for my keys as I ran to my car.

"Len, no!"

"Get in if you're coming!"

I yanked open the driver door and threw myself into the car, mashing the key into the ignition and pumping the gas as I cranked the sleepy engine. The car was cold and stank of burned plastic.

Ælven ran across the driveway in front of me, pursuing the alben. I pulled my trailing cloak into the car and slammed my door. Heard the other doors opening, felt the weight of passengers getting in, front and back.

The engine roared to life and I floored it, tires spinning in the snow until they got traction. I careened off down the driveway, trusting the ælven to stay out of my way. They had much faster reflexes.

"Damn that bastard! That sonofabitch! Can you see him?"

"No," Caeran said beside me. "They have reached the woods."

I was driving too fast, pissed because I knew I probably wasn't helping much, if at all. The alben could evade me by going cross-country. Best I could do was maybe limit his choices.

"I do not understand," said someone from the back seat. "Why did Madóran not fight?"

"Bastard probably zapped him," I said, glancing in the rear-view mirror at the two guys in the back—Nathrin and one of the others, Lomen maybe.

"Len!"

I looked back at the driveway and stomped on the brakes. I was nearly to the road.

The car fishtailed in the snow, throwing my unbelted

passengers around until I got it under control just short of ramming into Madóran's beautiful gatepost. I turned right, heading for Guadalupita down a highway that was slushy but mostly clear. The sand trucks had been out, and the warm day had melted most of the snow.

"You might want to fasten your seat belts," I said.

Murmuring voices from the back as Nathrin helped Lomen figure that out. I kept my eyes on the road, watching for any flicker of movement. The alben would probably stay in the trees as much as he could, avoiding the open fields and meadows. That would narrow his choices, too.

"Have they crossed the road?" I wondered aloud.

"I think not," Caeran said.

"Can you tell where they are?"

He closed his eyes, frowning in concentration. I slowed down as a pair of headlights approached from the south.

My heart was pumping. I didn't care how sentimental Madóran felt, that damn alben was going to die.

Caeran stirred. "They are heading south."

I looked away from the headlights as they passed, a white glare leaving the night darker behind it. What was south of here? Guadalupita, then Mora. Where could the alben be going?

A long chase wouldn't be advantageous for him, burdened with Madóran. He'd want to go to ground as soon as possible. I didn't think he'd try the bar, though—folks there would probably be unhappy to see Madóran unconscious over his shoulder. So where?

Human hostages were a complication he couldn't afford right now. One more thing to keep control of. So a barn or something would be better than a house.

It would be a standoff. The ælven were on him; they'd follow him until he stopped. He'd have to count on holding them off with a threat. Against Madóran's life?

Cold went through me as I thought of another possibility. Maybe he wanted to infect Madóran. Misery loves company.

"Sonofabitch," I whispered.

Caeran looked at me. I sped up, not that it would help, but because I felt helpless.

Guadalupita flashed by, the bar and the post office. I drove on toward Mora.

"Still moving?" I asked.

"Yes."

Caeran gazed out the window. The two in the back were silent.

The few miles to Mora zipped by. There wasn't much traffic, for which I was glad. Folks were either at home or at the bar.

When I began to see more buildings I slowed down. Mora was a bigger town, but if it had a bar I didn't know it. Barns, yes. There was some kind of big storage building on the raspberry ranch, I thought. It was too dark by now for me to see.

Caeran leaned forward. "They are just ahead. They have stopped moving."

We were coming up on the junction. I frowned, wondering where they might be. Not in the raspberry store...

The old mill! Nothing in there right now. Plans to make it a museum—it was already on the historic register. But unoccupied, and big.

I pulled into the parking lot at the raspberry store, just north of the mill. No sense in announcing our arrival. I got out, hugging my cloak around me. The air was sharp, but clean. I took a deep lungful and coughed at the cold.

The others followed me down the shoulder toward the mill. A pale form stood at the north end of the building—Bironan. He glanced at us and nodded, gesturing to the mill.

The building paralleled the highway, ending at the intersection. It was long and fairly narrow, built of huge dark beams of lumber that had once been massive and were now rickety.

I could see another ælven standing down by the junction, near the far end of the mill. Couldn't tell who.

Bironan pulled my passengers aside and conferred with

them in hushed voices. I held my cloak tight and paced to keep warm, angry at being excluded.

After a few minutes, Caeran came to me. The others began moving toward the mill.

"Len, please wait at the car."

I frowned. "Let me stand watch or something. I won't interfere. I'll feel safer with you."

"You will be a liability."

His tone was stern, almost sounding like Madóran. I hated knowing he was right. Stupid feeble human body.

"I'll wait here."

I stepped over to the corner of the newer building that held the raspberry store, and leaned against the stone wall. Caeran sighed.

"Do not move from there."

"Right. Hurry back."

I watched him catch up with the others, fast and silent. It was weird watching four men move without making a sound.

The alben must know he was surrounded. What would he do? What were they going to try?

The ælven disappeared against the darkness of the mill. The one I had seen earlier by the junction moved into shadow and I lost track of him as well. I strained to hear something, anything. They were too good; not even a creak from the old wooden building.

Since I couldn't see anything anyway, I closed my eyes and pictured Madóran, then surrounded him with white light. *Please*, I thought, not sure who I was asking—God or whatever —*please protect him.*

A shout made me jump. The alben's voice, harsh, imperative, speaking words I didn't know. A moment later someone called back. The alben interrupted, short and sharp. After that it was silent.

Long minutes went by. I stood straining to hear, but no more voices reached me. Maybe they were talking mentally, and I couldn't hear. Frustrated, I took a few steps forward.

No moon, and I couldn't see much by starlight. I wanted to go investigate, but I'd promised to stay put.

Caeran?

I bounced from foot to foot, hating inactivity. Finally a figure came toward me out of the darkness. Caeran.

"What's going on?" I whispered.

"It is a standoff. Gehmanin is holding Madóran at knife-point inside the building. He swears he will kill him if we do not leave."

"That's a lie. He doesn't want Madóran dead."

"We have no alternative."

"Yes you do. Let me talk to him."

"No! Absolutely not, Len."

"He can infect any of you, but not me."

"He will kill you without a thought."

"No, because he needs me. He just doesn't know it yet."

I could feel Caeran glaring at me, even though I couldn't see his face very well in the dark. I stepped closer and put a hand on his arm.

"I'll talk to him about the research. He seemed interested in that earlier."

"It was only a ruse to make Madóran come within reach."

"Partly, maybe. But I think I can make him listen."

"No." His voice held a flat, uncompromising tone. "It is too dangerous."

I ran my hand up his arm to his shoulder and leaned in. "*You* haven't hesitated to face danger. You've done it repeatedly in the last week. You saved my life a couple of times, for which thank you, by the way. Now it's my turn."

"Len, no." His voice was softer now, more pleading than ordering, and that was harder to resist. He put his arms around me. "I cannot bear to lose you so soon."

I drew a shaky breath. "You won't lose me. I'll stay by the door, I promise."

"He can compel you—"

"Why would he, though?"

Caeran's answer was a wall of darkness that I could feel. Was I sensing his khi? It didn't matter.

"He won't eat me. I'll make him curious before he has the chance."

I could feel Caeran's breathing, faster than usual. His confidence was shaken, something I hadn't observed before. I struggled to hide my own doubts.

"Please, just let me try. If he won't listen I'll get out of there."

"I will go with you."

"He won't let you."

"I will stay outside the door. If he makes a move against you...."

I swallowed. If the alben moved against me, all hell would break lose.

"OK," I said.

Suddenly Caeran was kissing me ravenously. I gave back with enthusiasm, so much so that my loins ached to be elsewhere, someplace warm with a bed. Finally I pulled away.

"We'd better explain to the others."

"I will do so," Caeran said. He offered his arm—the quaint formal gesture I'd come to love—and led me toward the mill.

He must have done his explaining on some mental plane that I wasn't in on. As we neared the mill, the other ælven gathered around the door. Tiruli was there; I could tell by her shape, and even by her khi a little, I thought.

Bironan came close to whisper to me. "We are grateful to you for making this attempt. We will defend you."

"Right. Thanks," I whispered. "Hopefully there won't be a need."

The door to the mill sagged, leaving gaps above and at the side. Darkness leaked out through them, and to my over-active mind it felt malevolent. I pushed on the door; it creaked.

"It's me," I called out, though I was sure the alben already knew. An ælven would have managed to open the door without making noise.

"Listen to me, please."

No answer. I drew a deep breath, feeling a lot less sure of myself than when I discussed this plan with Caeran a few minutes earlier. He put a hand on my shoulder from behind; he knew, of course, exactly what I was feeling. I hadn't bothered to try to shield my thoughts. It hardly mattered now.

"I'm coming in. I just want to talk to you."

The door groaned as I opened it enough to go in. The floor was uneven and I dreaded putting my foot through it. I moved with tiny steps, edging past the door and leaving it open behind me. The starlight from outside was bright compared with the interior of the mill. I could see slivers of gray where the boards of the walls had gapped apart, but there wasn't enough light for me to see Madóran or the alben.

"Madóran?"

"He cannot answer you."

I turned toward the voice, frowning. The alben wasn't close by, which was a relief. If he wanted to attack me, he'd have to get closer.

"Is he alive?" I asked.

"What does it matter to you?"

The sneer in his voice made me angry. I kept straining to see, to hear any movement. I hated this blindness.

Len.

Caeran's touch brought me vision; he was looking through a gap in the wall behind me. Everything in the mill was shades of gray, but I saw clearly. The alben was backed against a large, boxy structure, holding Madóran before him like a shield. Starlight glinted off the knife he held at Madóran's throat.

17

My anger flared. "It matters to you," I said. "If he's dead, there's no hope. You know that."

The alben didn't answer, just frowned back at me. Caeran's attention focused on Madóran and I stared at him, hoping to see him breathe.

"I came to tell you why you have to wait ten years," I said. "Madóran didn't say because he was protecting me, but you need to know. You need both of us, or there won't be a cure."

The alben gave a bark of scornful laughter. "If a cure was possible, he would have found it."

"He doesn't have access to our scientific technology. I will, but I've got to go through medical school first. Then I'll get into a research lab. Madóran has agreed to work with me. If human science can offer a cure, we'll find it."

The alben's eyes narrowed. Good, he was thinking.

"Let him go."

I took a step toward them. The alben tightened his grip, pressing the blade against Madóran's throat. I froze.

"What could I do to you?" I said. "Nothing. You're stronger, faster. I'm no threat. Let him go, and you can leave. Leave the country like he said. Come back in ten years."

"A pretty fantasy."

I shook my head. "Truth. You know Madóran wouldn't lie to you."

For a moment a look of anguished hunger crossed his face, then the frown returned. "Those others will never let me pass."

"Yes they will." I raised my voice. "Right, Bironan? If he lets Madóran go, he can leave?"

"Yes," came the grudging reply from outside.

"See? So let him go. We're your best chance. You'd like to be normal again, right?"

I'd said too much. He scowled and started to drag Madóran backward. That didn't look good.

I followed them to the south end of the building, past what was left of the machinery. Seeing through Caeran's eyes, I watched myself walk away; disorienting, but I could cope. Sort of like fun house mirrors.

The alben stopped near the back wall. Behind him, light came through a large gap in the boards.

"Let him go. You won't get far if you run, you know that."

"I don't need to get far," he whispered, his voice a hiss.

Madóran slumped to the floor. I had just enough time to realize the alben had vanished, then I was yanked backward, strangling.

I clawed at the cloak clasp and got it loose. The cloak fell away and I stumbled sideways, my foot tangling in the fabric. I almost fell.

Len! Get out!

I couldn't see what I was doing, still watching the show from a distance. I shoved my hands in my pockets, frantic for my keys, my only weapon. Came up with keys in one hand and a wad of cloth in the other. Napkin, I remembered.

A noise; I spun, but too late. An iron arm went around me from behind and I felt the knife at my throat.

I squeezed my eyes shut, gulped a breath, and flung the chile powder from the napkin over my shoulder.

The alben's short scream turned to coughing and horrible wheezing. He let me go; I felt wetness on my front, heard the blade fall.

The floor boards boomed as the ælven rushed in. I was on my knees, though I didn't remember how I got there. Cautiously I opened my eyes.

Dark again. I held still, panting, listening. The remnants of chile hanging in the air irritated my throat. I was cold—and wet. Oh, yeah. Bleeding.

Hands caught my shoulders. I gave a small shriek, then recognized Caeran.

Len. You're hurt!

Yeah, cut. Not too bad, I think.

I started shivering. There were footsteps, angry voices, but I was too freaked to sort them out.

A cloak draped around my shoulders, and a moment later something warm and soft pressed against my throat. Both smelled like Caeran.

Hold that there.

I took hold of the cloth—Caeran's shirt—and tried to stop shaking. The cloak was warm and wonderfully comforting. Gradually my shivering subsided.

The door opened wide, letting in enough light for me to see a little. The opening was blocked briefly by moving figures.

Madóran—is he alive?

Yes. Caeran's tone was grim.

Show me, please.

Caeran shared his view with me. Madóran lay not far from me—horribly still.

I struggled to get up, and the view shifted to me. I froze, blinking in confusion. I was a mess: hair every which way, blood all over my shirt, cloak slipping from my shoulders.

Caeran caught the cloak and tucked it around me, then helped me to Madóran's side. Clumsily because of the weird perspective, I laid a hand on the healer's cheek. It was icy.

No blood, no wound. What did that bastard do to him?

I could feel Caeran's anger. *He fed on Madóran's khi.*

They can do that?

Any ælven can draw upon khi, but it is forbidden.

He doesn't seem to care much about your taboos.

He will never break them again.

That sounded ominous. I turned my head toward Caeran, but the view didn't change.

What are you going to do?

It is already done.

I caught my breath, stunned at the swiftness of the ælven's retaliation. Not that I liked the alben much—he was a vicious bastard—but the ælven didn't seem like the kind of people to take a life so quickly.

They hadn't, I realized as I continued to gaze at Madóran. They had given the alben chance after chance—mostly because of Madóran's compassion—and they must have finally decided he wasn't going to be stopped any other way.

I touched Madóran's throat, looking for a pulse. I found it, but it was feathery and light.

We've got to get him warmed up. Can you carry him to the car?

Yes. Can you drive?

Um. I think so. Where are my keys?

Caeran knelt beside me and touched my right hand, which was clenched shut over my keychain. I sighed and leaned against him. His chest was bare, his skin warm. Shuddering, I clung to him.

Aren't you freezing?

No.

My cloak's here somewhere—

I see it.

With Caeran's help I got to my feet. He fetched my cloak and tossed it over his shoulders, then picked up Madóran.

The air outside was cold, setting me shivering again. Two ælven men stood waiting by my car. They helped Caeran load Madóran into the back seat, then exchanged a few words with him in ælven and took off running north.

I got in the car, glancing at Madóran lying across the back seat. His pallor frightened me. I started the car as Caeran got in, cranked the heater to high, and drove carefully back to the hacienda. As I came near the house I saw a bonfire in the field behind it. A big bonfire.

"What's that about?"

We burn our dead.

"Oh." I swallowed.

Made sense. Good way to dispose of a body.

I felt oddly sad about Gehmanin's death, though I sure never wanted to see him again. It was an opportunity missed.

He was the inspiration for Madóran's and my agreement, and now he'd never benefit. Of course, if anyone was going to benefit, we had to help Madóran.

Nathrin and Faranin were waiting at the door. They came out and carried Madóran into the house, laying him on the sofa in the front room. He looked terrible now that I could see him better, and my dread grew.

"Build up the fire."

I pulled off my cloak to drape over Madóran, and Caeran did the same. Gingerly, I pulled the shirt away from my neck. It stuck a little, making me wince. I couldn't see the cut but it had mostly stopped bleeding.

I pulled the hassock over beside the couch next to Madóran, and tried to figure out what to do. Panic rose in my chest. I wasn't a healer, just a wannabe.

Maybe I should just call 911, except how would I explain the problem? This guy's had his khi sucked out of him?

Remembering what I'd seen Madóran do in the treatment room, I held out my hands toward him. Heat flared in my palms, so fast I gave a startled yip. I moved them around over Madóran, trying to figure out where to put them. The heat increased when my hands passed over his heart, so I decided to try there.

I laid my hands side by side on his chest and closed my eyes. *Please, whoever can help, let your power go to him.*

Hands touched my shoulders from behind. Caeran, sharing his khi. I felt it pour down my arms and into Madóran's chest. It grew stronger and stronger, and I was vaguely aware that the others were joining in, putting their hands on Caeran's shoulders, on each other's. A pyramid took shape behind me, focusing khi through me to Madóran.

More aware of this amazing flow of energy than of anything else, I felt adrift in the warmth. How long we stayed that way I had no idea. I only came down when the intensity started to lighten and the furnace in my hands began to cool.

Opening my eyes, I saw that Madóran's face held color

again. Tears of relief ran down my cheeks. I wiped them away, sniffing, and became aware that my back was stiff. Caeran lifted his hands from my shoulders, only to wrap his arms around me as he sat beside me on the hassock, squishing close. Still shirtless, which was fine by me, and everyone else was politely ignoring it.

"Well done, healer," he said.

"Junior assistant healer in training, please. If that. I've never even taken CPR."

I felt Madóran's pulse. Much stronger, and his skin was warmer. Daring to hope he'd be all right, I drew a shuddering breath and looked around the room. The other ælven were all gathered there, even Mirali. Only Savhoran was missing.

"And it was all of you as much as me," I said.

Faranin shook his head. "You were the focus. That is a gift that few possess. We might have helped Madóran without you, but less effectively."

My cheeks went hot. Strange to be praised by these incredible immortals, who had been so indifferent to me at first. I felt undeserving, an impostor.

"Could someone go make some tea?" I said. "And maybe warm up some of the soup?"

Mirali and Nathrin headed for the kitchen at once. Lomen went to the fireplace and put more wood on the coals. That they had burned so low was an indication of how long we'd been here.

"Where is Gehmanin?"

I turned to see Madóran's eyes open, gazing at me. His voice was weak and he looked exhausted. Seeing the worry in his eyes, I couldn't answer. My throat tightened on the words.

"He is gone, my lord," said Bironan. "We had no choice."

Madóran's eyes glanced aside, then closed. A frown creased his brow, and I felt tears again. Even now, after the jerk had almost killed him, he still loved that bastard. I was sorry for his heartbreak.

Caeran's arms tightened around me. I leaned my head

against his, grateful for his support. I was luckier than Madóran had been.

Madóran looked at me again, his glance flicking to my throat. "Did he do that?"

I glanced at the blood on my shirt. "Uh, yeah. It isn't as bad as it looks."

He lifted a hand toward my throat. I felt the tingle of his khi.

"You should rest—"

"This is simple."

His hand was warm against my skin, and the khi took away the discomfort that I'd been aware of in the background, the raw edge of the cut made by the alben's knife. After only a moment, my skin felt whole again. Madóran's hand dropped away and I caught it, squeezing.

"Thank you."

"Thank you, Lenore. Your light led me back from the darkness."

"Was it that bad?"

"I have never been so close to quitting this world." He frowned in grief. "I do not understand Gehmanin's actions. We might have helped him."

"We can help others. You're still up for it, right?"

He met my gaze, and after a long moment, nodded. "We will have to find another—sufferer—to cooperate with our studies."

"We'll figure something out. That's down the road a ways. I've got a lot to learn first. Will you teach me?"

A tiny smile curved his lips, and he nodded. That more than anything told me he'd be all right.

Mirali and Nathrin came in, carrying soup and a tray with the teapot and cups. Caeran and I helped Madóran sit up while the others converged on the tea. I nabbed a cup of tea for Madóran, and watched while he sipped it and ate a little soup.

Bironan came and sat beside Madóran, asking him about what sort of property might be available nearby. Apparently

Caeran's family liked the area enough to stay. I suppressed an instinct to shoo him away. The distraction would probably do Madóran good.

The others gradually dispersed, some to find a late meal, others to the privacy of their rooms. When Madóran had finished his soup I collected the bowl and spoon and slipped away, Caeran shadowing me.

Tiruli was in the kitchen, stirring a small pot of soup that was heating on the stove. She glanced up, smiling.

"Savhoran asked for something to eat."

"Oh! I'm so glad!"

I wanted to hug her, but chickened out and went to the sink instead to wash the dishes. Shyness, and the fear of accidentally offending. The ælven had their own customs, and I didn't know what they were. I had a lot to learn.

I paused, gazing at the blue and white tiles of the counter, wondering if I could successfully live in two worlds. Here, in Madóran's house, my life at the university seemed distant, almost a dream. Would this place seem like that when I was back in school? Maybe, but I wouldn't let it slip away completely. I'd come back here, as often as Madóran would let me. To learn, and to be among the immortals.

Setting the clean bowl in the dish rack, I turned and found Caeran watching me, leaning on the end of the counter. His arms were folded across his bare chest. So gorgeous. I stood staring at him, the gold-green eyes, the auburn hair spilling over his shoulders. His smile widened and he held out his hand.

We headed out the back door, but when we reached the enclosed *portal* I was drawn to the courtyard. The moon had risen, painting the leftover snow blue-white. I went out and walked over to the fountain where I'd seen Madóran standing.

What was it that drew him here? Just the magic of moving water?

His footprints had worn a trail around the fountain. I followed it, wondering what he thought as he walked this circle, what it meant to him. As I reached the east side again I realized that Caeran had followed me. He was beaming.

"What?"

"Do you know what you just did? You walked around the world."

I glanced at the footprints in the snow. "I was just following Madóran's path."

"A good path to choose. You and he share a bond. I can see that."

Did I hear a hint of envy in his voice? I turned, reaching for him.

"A common interest. Oh, geez—you still don't have a shirt! Aren't you freezing?"

His smile widened. "Warm me, then."

His arms went around me and I hugged him back. He didn't seem to need more clothing—he felt wonderfully warm. I, on the other hand, had a wimpy mortal body and I wanted to be inside, by a fire.

Come, then.

His warmth filled my mind, my soul. Breathtaking. Though I treasured my growing friendship with Madóran, it was nothing to this. I let that thought float freely through my mind.

We walked slowly across the courtyard to the north door, and to my room. Caeran made a fire while I pulled off yet another bloodstained shirt. There was a pile of clean clothing on the dresser, including my socks. When Madóran had found the time to deal with laundry I had no clue.

I pulled on the ælven shirt and joined Caeran by the fire, settling into his arms with a sigh. "This is nice. No threats, no constraints. No hurry."

He smiled, gazing at me. *We have all the time in the world.*
No, not that. But we have a lifetime.

His smile widened as he bent to kiss me.
Then we had better get started.

About the Author

Pati Nagle was born and raised in the mountains of northern New Mexico. An avid student of music, history, and humans in general, she loves the outdoors but hides from the sun.

She writes in a variety of genres, but is most often drawn to fantasy or (as P.G. Nagle) historical fiction. Her stories have appeared in *Asimov's Science Fiction*, the *Magazine of Fantasy & Science Fiction*, and in various other magazines and anthologies, including *Elf Magic,* which featured "Kind Hunter," the story that sparked the ælven world. Her first ælven novel, *The Betrayal,* was released in 2009 by Del Rey Books. Its sequel, *Heart of the Exiled*, will come out in January 2011.

Pati Nagle still lives in the mountains in New Mexico, with her husband and two furry feline muses, where she loves to walk in the woods and look up at the stars.

Pati Nagle's websites:

patinagle.com
pgnagle.com

Other Books by Pati Nagle

Blood of the Kindred Series

Before the human race evolved, the ælven were locked in a war with their kindred and foes, the blood-drinking alben

The Betrayal

read a sample at aelven.com

Heart of the Exiled

read a sample at aelven.com

www.ingramcontent.com/pod-product-compliance
Lightning Source LLC
Chambersburg PA
CBHW020507120726
47904CB00003B/732